ALISTAIR MACLEAN

Alistair MacLean, the son of a Scots minister, was born in 1922 and brought up in the Scottish Highlands. In 1941 at the age of eighteen he joined the Royal Navy; two-and-a-half years spent aboard a cruiser was later to give him the background for HMS *Ulysses*, his first novel, the outstanding documentary novel on the war at sea. After the war, he gained an English Honours degree at Glasgow University, and became a school master. In 1983 he was awarded a D.Litt from the same university.

He is now recognized as one of the outstanding popular writers of the 20th century. By the early 1970s he was one of the top 10 bestselling authors in the world, and the biggest-selling Briton. He wrote twenty-nine worldwide bestsellers that have sold more than 30 million copies, and many of which have been filmed, including *The Guns of Navarone*, *Where Eagles Dare*, *Fear is the Key* and *Ice Station Zebra*. Alistair MacLean died in 1987 at his home in Switzerland.

By Alistair MacLean

ALISTAIR MACLEAN

Partisans

HARPER

Harper
An imprint of HarperCollins*Publishers*
77–85 Fulham Palace Road,
Hammersmith, London W6 8JB

www.harpercollins.co.uk

This paperback edition 2009
1

First published in Great Britain by
William Collins Sons & Co. Ltd 1982
then in paperback by Fontana 1983

Copyright © Alistair MacLean 1982

Alistair MacLean asserts the moral right to
be identified as the author of this work

A catalogue record for this book is
available from the British Library

ISBN 978-0-00-789234-1

Typeset in Meridien by Thomson Digital, India

Printed and bound in Great Britain by
Clays Ltd, St Ives plc

To Avdo and Inge

ONE

The chill night wind off the Tiber was from the north and carried with it the smell of snow from the distant Apennines. The sky was clear and full of stars and there was light enough to see the swirling of the dust-devils in the darkened streets and the paper, cardboard and assorted detritus that blew about every which way. The darkened, filthy streets were not the result of the electrical and sanitation departments of the Eternal City, as was their peacetime wont, staging one of their interminable strikes, for this was not peacetime: events in the Mediterranean theatre had reached a delicate stage where Rome no longer cared to advertise its whereabouts by switching on the street lights: the sanitation department, for the most part, was some way off to the south fighting a war it didn't particularly care about.

Petersen stopped outside a shop doorway – the nature of its business was impossible to tell for the windows were neatly masked in regulation blackout paper – and glanced up and down the Via Bergola. It appeared to be deserted as were most streets in the city at that time of night. He produced a hooded torch and a large bunch of peculiarly shaped keys and let himself in with a speed, ease and dexterity which spoke well for whoever had trained him in such matters. He took up position behind the opened door, removed the hood from the torch, pocketed the keys, replaced them with a silenced Mauser and waited.

He had to wait for almost two minutes, which, in the circumstances, can be a very long time, but Petersen didn't seem to mind. Two stealthy foot-steps, then there appeared beyond the edge of the door the dimly seen silhouette of a man whose only identifiable features were a peaked cap and a hand clasping a gun in so purposeful a grip that even in the half-light the faint sheen of the knuckles could be seen.

The figure took two further stealthy steps into the shop then halted abruptly as the torch clicked on and the silencer of the Mauser rammed none too gently into the base of his neck.

'Drop that gun. Clasp your hands behind your neck, take three steps forward and don't turn round.'

The intruder did as told. Petersen closed the shop door, located the light switch and clicked it on. They appeared to be in what was, or should have been, a jeweller's shop, for the owner, a man with little faith in the occupying forces, his fellow-countrymen or both, had prudently and totally cleared all his display cabinets.

'Now you can turn round,' Petersen said.

The man turned. The set expression on the youthful face was tough and truculent, but he couldn't do much about his eyes or the apprehension reflected in them.

'I will shoot you,' Petersen said conversationally, 'if you are carrying another gun and don't tell me.'

'I have no other gun.'

'Give me your papers.' The youngster compressed his lips, said nothing and made no move. Petersen sighed.

'Surely you recognize a silencer? I can just as easily take the papers off your body. Nobody will know a thing. What's more to the point, neither will you.'

The youngster reached inside his tunic and handed over a wallet. Petersen flicked it open.

'Hans Wintermann,' he read. 'Born August 24, 1924. Just nineteen. *And* a lieutenant. You must be a bright young man.' Petersen folded and pocketed the wallet. 'You've been following me around tonight. And most of yesterday. And the evening before that. I find such persistence tedious, especially when it's so obvious. Why do you follow me?'

'You have my name, rank, regiment – '

Petersen waved him to silence. 'Spare me. Well, I'm left with no option.'

'You're going to shoot me?' The truculence had left the youngster's face.

'Don't be stupid.'

The Hotel Splendide was anything but: but its dingy anonymity suited Petersen well enough. Peering through the cracked and stained glass of the front door he noted, with mild surprise, that the concierge, fat, unshaven and well stricken in years, was, for once, not asleep or, at least, wide enough awake to be able to tilt a bottle to his head. Petersen circled to the rear of the hotel, climbed the fire escape, let himself in to the third-floor passage, moved along this, turned into a left-hand corridor and let himself into his room with a skeleton key. He quickly checked cupboards and drawers, seemed satisfied, shrugged into a heavy coat, left and took up position on the fire escape. Despite the added protection of the coat his exposed position was considerably colder than it had been in the comparative shelter of the streets below and he hoped he would not have to wait too long.

The wait was even shorter than he had expected. Less than five minutes had passed when a German officer strode briskly along the corridor, turned left, knocked on a door, knocked again, this time peremptorily, rattled the handle then reappeared, frowning heavily. There came the creaking and clanking of the ancient elevator, a silence, more creaking and clanking, then the officer again hove into sight this time with the concierge, who had a key in his hand.

When ten minutes had passed with no sign of either man Petersen went inside, eased his way along the passage and peered round the corner to his left. Halfway along the corridor stood the concierge, obviously on guard. Just as obviously, he was an experienced campaigner prepared for any contingency for, as Petersen watched, he produced a hip flask from his pocket and was still savouring the contents, his eyes closed in bliss, when Petersen clapped him heartily on the shoulder.

'You keep a good watch, my friend.'

The concierge coughed, choked, spluttered and tried to speak but his larynx wasn't having any of it. Petersen looked past him and through the doorway.

'And good evening to you, Colonel Lunz. Everything is in order, I trust?'

'Ah, good evening.' Lunz was almost a look-alike for Petersen himself, medium height, broad shoulders, aquiline features, grey eyes and thin black hair: an older version, admittedly, but nevertheless the resemblance was startling. He didn't seem in any way put out. 'I've just this moment arrived and –'

'Ah, ah, Colonel.' Petersen wagged a finger. 'Officers, whatever their nationality, are officers and gentlemen the world over. Gentlemen don't tell lies. You've been here for exactly eleven minutes. I've timed you.' He turned to the still red-faced and gasping concierge who was making valiant efforts to communicate with them and clapped him encouragingly on the back. 'You were trying to say something?'

'You were out.' The convulsions were easing. 'I mean, you were in, but I saw you go out. Eleven minutes, you said? I didn't see – I mean, your key –'

'You were drunk at the time,' Petersen said kindly. He bent, sniffed and wrinkled his nose. 'You still are. Be off. Send us a bottle of brandy. Not that tearful rot-gut you drink: the French cognac you keep for the Gestapo. And two glasses – *clean* glasses.' He turned to Lunz. 'You will, of course, join me, my dear Colonel?'

'Naturally.' The Colonel was a hard man to knock off balance. He watched Petersen calmly as he took off his coat and threw it on the bed, lifted an eyebrow and said: 'A sudden chill snap outside, yes?'

'Rome? January? No time to take chances with one's health. It's no joke hanging about those fire escapes, I can tell you.'

'So that's where you were. I should have exercised more care, perhaps.'

'No perhaps about your choice of lookout.'

'True.' The Colonel brought out a briar pipe and began to fill it. 'I hadn't much choice.'

'You sadden me, Colonel, you really do. You obtain my key, which is illegal. You post a guard so that you won't be discovered breaking the law yet again. You ransack my belongings –'

'Ransack?'

'Carefully examine. I don't know what kind of incriminating evidence you were expecting to find.'

'None, really. You don't strike me as the kind of man who would leave –'

'And you had me watched earlier tonight. You must have done, otherwise you wouldn't have known that I had been out earlier without a coat. Saddens? It shocks. Where is this mutual trust that should exist between allies?'

'Allies?' He struck a match. 'I hadn't thought about it very much in that way.' Judging by his expression, he still wasn't thinking very much about it in that way.

'And more evidence of mutual trust.' Petersen handed over the wallet he had taken from the young lieutenant, together with a revolver. 'I'm sure you know him. He was waving his gun around in a very dangerous fashion.'

'Ah!' Lunz looked up from the papers. 'The impetuous young Lieutenant Wintermann. You were right to take this gun from him, he might have done himself an injury. From what I know of you I assume he's not resting at the bottom of the Tiber?'

'I don't treat allies that way. He's locked up in a jeweller's shop.'

'Of course.' Lunz spoke as if he had expected nothing else. 'Locked up. But surely he can –'

'Not the way I tied him up. You not only sadden me, Colonel, you insult me. Why didn't you give him a red flag to wave or a drum to beat? Something that would really attract my attention.'

Lunz sighed. 'Young Hans is well enough in a tank but subtlety is not really his métier. I did not, by the way, insult you. Following you was entirely his own idea. I knew what he was up to, of course, but I didn't try to stop him. For hardly won experience a sore head is little enough to pay.'

'He hasn't even got that. An ally, you see.'

'Pity. It might have reinforced the lesson.' He broke off as a knock came to the door and the concierge entered bearing brandy and glasses. Petersen poured and lifted his glass.

'To Operation Weiss.'

'*Prosit.*' Lunz sipped appreciatively. 'Not all Gestapo officers are barbarians. Operation Weiss? So you know? You're not supposed to.' Lunz didn't seem at all put out.

'I know lots of things that I'm not supposed to.'

'You surprise me.' Lunz's tone was dry. He sipped some more brandy. 'Excellent, excellent. Yes, you do have a penchant for picking up unconsidered – and classified – trifles. Which leads to your repeated use of the world "ally". Which leads, in turn, to what you possibly regard as our undue interest in you.'

'You don't trust me?'

'You'll have to improve on that injured tone of yours. Certainly we trust you. Your record –

8

and it is a formidable one – speaks for itself. What we – and especially myself – find difficult to understand is why such a man with such a record aligns himself with – well, I'm afraid I have to say it – with a quisling. I do not hurt your feelings?'

'You'd have to find them first. I would remind you that it was your Führer who forced our departed Prince Regent to sign this treaty with you and the Japanese two years ago. I assume he's the quisling you're talking about. Weak, certainly, vacillating, perhaps cowardly and no man of action. You can't blame a man for those things: nature's done its worst and there's nothing we can do about nature. But no quisling – he did what he thought was best for Yugoslavia. He wanted to spare it the horrors of war. "*Bolje grob nego rob*". You know what that means?'

Lunz shook his head. 'The intricacies of your language –'

' "Better death than slavery". That's what the Yugoslav crowds shouted when they learned that Prince Paul had acceded to the Tripartite Pact. That's what they shouted when he was deposed and the pact denounced. What the people didn't understand was that there was no "*nego*", no "than". It was to be death *and* slavery as they found out when the Führer, in one of his splendid rages, obliterated Belgrade and crushed the army. I was one of those who were crushed. Well, nearly.'

'If I might have some more of that excellent cognac.' Lunz helped himself. 'You don't seem greatly moved by your recollections.'

'Who can live with all his yesterdays?'

'Nor by the fact that you find yourself in the unfortunate position of having to fight your own countrymen.'

'Instead of joining them and fighting you? War makes for strange bed-fellows, Colonel. Take yourselves and the Japanese, for instance. Hardly entitles you to a holier-than-thou attitude.'

'A point. But at least we're not fighting our own people.'

'Not yet. I wouldn't bank on it. God knows, you've done it enough in the past. In any event, moralizing is pointless. I'm a loyalist, a Royalist, and when – and if ever – this damned war is over I want to see the monarchy restored. A man's got to live for something and if that's what I choose to live for, then that's my business and no-one else's.'

'All to hell our own way,' Lunz said agreeably. 'It's just that I have some difficulty in visualizing you as a Serbian Royalist.'

'What does a Serbian Royalist look like? Come to that, what does a Serbian look like?'

Lunz thought then said: 'A confession, Petersen. I haven't the slightest idea.'

'It's my name,' Petersen said kindly. 'And my background. There are Petersens all over. There's a village up in the Italian Alps where every second surname starts with "Mac". The remnants, so I'm told, of some Scottish regiment that got cut off in one of those interminable medieval wars. My great-great-great grandfather or whatever, was a soldier of fortune, which sounds a lot more romantic than the term "mercenary" they use today. Like a thousand others he arrived here and forgot to go home again.'

'Where was home? I mean, Scandinavian, Anglo-Saxon, what?'

'Genealogy bores me and, not only don't I care, I don't know either. Ask any Yugoslav what his ancestors five times removed were and he almost certainly wouldn't know.'

Lunz nodded. 'You Slavic people *do* have rather a chequered history. And then, of course, just to complicate matters, you graduated from Sandhurst.'

'Dozens of foreign countries have had their officers graduate from there. In my case, what more natural? My father was, after all, the military attaché in London. If he'd been the naval attaché in Berlin I'd probably have ended up in Kiel or Mürwik.'

'Nothing wrong with Sandhurst. I've been there, as a visitor only. But a bit on the conservative side as far as the courses offered are concerned.'

'You mean?'

'Nothing on guerrilla warfare. Nothing on espionage and counter-espionage. Nothing on code and cypher breaking. I understand you're a specialist on all three.'

'I'm self-educated in some things.'

'I'm sure you are.' Lunz was silent for some seconds, savouring his brandy, then said: 'Whatever became of your father?'

'I don't know. You may even know more than I do. Just disappeared. Thousands have done so since the spring of'41. Disappeared, I mean.'

'He was like you? A Royalist? A Četnik?' Petersen nodded. 'And very senior. Senior officers don't just disappear. He fell foul of the Partisans, perhaps?'

'Perhaps. Anything is possible. Again, I don't know.' Petersen smiled. 'If you're trying to suggest I'm carrying on a vendetta because of a blood feud, you'd better try again. Wrong country, wrong century. Anyway, you didn't come here to pry into my motives or my past.'

'And now *you* insult *me*. I wouldn't waste my time. You'd tell me just as much as you wanted me to know and no more.'

'And you didn't come here to carry out a search of my belongings – that was just a combination of opportunity and professional curiosity. You came here to give me something. An envelope with instructions for our commander. Another assault on what it pleases you to call Titoland.'

'You're pretty sure of yourself.'

'I'm not pretty sure. I'm certain. The Partisans have radio transceivers. British. They have skilled radio operators, both their own and British. And they have skilled code-crackers. You don't dare send secret and important messages any more by

12

radio. So you need a reliable message boy. There's no other reason why I'm in Rome.'

'Frankly, I can't think of any other, which saves any explanation on my part.' Lunz produced and handed over an envelope.

'This is in code?'

'Naturally.'

'Why "naturally"? In *our* code?'

'So I believe.'

'Stupid. Who do you think devised that code?'

'I don't think. I know. You did.'

'It's still stupid. Why don't you give me the message verbally? I've a good memory for this sort of thing. And there's more. I may be intercepted, and then two things may happen. Either I succeed in destroying it, in which case the message is useless. Or the Partisans take it intact and decipher it in nothing flat.' Petersen tapped his head. 'A clear case for a psychiatrist.'

Lunz took some more brandy and cleared his throat. 'You know, of course, of Colonel General Alexander von Löhr?'

'The German Commander in Chief for south-eastern Europe. Of course. Never met him personally.'

'Perhaps it is as well that you never do. I don't think General von Löhr would react too favourably to the suggestion that he is in need of psychiatric treatment. Nor does he take too kindly to subordinate officers – and, despite your nationality, you can take it that he very definitely regards

13

you as subordinate – who question far less disobey his orders. And those are his orders.'

'Two psychiatrists. One for von Löhr, one for the person who appointed him to his command. That would be the Führer, of course.'

Colonel Lunz said mildly: 'I do try to observe the essential civilities. It's not normally too difficult. But bear in mind that I am a German Regimental Commander.'

'I don't forget it and no offence was intended. Protests are useless. I have my orders. I assume that this time I will not be going in by plane?'

'You are remarkably well informed.'

'Not really. Some of your colleagues are re-markably garrulous in places where not only have they no right to be garrulous but have no right to be in the first place. In this case I am not well informed, but I can think, unlike – well, never mind. You'd have to notify my friends if you were sending in a plane and that message could be just as easily intercepted and deciphered as any other. You don't know how crazy those Partisans could be. They wouldn't hesitate to send a suicide com-mando behind our lines and shoot down the plane when it's still at an altitude of fifty or a hundred metres, which is an excellent way of ensuring that no-one gets out of that plane alive.' Petersen tapped the envelope. 'That way the message never gets delivered. So I go by boat. When?'

'Tomorrow night.'

'Where?'

'A little fishing village near Termoli.'

'What kind of boat?'

'You do ask a lot of questions.'

'It's my neck.' Petersen shrugged his indifference. 'If your travel arrangements don't suit me, I'll make my own.'

'It wouldn't be the first time you'd borrowed shall we say, a boat from your – ah – allies?'

'Only in the best interests of all.'

'Of course. An Italian torpedo boat.'

'You can hear one of those things twenty kilometres away.'

'So? You'll be landing near Ploče. That's in Italian hands, as you know. And even if you could be heard fifty kilometres away, what's the difference? The Partisans have no radar, no planes, no navy, nothing that could stop you.'

'So the Adriatic is your pond. The torpedo boat it is.'

'Thank you. I forgot to mention that you'll be having some company on the trip across.'

'You didn't forget. You just saved it for last.' Petersen refilled their glasses and looked consideringly at Lunz. 'I'm not sure that I care for this. You know I like to travel alone.'

'I know you *never* travel alone.'

'Ah! George and Alex. You know them, then?'

'They're hardly invisible. They attract attention – they have that look about them.'

'What look?'

'Hired killers.'

15

'You're half right. They're different. My insurance policy – they watch my back. I'm not complaining, but people are always spying on me.'

'An occupational hazard.' Lunz's airily dismissive gesture showed what he thought of occupational hazards. 'I would be grateful if you would allow those two people I have in mind to accompany you. More, I would regard it as a personal favour if you would escort them to their destination.'

'What destination?'

'Same as yours.'

'Who are they?'

'Two radio operator recruits for your Četniks. Carrying with them, I may say, the very latest in transceiver equipment.'

'That's not enough, and you know it. Names, background.'

'Sarina and Michael. Trained – highly trained, I might say – by the British in Alexandria. With the sole intent of doing what they are about to do – joining your friends. Let us say that we intercepted them en route.'

'What else? Male and female, no?'

'Yes.'

'No.'

'No what?'

'I'm a fairly busy person. I don't like being encumbered and I've no intention of acting as a shipborne chaperon.'

'Brother and sister.'

'Ah.' Petersen said. 'Fellow citizens?'

'Of course.'

'Then why can't they find their own way home?'

'Because they haven't been home for three years. Educated in Cairo.' Again the wave of a hand. 'Troubled times in your country, my friend. Germans here, Italians there, Ustaša, Četniks, Partisans everywhere. All very confusing. You know your way around your country in these difficult times. Better than any, I'm told.'

'I don't get lost much.' Petersen stood. 'I'd have to see them first, of course.'

'I would have expected nothing else.' Lunz drained his glass, rose and glanced at his watch. 'I'll be back in forty minutes.'

George answered Petersen's knock. Despite Lunz's unflattering description George didn't look a bit like a killer, hired or otherwise: genial buffoons, or those who look like them, never do. With a pudgy, jovial face crowned by a tangled thatch of grey-black hair, George, on the wrong side of fifty, was immense – immensely fat, that was: the studded belt strung tightly around what used to be his waist served only to emphasize rather than conceal his gargantuan paunch. He closed the door behind Petersen and crossed to the left-hand wall: like many very heavy men, as is so often seen in the case of overweight dancers, he was quick and light on his feet. He removed from the plaster a rubber suction cap with a central spike which was attached by a wire to a transformer and thence to a single earphone.

'Your friend seems to be a very pleasant man.' George sounded genuinely regretful. 'Pity we have to be on opposite sides.' He looked at the envelope Petersen had brought. 'Aha! Operational orders, no?'

'Yes. Hotfoot, you might say, from the presence of Colonel General von Löhr himself.' Petersen turned to the recumbent figure on one of the two narrow beds. 'Alex?'

Alex rose. Unlike George, he had no welcoming smile but that meant nothing, for Alex never smiled. He was of a height with George but there any resemblance ended. His weight was about half George's as were his years: he was thin-faced, swarthy and had black watchful eyes which rarely blinked. Wordlessly, for his taciturnity was almost on a par with the stillness of his face, he took the envelope, dug into a knapsack, brought out a small butane burner and an almost equally small kettle, and began to make steam. Two or three minutes later Petersen extracted two sheets of paper from the opened envelope and studied the contents carefully. When he had finished he looked up and regarded the two men thought-fully.

'This *will* be of great interest to a great number of people. It may be the depths of winter but things look like becoming very hot in the Bosnian hills in the very near future.'

George said: 'Code?'

'Yes. Simple. I made sure of that when I made it up. If the Germans never meant business before, they certainly mean it now. Seven divisions, no less. Four German, under General Lütters, whom we know, and three Italian under General Gloria, whom we also know. Supported by the Ustaša and, of course, the Četniks. Somewhere between ninety thousand and a hundred thousand troops.'

George shook his head. 'So many?'

'According to this. It's common knowledge of course that the Partisans are stationed in and around Bihać. The Germans are to attack from the north and east, the Italians from south and west. The battle plan, God knows, is simple enough. The Partisans are to be totally encircled and then wiped out to a man. Simple, but comprehensive. And just to make certain, both the Italians and Germans are bringing in squadrons of bomber and fighter planes.'

'And the Partisans haven't got a single plane.'

'Even worse for them they don't have anti-aircraft guns. Well, a handful, but they should be in a museum.' Petersen replaced the sheets and re-sealed the envelope. 'I have to go out in fifteen minutes. Colonel Lunz is coming to take me to meet a couple of people I don't particularly want to meet, two radio operator Četnik recruits who have to have their hands held until we get to Montenegro or wherever.'

'Or so Colonel Lunz says.' Suspicion was one of the few expressions that Alex ever permitted himself.

'Or so he says. Which is why I want you two to go out as well. Not with me, of course – behind me.'

'A little night air will do us good. These hotel rooms get very stuffy.' George was hardly exaggerating, his penchant for beer was equalled only by his marked weakness for evil-smelling, black cigars. 'Car or foot?'

'I don't know yet. You have your car.'

'Either way, tailing in a blackout is difficult. Chances are, we'd be spotted.'

'So? You've been spotted a long time ago. Even if Lunz or one of his men does pick you up it's most unlikely that he'll have you followed. What he can do, you can do.'

'Pick up *our* tail, you mean. What do you want us to do?'

'You'll see where I'm taken. When I leave find out what you can about those two radio operators.'

'A few details might help. It would be nice to know who we're looking for.'

'Probably mid-twenties, brother and sister, Sarina and Michael. That's all I know. No breaking down of doors, George. Discretion, that's what's called for. Tact. Diplomacy.'

'Our specialities. We use our Carabinieri cards?'

'Naturally.'

*   *   *

When Colonel Lunz had said that the two young radio operator recruits were brother and sister, that much, Petersen reflected, had been true. Despite fairly marked differences in bulk and colouring, they were unmistakably twins. He was very tanned, no doubt from all his years in Cairo, with black hair and hazel eyes: she had the flawless peach-coloured complexion of one who had no difficulties in ignoring the Egyptian sunshine, close-cropped auburn hair and the same hazel eyes as her brother. He was stocky and broad: she was neither, but just how slender or well proportioned she might have been it was impossible to guess as, like her brother, she was clad in shapeless khaki-coloured fatigues. Side by side on a couch, where they had seated themselves after the introductions, they were trying to look relaxed and casual, but their overly expressionless faces served only to accentuate their wary apprehensiveness.

Petersen leaned back in his arm-chair and looked appreciatively around the large living-room. 'My word. This is nice. Comfort? No. Luxury. You two young people do yourselves well, don't you?'

'Colonel Lunz arranged it for us,' Michael said.

'Inevitably. Favouritism. My spartan quarters —'

'Are of your own choosing,' Lunz said mildly. 'It is difficult to arrange accommodation for a person who is in town for three days before he lets anyone know that he's here.'

21

'You have a point. Not, mind you, that this place is perfect in all respects. Take, for instance, the matter of cocktail cabinets.'

'Neither my brother nor I drink.' Sarina's voice was low-pitched and quiet. Petersen noticed that the slender interlaced hands were ivory-knuckled.

'Admirable.' Petersen picked up a briefcase he had brought with him, extracted a brandy bottle and two glasses and poured for Lunz and himself. 'Your health. I hear you wish to join the good Colonel in Montenegro. You must, then, be Royalists. You can prove that?'

Michael said: 'Do we have to prove it? I mean, don't you trust us, believe us?'

'You'll have to learn and learn quickly – and by that I mean now – to adopt a different tone and attitude.' Petersen was no longer genial and smiling. 'Apart from a handful of people – and I mean a handful – I haven't trusted in or believed anyone for many years. Can you prove you're a Royalist?'

'We can when we get there.' Sarina looked at Petersen's unchanged expression and gave a helpless little shrug. 'And I know King Peter. At least, I did.'

'As King Peter is in London and London at the moment isn't taking any calls from the Wehrmacht, that would be rather difficult to prove from here. And don't tell me you can prove it when we get to Montenegro for that would be too late.'

22

Michael and Sarina looked at each other, momentarily at a loss for words, then Sarina said hesitatingly: 'We don't understand. When you say it would be too late –'

'Too late for me if my back is full of holes. Bullet wounds, stab wounds, that sort of thing.'

She stared at him, colour staining her cheeks, then said in a whisper: 'You must be mad. Why on earth should we –'

'I don't know and I'm not mad. It's just by liking to live a little longer that I manage to live a little longer.' Petersen looked at them for several silent moments, then sighed. 'So you want to come to Yugoslavia with me?'

'Not really.' Her hands were still clenched and now the brown eyes were hostile. 'Not after what you've just said.' She looked at her brother, then at Lunz, then back at Petersen. 'Do we have any options?'

'Certainly. Any amount. Ask Colonel Lunz.'

'Colonel?'

'Not any amount. Very few and I wouldn't recommend any of them. The whole point of the exercise is that you both get there intact and if you go by any other means the chances of your doing just that are remote: if you try it on your own the chances don't exist. With Major Petersen you have safe conduct and guaranteed delivery – alive, that is.'

Michael said, doubt in his voice: 'You have a great deal of confidence in Major Petersen.'

'I do. So does Major Petersen. He has every right to, I may add. It's not just that he knows the country in a way neither of you ever will. He moves as he pleases through any territory whether it's held by friend or enemy. But what's really important is that the fields of operations out there are in a state of constant flux. An area held by the Četniks today can be held by the Partisans tomorrow. You'd be like lambs in the fold when the wolves come down from the hills.'

For the first time the girl smiled slightly. 'And the Major is another wolf?'

'More like a sabre-toothed tiger. And he's got two others who keep him constant company. Not, mind you, that I've ever heard of sabre-toothed tigers meeting up with wolves but you take my point, I hope.'

They didn't say whether they took his point or not. Petersen looked at them both in turn and said: 'Those fatigues you're wearing – they're British?'

They both nodded.

'You have spares?'

Again they nodded in unison.

'Winter clothing? Heavy boots?'

'Well, no.' Michael looked his embarrassment. 'We didn't think we would need them.'

'You didn't think you would need them.' Petersen briefly contemplated the ceiling then returned his gaze to the uncomfortable pair on the couch. 'You're going up the mountains, maybe

24

two thousand metres, in the depths of winter, not to a garden party in high summer.'

Lunz said hastily: 'I shouldn't have much trouble in arranging for these things by morning.'

'Thank you, Colonel.' Petersen pointed to two fairly large, canvas-wrapped packages on the floor. 'Your radios, I take it. British?'

'Yes,' Michael said. 'Latest models. Very tough.'

'Spares?'

'Lots. All we'll ever need, the experts say.'

'The experts have clearly never fallen down a ravine with a radio strapped to their backs. You're British-trained, of course.'

'No. American.'

'In Cairo?'

'Cairo is full of them. This was a staff sergeant in the US Marines. An expert in some new codes. He taught quite a few Britishers at the same time.'

'Seems fair enough. Well, a little cooperation and we should get along just fine.'

'Cooperation?' Michael seemed puzzled.

'Yes. If I have to give some instructions now and again I expect them to be followed.'

'Instructions?' Michael looked at his sister. 'Nobody said anything –'

'I'm saying something now. I must express myself more clearly. Orders will be implicitly obeyed. If not, I'll leave you behind in Italy, jettison you in the Adriatic or just simply abandon you in Yugoslavia. I will not jeopardize my mission

25

for a couple of disobedient children who won't do as they're told.'

'Children!' Michael actually clenched his fists. 'You have no right to –'

'He has every right to.' Lunz's interruption was sharp. 'Major Petersen was talking about garden parties. He should have been talking about kindergartens. You're young, ignorant and arrogant and are correspondingly dangerous on all three counts. Whether you've been sworn in or not, you're now members of the Royal Yugoslav Army. Other rankers, such as you, take orders from officers.'

They made no reply, not even when Petersen again regarded the ceiling and said: 'And we all know the penalty for the wartime disobedience of orders.'

In Lunz's staff car Petersen sighed and said: 'I'm afraid I didn't quite achieve the degree of rapport back there that I might have. They were in a rather unhappy frame of mind when we left.'

'They'll get over it. Young, as I said. Spoilt, into the bargain. Aristocrats, I'm told, even some royal blood. Von Karajan or something like that. Odd name for a Yugoslav.'

'Not really. Almost certainly from Slovenia and the descendants of Austrians.'

'Be that as it may, they come from a family that's clearly not accustomed to taking orders and even less accustomed to being talked to the way you did.'

'I daresay they'll learn very quickly.'

'I daresay they will.'

Half an hour after returning to his room, Petersen was joined by George and Alex. George said, 'Well, at least we know their name.'

'So do I. Von Karajan. What else?'

George was in no way put out. 'The reception clerk, very old but sharp, told us he'd no idea where they'd arrived from – they'd been brought there by Colonel Lunz. He gave us their room number – no hesitation – but said that if we wanted to see them he'd have to announce us, ask permission and then escort us. Then we asked him if either of the rooms next to the number he had given us was vacant and when he told us those were their bedrooms we left.'

'You took your time about getting back.'

'We are accustomed to your injustices. We went round to the back of the hotel, climbed a fire escape and made our way along a narrow ledge. A very narrow ledge. No joke, I can tell you, especially for an old man like me. Perilous, dizzying heights –'

'Yes, yes.' Petersen was patient. The von Karajans had been staying on the first floor. 'Then?'

'There was a small balcony outside their room. Net curtains on their French windows.'

'You could see clearly?'

'And hear clearly. Young man was sending a radio message.'

'Interesting. Hardly surprising, though. Morse?'

'Plain language.'

'What was he saying?'

'I have no idea. Could have been Chinese for all I knew. Certainly no European language I've ever heard. A very short message. So we came back.'

'Anyone see you on the fire escape, ledge or balcony?'

George tried to look wounded. 'My dear Peter –'

Petersen stopped him with an upraised hand. Not many people called him "Peter" – which was his first name – but, then, not many people had been pre-war students of George's in Belgrade University where George had been the vastly respected Professor of Occidental Languages. George was known – not reputed, but known – to be fluent in at least a dozen languages and to have a working knowledge of a considerable number more.

'Forgive me, forgive me.' Petersen surveyed George's vast bulk. 'You're practically invisible anyway. So tomorrow morning, or perhaps even within minutes, Colonel Lunz will know that you and Alex have been around asking questions – he would have expected nothing less of me – but he won't know that young Michael von Karajan has been seen and heard to be sending radio messages soon after our departure. I do wonder about the nature of that message.'

George pondered briefly then said: 'Alex and I could find out on the boat tomorrow night.'

Petersen shook his head. 'I promised Colonel Lunz that we would deliver them intact.'

'What's Colonel Lunz to us or your promise to him?'

'*We* want them delivered intact too.'

George tapped his head. 'The burden of too many years.'

'Not at all, George. Professorial absent-mindedness.'

TWO

The Wehrmacht did not believe in limousines or luxury coaches for the transportation of its allies: Petersen and his companions crossed Italy that following day in the back of a vintage truck that gave the impression of being well enough equipped with tyres of solid rubber but sadly deficient in any form of springing. The vibration was of the teeth-jarring order and the rattling so loud and continuous as to make conversation virtually impossible. The hooped canvas covering was open at the back, and at the highest point in the Apennines the temperature dropped below freezing point. It was, in some ways, a memorable journey but not for its creature comforts.

The stench of the diesel fumes would normally have been overpowering enough but on that particular day faded into relative insignificance compared to the aroma, if that was the word, given off by George's black cigars. Out of deference to his fellow-travellers' sensibilities he had seated himself at the very rear of the truck and on the rare occasion when he wasn't smoking, kept himself busy and contented enough with the contents of a crate of beer that lay at his feet. He seemed immune to the cold and probably was: nature had provided him with an awesome insulation.

The von Karajans, clad in their newly acquired winter clothing, sat at the front of the left-hand unpadded wooden bench. Withdrawn and silent they appeared no happier than when Petersen had left them the previous night: this could have been an understandable reaction to their current sufferings but more probably, Petersen thought, their injured feelings had not yet had time to mend. Matters were not helped by the presence of Alex, whose totally withdrawn silence and dark, bitter and brooding countenance could be all too easily misinterpreted as balefulness: the von Karajans were not to know that Alex regarded his parents, whom he held in vast respect and affection, with exactly the same expression.

They stopped for a midday meal in a tiny village in the neighbourhood of Corfinio after having safely, if at times more or less miraculously, negotiated the hazardous hair-pin switch-backs of the Apennine spine. They had left Rome at seven o'clock that morning and it had taken over five hours to cover a hundred miles. Considering the incredibly dilapidated state of both the highway and the ancient Wehrmacht truck – unmarked as such and of Italian make – an average of almost twenty miles an hour was positively creditable. Not without difficulty for, with the exception of George, the passengers' limbs were stiff and almost frozen, they climbed down over the tailboard and looked around them through the thinly falling snow.

There was miserably little to see. The hamlet – if it could even be called that, it didn't as much as have a name – consisted of a handful of stone cottages, a post office store and a very small inn. Nearby Corfinio, if hardly ranking as a metropolis, could have afforded considerably more in the way of comfort and amenities: but Colonel Lunz, apart from a professional near-mania for secrecy, shared with his senior Wehrmacht fellow-officers the common if unfair belief that all his Italian allies were renegades, traitors and spies until proved otherwise.

In the inn itself, the genial host was far from being that. He seemed diffident, almost nervous, a markedly unusual trait in mountain innkeepers. A noticeably clumsy waiter, civil and helpful in his own way, volunteered only the fact that he was called Luigi but thereafter was totally uncommunicative. The inn itself was well enough, both warmed and illuminated by a pine log fire in an open hearth that gave off almost as much in the way of sparks as it did heat. The food was simple but plentiful, and wine and beer, into which George made his customary inroads, appeared regularly on the table without having to be asked for. Socially, however, the meal was a disaster.

Silence makes an uncomfortable table companion. At a distant and small corner table, the truck-driver and his companion – really an armed guard who travelled with a Schmeisser under his seat and a Luger concealed about his person – talked almost continuously in low voices; but of the five at Petersen's table, three seemed afflicted with an almost permanent palsy of the tongue. Alex, remote and withdrawn, seemed, as was his wont, to be contemplating a bleak and hopeless future: the von Karajans who, by their own admission, had had no breakfast, barely picked at their food, had time and opportunity to talk, but rarely ventured a word except when directly addressed: Petersen, relaxed as ever, restricted himself to pleasantries and civilities but otherwise showed no signs of wishing to alleviate the conversational awkwardness or, indeed, to be aware of it: George, on the other hand, seemed to be acutely aware of it and did his talkative best to dispel it, even to the point of garrulity.

His conversational gambit took the form of questions directed exclusively at the von Karajans. It did not take him long to elicit the fact that they were, as Petersen had guessed, Slovenians of Austrian ancestry. They had been to primary school in Ljubljana, secondary school in Zagreb and thence to Cairo University.

'Cairo!' George tried to make his eyebrows disappear into his hairline. 'Cairo! What on earth induced you to go to that cultural backwater?'

'It was our parents' wish,' Michael said. He tried to be cold and distant but he only succeeded in sounding defensive.

'Cairo!' George repeated. He shook his head in slow disbelief. 'And what, may one ask, did you study there?'

'You ask a lot of questions,' Michael said.

'Interest,' George explained. 'A paternal interest. And, of course, a concern for the hapless youth of our unfortunate and disunited country.'

For the first time Sarina smiled, a very faint smile, it was true, but enough to give some indication of what she could do if she tried. 'I don't think such things would really interest you, Mr – ah –'

'Just call me George. How do you know what would interest me? All things interest me.'

'Economics and politics.'

'Good God!' George clapped a hand to his forehead. As a classical actor he would have starved: as a ham actor he was a nonpareil. 'Good heavens, girl, you go to Egypt to learn matters of such importance? Didn't they even teach you enough to make you realize that theirs is the poorest country in the Middle East, that their economy is not only a shambles but is in a state of total collapse and that they owe countless millions, sterling, dollars, any currency you care to name, to practically any country you care to name. So much for their economy. As for politics, they're no more than a political football for any country that

34

wants to play soccer on their arid and useless desert sands.'

George stopped briefly, perhaps to admire the eloquence of his own oratory, perhaps to await a response. None was forthcoming so he got back to his head-shaking.

'And what, one wonders, did your parents have against our premier institute of learning. I refer, of course, to the University of Belgrade.' He paused, as if in reflection. 'One admits that Oxford and Cambridge have their points. So, for that matter, does Heidelberg, the Sorbonne, Padua and one or two lesser educational centres. But, no, Belgrade is best.'

Again the faint smile from Sarina. 'You seem to know a great deal about universities, Mr – ah – George.'

George didn't smirk. Instead, he achieved the near impossible – he spoke with a lofty diffidence. 'I have been fortunate enough, for most of my adult life, to be associated with academics, among them some of the most eminent.' The von Karajans looked at each other for a long moment but said nothing: it was unnecessary for them to say that, in their opinion, any such association must have been on a strictly janitorial level. They probably assumed that he had learned his mode of speech when cleaning out common rooms or, it may have been, while waiting on high table. George gave no indication that he had noticed anything untoward, but, then, he never did.

'Well,' George said in his best judicial tones, 'far be it from me to visit the sins of the fathers upon their sons or, come to that, those of mothers upon their daughters.' Abruptly, he switched the subject. 'You are Royalists, of course.'

'Why "of course"?' Michael's voice was sharp.

George sighed. 'I would have hoped that that institute of lower learning on the Nile hadn't driven all the native sense out of your head. If you weren't a Royalist you wouldn't be coming with us. Besides, Major Petersen told me.'

Sarina looked briefly at Petersen. 'This is the way you treat confidences?'

'I wasn't aware it was a confidence.' Petersen gestured with an indifferent hand. 'It was too unimportant to rate as a confidence. In any event, George is my confidant.'

Sarina looked at him uncertainly, then lowered her eyes: the rebuke could have been real, implied or just imagined. George said: 'I'm just puzzled, you see. You're Royalists. Your parents, one must assume, are the same. It's not unusual for the royal family and those close to them to send their children abroad to be educated. But not to Cairo. To Northern Europe. Specifically, to England. The ties between the Yugoslav and British royal families are very close – especially the blood ties. What place did King Peter choose for his enforced exile? London, where he is now. The Prince Regent, Prince Paul, is in the care of the British.'

'They say in Cairo that he's a prisoner of the British.' Michael didn't seem particularly concerned about what they said in Cairo.

'Rubbish. He's in protective custody in Kenya. He's free to come and go. He makes regular withdrawals from a bank in London. Coutts, it's called – it also happens to be the bank of the British royal family. Prince Paul's closest friend in Europe – and his brother-in-law – is the Duke of Kent: well, he was until the Duke was killed in a flying-boat accident last year. And it's common knowledge that very soon he's going to South Africa, whose General Smuts is a particularly close friend of the British.'

'Ah, yes,' Michael said. 'You said you're puzzled. I'm puzzled too. This General Smuts has two South African divisions in North Africa fighting alongside the Eighth Army, no?'

'Yes.'

'Against the Germans?'

George showed an unusual trace of irritation. 'Who else would they be fighting?'

'So our royal family's friends in North Africa are fighting the Germans. We're Royalists, and we're fighting with the Germans, not against them. I mean it's all rather confusing.'

'I'm sure *you're* not confused.' Again Sarina's little smile. Petersen was beginning to wonder whether he would have to revise his first impression of her. 'Are you, George?'

'No confusion.' George waved a dismissive hand. 'Simply a temporary measure of convenience and expediency. We are fighting *with* the Germans, true, but we are not fighting *for* them. We are fighting for ourselves. When the Germans have served their purpose it will be time for them to be gone.' George refilled his beer mug, drained half the contents and sighed either in satisfaction or sorrow. 'We are consistently underestimated, a major part, as the rest of Europe sees it, of the insoluble Balkan problem. To me, there is no problem just a goal.' He raised his glass again. 'Yugoslavia.'

'Nobody's going to argue with that,' Petersen said. He looked at the girl. 'Speaking – as George has been doing at some length – of royalty, you mentioned last night you knew King Peter. How well?'

'He was Prince Peter then. Not well at all. Once or twice on formal occasions.'

'That's about how it was for me. I don't suppose we've exchanged more than a couple of dozen words. Bright lad, pleasant, should make a good king. Pity about his limp.'

'His what?'

'You know, his left foot.'

'Oh, that. Yes. I've wondered –'

'He doesn't talk about it. All sorts of sinister stories about how he was injured. All ridiculous. A simple hunting accident.' Petersen smiled. 'I shouldn't imagine there's much of a diplomatic future for a courtier who mistakes his future sovereign for a wild boar.' He lifted his eyes and right arm at the same time: the innkeeper came hurrying towards him. 'The bill, if you please.'

'The bill?' Momentarily the innkeeper gave the impression of being surprised, even taken aback. 'Ah, the bill. Of course. The bill. At once.' He hurried off.

Petersen looked at the von Karajans. 'Sorry you didn't have a better appetite – you know, stoked the furnaces for the last part of the trip. Still, it's downhill now all the way and we're heading for the Adriatic and a maritime climate. Should be getting steadily warmer.'

'Oh, no, it won't.' It was the first time Alex had spoken since they had entered the inn and, predictably, it was in tones of dark certainty. 'It's almost an hour since we came in here and the wind has got stronger. Much stronger. Listen and you can hear it.' They listened. They heard it, a deep, low-pitched, ululating moaning that boded no good at all. Alex shook his head gravely. 'An east-north-easter. All the way from Siberia. It's going to be very cold.' His voice sounded full of gloomy satisfaction but it meant nothing, it was the only way he knew how to talk. 'And when the sun goes down, it's going to be very *very* cold.'

'Job's comforter,' Petersen said. He looked at the bill the innkeeper had brought, handed over some notes, waved away the proffered change and said: 'Do you think we could buy some blankets from you?'

'Blankets?' The innkeeper frowned in some puzzlement: it was, after all, an unusual request.

'Blankets. We've a long way to go, there's no heating in our transport and the afternoon and evening are going to be very cold.'

'There will be no problem.' The innkeeper disappeared and was back literally within a minute with an armful of heavy coloured woollen blankets which he deposited on a nearby empty table. 'Those will be sufficient?'

'More than sufficient. Most kind of you.' Petersen produced money. 'How much, please?'

'Blankets?' The innkeeper lifted his hands in protest. 'I am not a shopkeeper. I do not charge for blankets.'

'But you must. I insist. Blankets cost money.'

'Please.' The truckdriver had left his table and approached them. 'I shall be passing back this way tomorrow. I shall bring them with me.'

Petersen thanked them and so it was arranged. Alex, followed by the von Karajans, helped the innkeeper carry the blankets out to the truck. Petersen and George lingered briefly in the porch, closing both the inner and outer doors.

'You really are the most fearful liar, George,' Petersen said admiringly. 'Cunning. Devious. I've said it before, I don't think I'd care to be interrogated by you. You ask a question and whether people say yes, no or nothing at all you still get your answer.'

'When you've spent twenty-five of the best years of your life dealing with dim-witted students – ' George shrugged as if there were no more to say.

'I'm not a dim-witted student but I still wouldn't care for it. You have formed an opinion about our young friends?'

'I have.'

'So have I. I've also formed another opinion about them and that is that while Michael is no intellectual giant, the girl could bear watching. I think she could be clever.'

'I've often observed this with brother and sister, especially when they're twins. I share your opinion. Lovely and clever.'

Petersen smiled. 'A dangerous combination?'

'Not if she's nice. I've no reason to think she's not nice.'

'You're just middle-aged and susceptible. The innkeeper?'

'Apprehensive and unhappy. He doesn't look like a man who should be apprehensive and unhappy, he looks a big tough character who would be perfectly at home throwing big tough drunks out of his inn. Also, he seemed caught off-balance when you offered to pay for the meal. One got the unmistakable impression that there are some travellers who do not pay for their meals. Also his refusal to accept money for the blankets was out of character. Out of character for an Italian, I mean, for I've never known of an

Italian who wasn't ready, eager rather, to make a deal on some basis or other. Peter, my friend, wouldn't even you be slightly nervous if you worked for, or were forced to work for the German SS?'

'Colonel Lunz casts a long shadow. The waiter?'

'The Gestapo have fallen in my estimation. When they send in an espionage agent in the guise of a waiter they should at least give him some training in the rudiments of table-waiting. I felt positively embarrassed for him.' George paused, then went on: 'You were talking about King Peter a few minutes ago.'

'You introduced that subject.'

'That's irrelevant and don't hedge. As a departmental head in the university I was regarded – and rightly – as being a man of culture. Prince Paul was nothing if not a man of culture although his interests lay more in the world of art than in philology. Never mind. We met quite a few times, either in the university or at royal functions in the city. More to the point, I saw Prince Peter – as he was then – two or three times. He didn't have a limp in those days.'

'He still doesn't.'

George looked at him then nodded slowly. 'And you called me devious.'

Petersen opened the outer door and clapped him on the shoulder. 'We live in devious times, George.'

*   *   *

The second half of the trip was an improvement on the first but just marginally. Cocooned, as they were, to the ears in heavy blankets, the von Karajans were no longer subject to involuntary bouts of shivering and teeth-chattering but otherwise looked no happier and were no more communicative than they had been in the morning, which meant that they were both totally miserable and silent. They didn't even speak when George, shouting to make himself heard above the fearful mechanical din, offered them brandy to relieve their sufferings. Sarina shuddered and Michael shook his head. They may have been wise for what George was offering them was no French cognac but his own near-lethal form of slivovitz, his native plum brandy.

Some twelve kilometres from Pescara they bore right off the Route 5 near Chieti, reaching the Adriatic coast road at Francavilla as a premature dusk was falling – premature, because of gathering banks of dark grey cloud which Alex, inevitably, said could only presage heavy snow. The coastal road, Route 16 was an improvement over the Apennines road – it could hardly have failed to be otherwise – and the relatively comfortable though still cacophonous ride to Termoli took no more than two hours. Wartime Termoli, on a winter's night, was no place to inspire a rhapsody in the heart of the poet or composer: the only feelings it could reasonably expect to give rise to were gloom and depression. It was grey, bleak, bare, grimy and seemingly uninhabited except for a very few half-heartedly blacked-out premises which were presumably cafés or taverns. The port area itself, however, was an improvement on Rome: here was no blackout, just a dimout which probably didn't vary appreciably from the normal. As the truck stopped along a wharf-side there was more than enough light from the shaded yellow overhead lamps to distinguish the lines of the craft alongside the wharf, their transport to Yugoslavia.

That it was a motor torpedo boat was beyond question. Its vintage was uncertain. What was certain was that it had been in the wars. It had sustained considerable, though not incapacitating, damage to both hull and superstructure. No attempt had been made at repair: no-one had even thought it worthwhile to repaint the numerous dents and scars that pockmarked its side. It carried no torpedoes, for the sufficient reason that the torpedo tubes had been removed; nor had it depth-charges, for even the depth-charge racks had been removed. The only armament, if such it could be called, that it carried was a pair of insignificant little guns, single-barrelled, one mounted for'ard of the bridge, the other on the poop. They looked suspiciously like Hotchkiss repeaters, one of the most notoriously inaccurate weapons ever to find its mistaken way into naval service.

A tall man in a vaguely naval uniform was standing on the wharf-side at the head of the

MTB's gangway. He wore a peaked badgeless naval cap which shaded his face but could not conceal his marked stoop and splendid snow-white Buffalo Bill beard. He raised his hand in half-greeting, half-salute as Petersen, the others following close behind, approached him.

'Good evening. My name is Pietro. You must be the Major we are expecting.'

'Good evening and yes.'

'And four companions, one a lady. Good. You are welcome aboard. I will send someone for your luggage. In the meantime, it is the commanding officer's wish that you see him as soon as you arrive.'

They followed him below and into a compartment that could have been the captain's cabin, a chart-room, an officers' mess-room and was probably all three: space is at a premium on MTBs. The captain was seated at his desk, writing, as Pietro entered without benefit of knocking. He swung round in his swivel-chair which was firmly bolted to the deck as Pietro stood to one side and said: 'Your latest guests, Carlos. The Major and the four friends we were promised.'

'Come in, come in, come in. Thank you, Pietro. Send that young ruffian along, will you?'

'When he's finished loading the luggage?'

'That'll do.' Pietro left. The captain was a broad-shouldered young man with thick curling black hair, a deep tan, very white teeth, a warm smile and warm brown eyes. He said: 'I'm Lieutenant

Giancarlo Tremino. Call me Carlos. Nearly everyone else does. No discipline left in the Navy.' He shook his head and indicated his white polo neck jersey and grey flannel trousers. 'Why wear uniform? No-one pays any attention to it anyway.' He extended his hand – his left hand – to Petersen. 'Major, you are very welcome. I cannot offer you Queen Mary type accommodation – peacetime accommodation, that is – but we have a very few small cabins, washing and toilet facilities, lots of wine and can guarantee safe transit to Ploče. The guarantee is based on the fact that we have been to the Dalmatian coast many times and haven't been sunk yet. Always a first time, of course, but I prefer to dwell on happier things.'

'You are very kind,' Petersen said. 'If it's to be first name terms, then mine is Peter.' He introduced the other four, each by their first name. Carlos acknowledged each introduction with a handshake and smile but made no attempt to rise. He was quick to explain this seeming discourtesy and quite unembarrassed about doing so.

'I apologize for remaining seated. I'm not really ill-mannered or lazy or averse to physical exertion.' He moved his right arm and, for the first time, brought his glove-sheathed right hand into view. He bent and tapped his right hand against his right leg, about halfway between knee and ankle. The unmistakable sound of hollow metal meeting hollow metal made the onlookers wince. He straightened and tapped the tips of his left fingers against the back of his right glove. The sound was against unmistakable although different – flesh meeting metal. 'Those metal appliances take some getting used to.' Carlos was almost apologetic. 'Unnecessary movement – well, any movement – causes discomfort and who likes discomfort? I am not the noblest Roman of them all.'

Sarina gnawed her lower lip. Michael tried to look as if he weren't shocked but was. The other three, with eighteen months of vicious and bitter warfare in the Yugoslav mountains behind them, predictably showed no reaction. Petersen said: 'Right hand, right leg. That's quite a handicap.'

'Just the right foot really – blown off at the ankle. Handicap? Have you heard of the English fighter pilot who got both legs destroyed? Did he shout for a bath-chair? He shouted to get back into the cockpit of his Spitfire or whatever. He did, too. Handicap!'

'I know of him. Most people do. How did you come by those two – um – trifling scratches?'

'Perfidious Albion,' Carlos said cheerfully. 'Nasty, horrible British. Never trust them. To think they used to be my best friends before the war – sailed with them in the Adriatic and the Channel, raced against them at Cowes – well, never mind. We were in the Aegean going, as the lawyers say, about our lawful occasions and bothering no-one. Dawn, lots of heavy mist about when suddenly, less than two kilometres away, this great big British warship appeared through a gap in the mist.'

Carlos paused, perhaps for effect, and Petersen said mildly: 'It was my understanding that the British never risked their capital ships north of Crete.'

'Size, like beauty, is in the eye of the beholder. It was, in fact, a very small frigate, but to us, you understand, it looked like a battleship. We weren't ready for them but they were ready for us – they had their guns already trained on us. No fault of ours – we had four men, not counting myself, on lookout: they must have had radar, we had none. Their first two shells struck the water only a few metres from our port side and exploded on contact: didn't do our hull much good, I can tell you. Two other light shells, about a kilo each, I should think – pom-poms, the British call them – scored direct hits. One penetrated the engine-room and put an engine out of action – I regret to say it's still out of action but we can get by without it – and the other came into the wheelhouse.'

'A kilo of explosives going off in a confined space is not very nice,' Petersen said. 'You were not alone?'

'Two others. They were not as lucky as I was. Then I had more luck – we ran into a fog bank.' Carlos shrugged. 'That's all. The past is past.'

A knock came at the door. A very young sailor entered, stood at attention, saluted and said: 'You sent for me, Captain.'

'Indeed. We have guests, Pietro. Tired, thirsty guests.'

'Right away, Captain.' The boy saluted and left.

Petersen said: 'What's all this you were saying about no discipline?'

Carlos smiled: 'Give him time. He's been with us for only a month.'

George looked puzzled. 'He is a truant from school, no?'

'He's older than he looks. Well, at least three months older.'

'Quite an age span you have aboard,' Petersen said. 'The elder Pietro. He can't be a day under seventy.'

'He's a great number of days over seventy.' Carlos laughed. The world seemed to be a source of constant amusement to him. 'A so-called captain with only two out of four functioning limbs. A beardless youth. An old age pensioner. What a crew. Just wait till you see the rest of them.'

Petersen said: 'The past is past, you say. Accepted. One may ask a question about the present?' Carlos nodded. 'Why haven't you been retired, invalided out of the Navy or at very least given some sort of shore job? Why are you still on active service?'

'Active service?' Carlos laughed again. 'Highly inactive service. The moment we run into anything resembling action I hand in my commission. You saw the two light guns we have mounted fore and aft? It was just pride that made me keep them there. They'll never be used for either attack or defence for the perfectly adequate reason that neither works. This is a very undemanding assignment and I do have one modest qualification for it. I was born and brought up in Pescara where my father had a yacht – more than one. I spent my boyhood and the ridiculously long university vacations sailing. Around the Mediterranean and Europe for part of the time but mainly off the Yugoslav coast. The Adriatic coast of Italy is dull and uninteresting, with not an island worth mentioning between Bari and Venice: the thousand and one Dalmatian islands are a paradise for the cruising yachtsman. I know them better than I know the streets of Pescara or Termoli. The Admiralty finds this useful.'

'On a black night?' Petersen said. 'No lighthouses, no lit buoys, no land-based navigational aids?'

'If I required those I wouldn't be much use to the Admiralty, would I? Ah! Help is at hand.'

It took young Pietro an heroic effort not to stagger under the weight of his burden, a vertically-sided, flat-bottomed wicker basket holding the far from humble nucleus of a small but well-stocked bar. In addition to spirits, wines and liqueurs, Pietro had even gone to the length of providing a soda syphon and a small ice-bucket.

'Pietro hasn't yet graduated to bar-tender and I've no intention of leaving this chair,' Carlos said. 'Help yourselves, please. Thank you, Pietro. Ask our two passengers to join us at their convenience.' The boy saluted and left. 'Two other Yugoslav-bound passengers. I don't know their business as I don't know yours. You don't know theirs and they don't know yours. Ships that pass in the night. But such ships exchange recognition signals. Courtesy of the high seas.'

Petersen gestured at the basket from which George was already helping the von Karajans to orange juice. 'Another courtesy of the high seas. Lessens the rigours of total war, I must say.'

'My feeling exactly. No thanks, I may say, to our Admiralty who are as stingy as Admiralties the world over. Some of the supplies come from my father's wine cellars – they would have your three-star sommeliers in raptures, I can tell you – some are gifts from foreign friends.'

'Kruškovac.' George touched a bottle. 'Grappa. Pelinkovac. Stara Šljivovica. Two excellent vintages from the Neretva delta. Your foreign friends. All from Yugoslavia. Our hospitable and considerate young friend, Pietro. Clairvoyant? He thinks we go to Yugoslavia? Or has he been informed?'

'Suspicion, one would suppose, is part of your stock-in-trade. I don't know what Pietro thinks. I don't even know if he *can* think. He hasn't been informed. He knows.' Carlos sighed. 'The romance and glamour of the cloak-and-dagger, sealed-orders missions are not, I'm afraid, for us. Search Termoli and you might find a person who is deaf, dumb and blind, although I much doubt it. If you did, he or she would be the only person in Termoli who doesn't know that the *Colombo* – that's the name of this crippled greyhound – plies a regular and so far highly dependable ferry-service to the Yugoslav coast. If it's any consolation, I'm the only person who knows *where* we're going. Unless, of course, one of you has talked.' He poured himself a small scotch. 'Your health, gentlemen. And yours, young lady.'

'We don't talk much about such things, but about other things I'm afraid I talk too much.' George sounded sad but at once refuted himself. 'University, eh? Some kind of marine school?'

'Some kind of medical school.'

'Medical school.' With the air of a man treating himself for shock George poured some more grappa. 'Don't tell me you're a doctor.'

'I'm not telling you anything. But I have a paper that says so.'

Petersen waved a hand. 'Then why this?'

'Well you might ask.' Momentarily, Carlos sounded as sad as George had done. 'The Italian Navy. Any navy. Take a highly skilled mechanic, obvious material for an equally highly skilled engine-room-artificer. What does he become? A cook. A cordon bleu chef? A gunner.' He waved his hand much as Petersen had done. 'So, in their all-knowing wisdom, they gave me this. Dr Tremino, ferryman, first class. Considering the state of the ferry, make that second class.

Come in, come in.' A knock had come on the door.

The young woman who stepped over the low coaming – she could have been anything between twenty and thirty-five – was of medium height, slender and dressed in a jersey, jacket and skirt, all in blue. Pale-complexioned, without a trace of make-up, she was grave and unsmiling. Her hair was black as night and swooped low, like a raven's wing, over the left forehead, quite obscuring the left eyebrow. The pock-marking, for such it seemed to be, high up on the left cheekbone, served only to accentuate, not diminish, the classical, timeless beauty of the features: twenty years on, just as conceivably thirty, she would still be as beautiful as she was at that moment. Nor, it seemed certain, would time ever change the appearance of the man who followed her into the cabin, but the sculpted perfection of features had nothing to do with this. A tall, solidly built, fair-haired character, he was irredeemably ugly. Nature had had no hand in this. From the evidence offered by ears, cheeks, chin, nose and teeth he had been in frequent and violent contact with a variety of objects, both blunt and razor-edged, in the course of what must have been a remarkably chequered career, It was, withal, an attractive face, largely because of the genuine warmth of his smile: as with Carlos, an almost irrepressible cheerfulness was never far from the surface.

'This,' Carlos said, 'is Lorraine and Giacomo.' He introduced Petersen and the other four in turn. Lorraine's voice was soft and low, in tone and timbre remarkably like that of Sarina: Giacomo's, predictably, was neither soft nor low and his hand-clasp fearsome except when it came to Sarina: her fingers he took in his finger and thumb and gallantly kissed the back of her hand. Such a gesture from such a man should have appeared both affected and stagey: oddly enough, it did neither. Sarina didn't seem to think so either. She said nothing, just smiled at him, the first genuine smile Petersen had seen from her: it came as no surprise that her teeth would have been a dentist's delight or despair, depending upon whether aesthetic or financial considerations were uppermost in his mind.

'Help yourselves,' Carlos gestured to the wicker basket. Giacomo, leaving no doubt that he was decisive both as to cast of mind and action, needed no second urging. He poured a glass of Pellegrino for Lorraine, evidence enough that this was not the first time he had met her and that she shared the von Karajans' aversion towards alcohol, and then half-filled a tumbler with scotch, topping it up with water. He took a seat and beamed around the company.

'Health to all.' He raised his brimming glass. 'And confusion to our enemies.'

'Any particular enemies?' Carlos said.

'It would take too long.' Giacomo tried to look sad but failed. 'I have too many.' He drank deeply to his own toast. 'You have called us to a conference, Captain Carlos?'

'Conference, Giacomo? Goodness me, no.' It didn't require any great deductive powers, Petersen reflected, to realize that those two had met before and not just that day. 'Why should I hold a conference? My job is to get you where you're going and you can't help me in that. After you land I can't help you in whatever you're going to do. Nothing to confer about. As a ferryman, I'm a great believer in introductions. People in your line of business are apt to react over-quickly if, rightly or wrongly, they sense danger in meeting an unknown on a dark deck at night. No such danger now. And there are three things I want to mention briefly.

'First, accommodation. Lorraine and Giacomo have a cabin each, if you can call something the size of a telephone box a cabin. Only fair. First come, first served. I have two other cabins, one for three, one for two.' He looked at Michael. 'You and – yes, Sarina – are brother and sister?'

'Who told you?' Michael probably didn't mean to sound truculent, but his nervous system had suffered from his encounter with Petersen and his friends, and that was the way it came out.

Carlos lowered his head briefly, looked up and said, not smiling, 'The good Lord gave me eyes and they say "twins".'

'No problem.' Giacomo bowed towards the embarrassed girl. 'The young lady will do me the honour of switching cabins with me?'

She smiled and nodded. 'You are very kind.'

'Second. Food. You could eat aboard but I don't recommend it. Giovanni cooks only under duress and protest. I don't blame him. He's our engineer. Everything that comes out of that galley, even the coffee, tastes and smells of oil. There's a passable café close by – well, barely passable, but they do know me.' He half-smiled at the two women in turn. 'It will be a hardship and a sacrifice but I think I'll join you.

'Third. You're free to go ashore whenever you wish, although I can't imagine why anyone should want to go ashore on a night like this – except, of course, to escape Giovanni's cooking. There are police patrols but their enthusiasm usually drops with the temperature. If you do run into any, just say you're from the *Colombo*: the worst that can happen is that they'll escort you back here to check.'

'I think I'll take my chance on both weather and the police,' Petersen said. 'Advancing years or too many hours in that damned truck or maybe both, but I'm as stiff as a board.'

'Back inside an hour, please, then we'll leave for the meal.' He looked at the bulkhead clock. 'We should be back at ten. We sail at one o'clock in the morning.'

'Not till then?' Michael looked his astonishment. 'Why, that's hours away. Why don't we –'

'We sail at 1.00 a.m.' Carlos was patient.

'But the wind's getting stronger. It must be rough now. It'll be getting rougher.'

'It will not be too comfortable. Are you a bad sailor, Michael?' The words were sympathetic, the expression not.

'No. Yes. I don't know. I don't see – I mean, I can't understand –'

'Michael.' It was Petersen, his voice gentle. 'It really doesn't matter what you can't see or can't understand. Lieutenant Tremino is the captain. The captain makes the decisions. No-one *ever* questions the captain.'

'It's very simple, really.' It was noticeable that Carlos spoke to Petersen not Michael. 'The garrison that guard such port installations as they have at Ploče are not first-line troops. As soldiers go, they are either superannuated or very very young. In both cases they're nervous and trigger-happy and the fact that they have radio notification of my arrival seems to have no effect on them. Experience and a few lucky escapes have taught me that the wisest thing is to arrive at sunrise so that even the most rheumy eyes can see that the gallant Captain Tremino is flying the biggest Italian flag in the Adriatic.'

The wind, as Michael had said, had indeed strengthened, and was bitingly cold but Petersen and his two companions were not exposed to it for long, for George's homing instinct was unerring.

The tavern in which they fetched up was no more or less dingy than any other dockside tavern and it was at least warm.

'A very short stroll for such stiff legs,' George observed.

'Nothing wrong with my legs. I just wanted to talk.'

'What was wrong with our cabin? Carlos has more wine and grappa and slivovitz than he can possibly use –'

'Colonel Lunz, as we've said, has a long arm.'

'Ah! So! A bug?'

'Would you put anything past him? This could be awkward.'

'Alas, I'm afraid I know what you mean.'

'I don't.' Alex wore his suspicious expression.

'Carlos,' Petersen said. 'I know him. Rather, I know who he is. I knew his father, a retired naval captain but on the reserve list: almost certainly on the active list now, a cruiser captain or such. He became a reserve Italian naval captain at the same time as my father became a reserve Yugoslav army colonel. Both men loved the sea and both men set up chandlers' businesses: both were highly successful. Inevitably, almost, their paths crossed and they became very good friends. They met frequently, usually in Trieste and I was with them on several occasions. Photographs were taken. Carlos may well have seen them.'

'If he has seen them,' George said, 'let it be our pious hope that the ravages of time and the dissipation of years make it difficult for Carlos to identify Major Petersen with the carefree youth of yesteryear.'

Alex said: 'Why is it so important?'

'I have known Colonel Petersen for many years,' George said. 'Unlike his son, he is, or was, a very outspoken man.'

'Ah!'

'A pity about Carlos, a great pity.' George sounded, and may well have been, profoundly sad. 'An eminently likeable young man. And you can say the same about Giacomo – except, of course, not so young. An excellent pair to have by one's side, one would have thought, in moments of trouble and strife, which are the only ones we seem to have.' He shook his head. 'Where, oh where, are my ivory towers?'

'You should be grateful for this touch of realism, George. Exactly the counter-balance you academics need. What do you make of Giacomo? An Italian counterpart of the British commando?'

'Giacomo has been savagely beaten up or savagely tortured or perhaps both at the same time. Commando material unquestionably. But not Italian. Montenegrin.'

'Montenegrin!'

'You know. Montenegro.' George, on occasion, was capable of elaborate sarcasm, an unfortunate gift honed and refined by a lifetime in the groves of academe. 'A province in our native Yugoslavia.'

'With that fair hair and impeccable Italian?'

'Fair hair is not unknown in Montenegro and though his Italian is very good the accent overlay is unmistakable.'

Petersen didn't doubt him for a moment. George's ear for languages, dialects, accents and nuances of accent was, in philological circles, a byword far beyond the Balkans.

The evening meal was more than passable, the café more than presentable. Carlos was not only known there, as he had said, but treated with some deference. Lorraine spoke only occasionally and then to no-one except Carlos, who sat beside her. She, too, had, it seemed been born in Pescara. Predictably, neither Alex nor Michael nor Sarina contributed a word to the conversation but that didn't matter. Both Carlos and Petersen were relaxed and easy talkers but even that didn't matter very much: when Giacomo and George were in full cry, more often than not at the same time, even the possibility of a conversational hiatus seemed preposterous: both men talked a great deal without saying anything at all.

On the way back to the ship they had to face not only a perceptibly stronger wind but a thinly driving snow. Carlos, who had drunk little enough, was not so sure on his feet as he thought or, more likely, would have others think. After the second stumble he was seen to be walking arm in arm with Lorraine: who had taken whose arm could only be guessed at. When they arrived at the gangway, the *Colombo* was rocking perceptibly at its moorings: the harbour swell responsible bespoke much worse conditions outside.

To Petersen's surprise and an ill-concealed irritation that amounted almost to anger, five more men were awaiting their arrival down below. Their leader, who was introduced as Alessandro, and for whom Carlos showed an unusual degree of respect, was a tall, thin, grey-haired man with a beaked nose, bloodless lips and only the rudimentary vestiges of eyebrows. Three of his four men, all about half his age, were introduced as Franco, Cola and Sepp, which names were presumably abbreviations for Francesco, Nicholas and Giuseppe: the fourth was called Guido. Like their leader, they wore nondescript civilian clothes. Like their leader they gave the distinct impression that they would have been much happier in uniform: like their leader they had cold, hard, expressionless faces.

Petersen glanced briefly at George, turned and left the cabin, George following with Alex, inevitably, close behind. Petersen had barely begun to speak when Carlos appeared in the passage-way and walked quickly towards them.

'You are upset, Major Petersen?' No 'Peter'. The trace of anxiety was faint but it was there.

'I'm unhappy. It is true, as I told Michael, that one never questions the captain's decisions but this is a different matter entirely. I take it those men are also passengers to Ploče?' Carlos nodded. 'Where are they sleeping?'

'We have a dormitory for five in the bows. I did not think that worth mentioning, any more than I thought their arrival worth mentioning.'

'I am also unhappy at the fact that Rome gave me the distinct impression that we would be travelling alone. I did not bargain for the fact that we would be travelling with five – seven now – people who are totally unknown to me.

'I am unhappy about the fact that you know them or, at least, Alessandro.' Carlos made to speak but Petersen waved him to silence. 'I'm sure you wouldn't think me such a fool as to deny it. It's just not in your nature to show a deference amounting almost to apprehension towards a total stranger.

'Finally, I'm unhappy about the fact that they have the appearance of being a bunch of hired, professional assassins, tough ruthless killers. They are, of course, nothing of the kind, they only think they are, which is why I use the word "appearance". Their only danger lies in their lack of predictability. For your true assassin, no such word as unpredictability exists in his vocabulary. He does precisely what he intends to do. And it is to be borne in mind, when it comes to the far from gentle art of premeditated and authorized murder, your true assassin never, never, never looks like one.'

'You seem to know a lot about assassins.' Carlos smiled faintly. 'I could be speaking to three of them.'

'Preposterous!' George was incapable of snorting but he came close.

'Giacomo, then?'

'One is left with the impression that Giacomo is a one-man panzer division,' Petersen said. 'Cold-blooded stealth is not his forte. He doesn't even begin to qualify. You should know – you know him much better than we do.'

'What makes you say that?'

'Because acting isn't *your* forte.'

'So our school drama teacher said. Lorraine?'

'You're mad.' George spoke with conviction.

'He doesn't mean you are.' Petersen smiled. 'Just the suggestion. Classically beautiful women almost never have gentle eyes.'

Carlos confirmed what seemed to be the growing opinion that he was indeed no actor. He was pleased, and not obscurely. He said: 'If you're unhappy, then I apologize for that although I really don't know why I'm apologizing. I have orders to carry out and it's my duty to follow orders. Beyond that, I know nothing.' He still wasn't a very good actor, Petersen thought, but there was nothing to be gained in saying so. 'Won't you come back to my cabin? Three hours before we sail yet. Ample time for a nightcap. Or two. Alessandro and his men, as you say, aren't so ferocious as they look.'

'Thank you,' Petersen said. 'But no. I think we'll just take a turn on the upper deck and then retire. So we'll say goodnight now.'

'The upper deck? This weather? You'll freeze.'

'Cold is an old friend of ours.'

'I prefer other company. But as you wish, gentlemen.' He reached out a steadying hand as the *Colombo* lurched sharply. 'A rather rough passage tonight, I'm afraid. Torpedo boats may have their good points – I may find one some day – but they are rather less than sea-kindly. I hope you are also on friendly terms with Father Neptune.'

'Our next of kin,' George said.

'That apart, I can promise you a quiet and uneventful trip. Never had a mutiny yet.'

In the lee of the superstructure Petersen said: 'Well?'

'Well?' George said heavily. 'All is not well. Seven total strangers aboard this boat and the worthy young Carlos seems to know all seven of them. Every man's hand against us. Not, of course, that that's anything new.' The tip of his nauseous cigar glowed redly in the gloom. 'Would it be naïve of me to wonder whether or not our good friend Colonel Lunz is acquainted with the passenger list of the *Colombo*?'

'Yes.'

'We are, of course, prepared for all eventualities?'

'Certainly. Which ones did you have in mind?'

'None. We take turns to keep watch in our cabin?'

'Of course. If we stay in our cabin.'

'Ah! We have a plan?'

'We have no plan. What do you think about Lorraine?'

'Charming. I speak unhesitatingly. A delightful young lady.'

'I've told you before, George. About your advanced years and susceptibility. That wasn't what I meant. Her presence aboard puzzles me. I can't see that she belongs in any way to this motley bunch that Carlos is transporting to Ploče.'

'Motley, eh? First time I've ever been called motley. How does she differ?'

'Because every other passenger on this vessel is up to no good or I strongly suspect them of being up to no good. I suspect her of nothing.'

'My word!' George spoke in tones of what were meant to be genuine awe. 'That makes her unique.'

'Carlos let us know – he could have been at pains to let us know – that she, too, came from Pescara. Do you think she comes from Pescara, George?'

'How the devil should I tell? She could come from Timbuktu for all I know.'

'You disappoint me, George. Or wilfully misunderstand me. I shall be patient. Your unmatched command of the nuances of all those European languages. Was she born or brought up in Pescara?'

'Neither.'

'But she is Italian?'

'No.'

'So we're back in Yugoslavia again?'

'Maybe you are. I'm not. I'm in England.'

'What! England?'

'The overlay of what it pleases the British Broadcasting Corporation to call Southern Standard English is unmistakable.' George coughed modestly, his smugness could occasionally verge on the infuriating. 'To the trained ear, of course.'

THREE

Both Alex and Carlos had made predictions and both had turned out to be wrong or, in Alex's case, half wrong. He had said, gloomily and accurately, that it was going to be very very cold and at three a.m. that morning none of the passengers on the *Colombo* would have disagreed with him. The driving snow, so heavy as to reduce visibility to virtually zero, had an uncommonly chilling effect on the torpedo boat, which would have been of no concern to those in an adequately central-heated boat but on this particular one the central-heating unit, as became practically everything else aboard, was functioning at about only one-third degree efficiency and, moreover, had been of a pathetically ancient design in the first place so that for the shivering passengers – and crew – the snow had become a matter for intense concern.

Alex had been wrong, even if only slightly – and what he had said had been a statement, really, not a fact – when he spoke of an east-north-east wind. It was a north-east wind. To a layman or, indeed, anybody not aboard an elderly torpedo boat, a paltry twenty-three degree difference in wind direction might seem negligible: to a person actually aboard such a boat the difference is crucial, marking, as it did for those with inbuilt queasiness, the border-line between the uncomfortable and the intolerable. Had the *Colombo* been head-on to wind and seas, the pitching would have been uncomfortable: had the seas been on the beam, the rolling would have been even more uncomfortable: but, that night, with the seas two points off the port bow, the resultant wicked corkscrewing was, for the less fortunate, the last straw. For some people aboard the torpedo boat that night, the degree of sea-sickness ranged from the unpleasant to the acute.

Carlos had predicted that the trip would be quiet and uneventful. At least two people, both, at least outwardly, immune to the effects of sea and cold, did not share Carlos' confidence. The door to the bo'sun's store, which lay to the port hand of the stairway leading down to the engine-room, had been hooked open and Petersen and Alex, standing two feet back in the unlit store, were only dimly visible. There was just enough light to see that Alex was carrying a semi-automatic machine-pistol while Petersen, using one hand to steady himself on the lurching deck had the other in his coat pocket. Petersen had long ago learned that with Alex by his side when confronting minimal forces, it was quite superfluous for him to carry a weapon of any kind.

Their little cabin, almost directly opposite them on the starboard side of the ill but sufficiently lit passage-way, had its door closed. George, Petersen knew, was still behind that door: and George, Petersen also knew, would be as wide awake as themselves. Petersen looked at his luminous watch. For just over ninety minutes he and Alex had been on station with no signs of weariness or boredom or awareness of the cold and certainly with no signs of their relaxed vigilance weakening at any time: a hundred times they had waited thus on the bleak and often icy mountains of Bosnia and Serbia and Montenegro, most commonly for much longer periods than this: and always they had survived. But that night was going to be one of their shorter and more comfortable vigils.

It was in the ninety-third minute that two men appeared at the for'ard end of the passage-way. They moved swiftly aft, crouched low as if making a stealthy approach, an attempt in which they were rather handicapped by being flung from bulkhead to bulkhead with every lurch of the *Colombo*: they had tried to compensate for this by removing their boots, no doubt to reduce the noise level of their approach, a rather ludicrous tactic in the circumstances because the torpedo boat was banging and crashing about to such a high decibel extent that they could have marched purposefully along in hob-nailed boots without anyone being any way the wiser. Each had a pistol stuck in his belt: more ominously, each carried in his right hand an object that looked suspiciously like a hand-grenade.

They were Franco and Cola and neither was looking particularly happy. That their expressions were due to the nature of the errand on hand or to twinges of conscience Petersen did not for a moment believe: quite simply, neither had been born with the call of the sea in his ear and, from the lack of colour in their strained faces, both would have been quite happy never to hear it again. On the logical assumption that Alessandro would have picked his two fittest young lieutenants, for the job on hand, Petersen thought, their appearance didn't say too much for the condition of those who had been left behind. Their cabin was right up in the bows of the vessel and in a cork-screwing sea that was the place to be avoided above all. They halted outside the door behind which George was lurking and looked at each other. Petersen waited until the boat was on even keel, bringing with it a comparative, if brief, period of silence.

'Don't move!'

Franco, at least, had some sense: he didn't move. Cola, on the other hand, amply demonstrated Petersen's assertion that they weren't hired assassins but only tried to look like ones, by dropping his grenade – he had to be right-handed – reaching for his pistol and swinging round, all in what he plainly hoped was one swift coordinated movement: for a man like Alex it was a scene in pathetically slow motion. Cola had just cleared the pistol from his left waistband when Alex fired, just once, the sound of the shot shockingly loud in the metallic confines. Cola dropped his gun, looked uncomprehendingly at his shattered right shoulder then, back to the bulkhead, he slid to the deck in a sitting position.

'They never learn,' Alex said gloomily. Alex was not one to derive childish pleasure from such childishly simply exercises.

'Maybe he's never had the chance to learn,' Petersen said. He relieved Franco of his armoury and had just picked up Cola's pistol and grenade when George appeared in the cabin doorway. He, too, carried a weapon but had had no expectation of using it: he held his semi-automatic loosely by the stock, its muzzle pointing towards the deck. He shook his head just once, resignedly, but said nothing.

Petersen said: 'Mind our backs, George.'

'You are going to return those unfortunates to the bosom of their family?' Petersen nodded. 'A Christian act. They're not fit to be out alone.'

Petersen and Alex moved back up the passage-way preceded by Franco and Cola, the former supporting his stricken comrade. They had taken only four steps when a door on the port side, just aft of where George was standing, opened and Giacomo stepped out into the passage-way, brandishing a Biretta.

'Put that thing away,' George said. His machine-pistol was still pointing at the deck. 'Don't you think there has been enough noise already?'

'That's why I'm here.' Giacomo had already lowered his gun. 'The noise, I mean.'

'Took your time, didn't you?'

'I had to get dressed first,' Giacomo said with some dignity. He was clad only in a pair of khaki trousers, displaying a tanned chest rather impressively criss-crossed with scars. 'But I notice you are fully dressed, so I take it you were expecting whatever did happen.' He looked in the direction of the quartet making their slow way along the passage-way. 'What exactly did happen?'

'Alex has just shot Cola.'

'Good for Alex.' If Giacomo was moved by the news he hid it well. 'Hardly worth wakening a man for.'

'Cola might view matters differently.' George coughed delicately. 'You are not, then, one of them?'

'You must be mad.'

'Not really. I don't know any of you, do I? But you don't *look* like them.'

'You're very kind, George. And now?'

'We won't find out just by standing here.'

They caught up with the others in just a matter of seconds which was easily enough done as the now moaning Cola could barely drag his feet along. A moment afterwards a door at the for'ard end of the passage-way opened and an armed figure came – or lurched – into view. It was Sepp and he wasn't looking at all like the ruthless killer of a few hours ago. It required no imagination to see the slightly greenish pallor on his face, for slightly green he indisputably was: time and the seaway had wrought its effect. It was not difficult to understand why Alessandro had selected Franco and Cola for the mission.

'Sepp.' Petersen's tone was almost kindly. 'We have no wish to kill you. Before you can reach us, you would have to kill your two friends, Franco and Cola. That would be bad enough, wouldn't it, Sepp?' From Sepp's pallor and general demeanour of uncertainty it seemed, that for him, things were quite bad enough as they were. 'Even worse, Sepp, before you could get around to killing the second of your friends, you yourself would be dead. Drop that gun, Sepp.'

Whatever other parts of Sepp's physiology were in a state of temporary dysfunction there was nothing wrong with his hearing. His elderly Lee Enfield .303 clattered to the deck.

'Who fired that shot?' Carlos, his habitual smile in momentary abeyance, had come limping up behind them, a pistol in hand. 'What goes on?'

'It would help if you could tell us.' Petersen looked at the gun in Carlos' hand. 'You don't require that.'

'I require it as long as I am the master of this vessel. I asked' – he broke off with an exclamation

73

of pain as George's massive hand closed over his gun-wrist. He struggled to free his hand, an expression of incomprehension spread over his face and he bit his lips as if to hold back another cry of pain. George removed the gun from the suddenly nerveless fingers.

'So that's it,' Carlos said. His face, not without reason, was pale. 'So I was right. *You* are the assassins. It is your intention to take over my vessel, perhaps?'

'Goodness gracious, no.' It was George who answered. 'Your forefinger has gone white at the knuckles. Precipitate action isn't going to help anyone.' He handed the pistol back to Carlos and went on pontifically: 'Unnecessary violence never helped anyone.'

Carlos took the pistol, hesitated, stuck it in his waistband and began to massage his right wrist. The demonstration of pacific intentions had had an unsettling effect. He said uncertainly: 'I still don't understand –'

'Neither do we, Carlos,' Petersen said, 'neither do we. That's what we're trying to do at this moment – understand. Perhaps you could help us. Those two men, Franco and Cola – Cola, I'm afraid is going to require your peacetime professional skills quite soon – came to attack us. Perhaps they came to kill us but I don't think so. They bungled it.'

'Amateurs,' George said by way of explanation.

'Amateurs, agreed. But the effect of an amateur bullet can be just as permanent as a professional one. I want to know why those two came for us in the first place. Perhaps you can help explain this, Carlos?'

'How should I be able to help you?'

'Because you know Alessandro.'

'I do but not well. I have no idea why he should seek to do you harm. I do not permit my passengers to carry out guerrilla warfare.'

'I'm sure you don't. But I'm equally sure that you know who Alessandro is and what he does.'

'I don't know.'

'I don't believe you. I suppose I should sigh and say how much trouble it would save all round if you were to tell the truth. Not, of course, that you are telling lies. You're just not telling anything. Well, if you don't help us, I'll just have to help myself.' Petersen raised his voice. 'Alessandro!'

Seconds passed without reply.

'Alessandro. I have three of your men prisoner, one of them badly injured. I want to know why those men came to attack us.' Alessandro made no reply and Petersen went on: 'You don't leave me any option. In wartime, people are either friends or enemies. Friends are friends and enemies die. If you're a friend, step out into the passage-way: if you're not, then you'll just have to stay there and die.'

Petersen didn't show any particular emotion but his tone sounded implacable enough. Carlos, his pain forgotten, laid a hand on Petersen's forearm.

'People don't commit murder aboard my ship.'

'Haven't committed. And murder is for peace-time. In wartime we call it execution.' For those listening inside the cabin the tone of his voice could have lent little encouragement. 'George, Alex. Help Franco and Sepp into the cabin. Keep out of any line of fire.'

Franco and Sepp didn't need any kind of helping. Execution chamber or not they couldn't get inside it fast enough. The door banged shut and a watertight clip came down. Petersen examined the pear-shaped object in his hand.

Carlos said apprehensively: 'What's that?'

'You can see. A hand-grenade of sorts. George?' George didn't need telling what to do. He never did. He took up position by the cabin door, his hand reaching up for the closed watertight clip. With one hand Petersen took a grip on the door handle, with the other he pressed a lever on the bottom of the grenade as he glanced at George who immediately opened the clip. Petersen jerked open the door the requisite few inches, dropped the grenade inside and banged shut the door as George closed the clip again. They could have rehearsed it a hundred times.

'Jesus!' Carlos' face was white. 'In that confined space –' He stopped, his face puzzled now, and said: 'The explosion. The bang.'

'Gas-grenades don't go bang. They go hiss. Reactions, George?' George had taken his hand away from the clip.

'Five seconds and then whoever it was gave up. Quick-acting stuff, is it not?'

Carlos was still almost distraught. 'What's the difference? Explosives or poison gas –'

Petersen spoke with patience. 'It was not poison gas, George.' He spoke a few words in the ear of his giant Lieutenant, who smiled and moved quickly aft. Petersen turned to Carlos. 'Is it your intention to let your friend Cola die?'

'He's not my friend and he's in no danger of dying.' He turned to the elder Pietro who had just arrived on the scene. 'Get my medicine box and bring along two of your boys.' To Petersen he said: 'I'll give a sedative, a knockout one. Then a coagulant. A few minutes later and I'll bandage him up. There'll be a broken bone or bones. It may be that his shoulder is shattered beyond repair, but whatever it is there's nothing I can do about it in this seaway.' He glanced aft, passed his hand over his forehead and looked as if he would like to moan. 'More trouble.'

Michael von Karajan was approaching them, closely followed by George. Michael was trying to look indignant and truculent but succeeded only in looking miserable and frightened. George was beaming.

'By heavens, Major, there's nothing wrong with this new generation of ours. You have to admire their selfless spirit. Here we are with the good ship *Colombo* trying to turn somersaults but does that

77

stop our Michael in the polishing of his skills? Not a bit of it. There he was, crouched over his transceiver in this appalling weather, headphones clamped over his ears –'

Petersen held up his hand. When he spoke his face was as cold as his voice. 'Is this true, von Karajan?'

'No. What I mean is –'

'You're a liar. If George says it's true, it's true. What message were you sending?'

'I wasn't sending any message. I –'

'George?'

'He wasn't transmitting any message when I arrived.'

'He would hardly have had time to,' Giacomo said. 'Not between the time I left our cabin and when George got there.' He eyed the now visibly shaking Michael with open distaste. 'He's not only a coward, he's a fool. How was he to know that I wasn't going to return at any moment? Why didn't he lock his door to make sure that he wasn't disturbed?'

Petersen said: 'What message were you going to transmit?'

'I wasn't going to transmit any –'

'That makes you doubly a liar. Who were you transmitting to or about to transmit to?'

'I wasn't going to –'

'Oh, do be quiet. That makes you three times a liar. George, confiscate his equipment. For good measure confiscate his sister's as well.'

'You can't do that.' Michael was aghast. 'Take away our radios? They're our equipment.'

'Good God in heaven!' Petersen stared at him in disbelief. Whether the disbelief were real or affected didn't matter. The effect was the same. 'I'm your commanding officer, you young fool. I can not only lock up your equipment, I can lock you up too, on charges of mutiny. In irons, if need be.' Petersen shook his head. ' "Can't", he says, "can't". Another thing, von Karajan. Can it be that you're so stupid as not to know that, in wartime at sea, the use of radio by unauthorized personnel is a very serious offence.' He turned to Carlos. 'Is that not so, Captain Tremino?' Petersen's use of formal terms lent to his enquiry all the gravity of a court-martial.

'Very much so, I'm afraid.' Carlos wasn't too happy to say it but he said it all the same.

'Is this young fellow authorized personnel?'

'No.'

'You see how it is, von Karajan? The Captain would also be justified in locking you up. George, put the sets in our cabin. No, wait a minute. This is primarily a naval offence.' He looked at Carlos. 'Do you think –'

'I have a very adequate safe in the office,' Carlos said. 'And I have the only key.'

'Splendid.' George moved off, a disconsolate Michael trailing behind him, passing by Pietro, bearing a black metal box and accompanied by two seamen. Carlos opened the medicine chest – it appeared to be immaculately equipped – and administered two injections to the hapless Cola. The box was closed and removed: so was Cola.

'Well, now,' Petersen said. 'Let's see what we have inside.' Alex, not without considerable effort, managed to free the watertight clip – when George heaved a watertight clip home it tended to stay heaved – then levelled his machine-pistol on the door. Giacomo did the same with his pistol, clearly demonstrating that whoever's side, if any, he was on it clearly was not that of Alessandro and his henchmen. Petersen didn't bother about any weapon, although he had a Luger on his person: he just pushed the door open.

The guns were unnecessary. The four men were not unconscious but, on the other hand, they weren't very conscious either, although they would be very soon. No coughing, no spluttering, no tears running down their cheeks: they were just slightly dazed, slightly woozy, slightly apathetic. Alex laid down his machine-pistol, collected the several weapons that were lying around, then searched the four men thoroughly, coming up with two more hand-guns and no fewer than four very unpleasant knives. All these he threw out into the passage-way.

'Well.' Carlos was almost smiling. 'That wasn't very clever of me, was it? I mean, if you had wished to dispose of all of them you'd have thrown Cola in here, too. I missed that.' He sniffed the air professionally. 'Nitrous oxide, I'd say. You know, laughing gas.'

'Not bad for a doctor,' Petersen said. 'I thought that gas was confined only to dentists' surgeries. Nitrous oxide, a refined form of. With this, you don't come out of the anaesthetic with tears in your eyes, laughing, singing and generally making a fool of yourself. Normally, you don't come out of it at all, by which I mean you'd just keep on sleeping until you woke up at your usual time, quite unaware that anything untoward had happened to you. But I'm told that if you've recently undergone some sort of traumatic experience immediately before you've been gassed, the tendency is to wake up directly the effects of the gas have worn off. They also say that if you had something weighing on your mind, such as a nagging conscience, the same thing happens.'

Carlos said: 'That's a strange sort of thing for a soldier to know about.'

'I'm a strange sort of soldier. Alex, take up your gun while I have a look around.'

'Look around?' Carlos did just that. The cabin, if one could call it such, held five canvas cots and that was all: there wasn't as much as even a cupboard for clothes. 'There's nothing to look around for.'

Petersen didn't bother to reply. He ripped blankets from the cots and flung them on the deck. Nothing had lain beneath the blankets. He picked up a rucksack – there were five of them in the cabin – and unceremoniously dumped the contents on a cot. They were innocuous. Among some clothes and a rudimentary toilet kit there was a considerable amount of ammunition, some loose, some in magazines, but those, too, Petersen considered innocuous: he would have expected nothing else. The second rucksack yielded the same results. The third was padlocked. Petersen looked at Alessandro, who was sitting on the deck, his ravaged face expressionless: the effect was chilling, even a hint of balefulness would have been preferable to this emptiness but Petersen was not the man to be moved by expressions or lack of them.

'Well, now, Alessandro, that wasn't very clever, was it? If you want to hide a thing you do it inconspicuously: a padlock is conspicuous. The key.'

Alessandro spat on the deck and remained silent.

'Spitting.' Petersen shook his head. 'Unpleasant, for second-rate villains. Alex.'

'Search him?'

'Don't bother. Your knife.'

Alex's knife, as one would have expected of Alex, was razor sharp. It sliced through the tough canvas of the rucksack as if through paper. Petersen peered at the contents.

'Yes, indeed, twinges of conscience.' He extracted a very small butane burner and an equally small kettle. The kettle had no top – the spout had a screwed top. Petersen shook the kettle: the glugging of water inside was unmistakable. Petersen turned to Carlos.

'Doesn't say much for the hospitality of the *Colombo*, does it, when a man has to bring along his own equipment for making tea or coffee or whatever.'

Carlos looked slightly puzzled. 'Any passenger aboard this ship can have as much tea or coffee or any other drink that he wants.' Then his face cleared. 'For shore use, of course.'

'Of course.' Petersen tipped the remainder of the contents of the rucksack on to another cot, rummaged briefly around, then straightened. 'Although, mind you, it's difficult to see how we can make any of those refreshing beverages without any tea or coffee to make them. I've found out all I want to know even although I knew in advance anyway.' He turned his attention to the fourth rucksack.

Carlos said: 'If you've already found out what you want to know why keep on?'

'Natural curiosity together with the fact that Alessandro, I'm afraid, is not a very trustworthy man. Who knows, this bag might contain a nest of vipers.'

There were no vipers but there were two more gas-grenades and a Walther with a screwed-on silencer.

'And a stealthy killer to boot,' Petersen said. 'I've always wanted one of those.' He put it in his pocket and opened up the last rucksack: this yielded only a small metal case about half the size of a shoe-box. Petersen turned to the nearest of his prisoners who happened to be Franco.

'You know what's inside this?'

Franco didn't say whether he did not not.

Petersen sighed, placed the muzzle of his Luger against Franco's knee-cap and said: 'Captain Tremino, if I pull the trigger, will he walk again?'

'Good God!' Carlos was used to war but not this kind of war. 'He might. He'll be a cripple for life.'

Petersen took two steps back. Franco looked at Alessandro but Alessandro wasn't looking at him. Franco looked at Petersen and the levelled Luger.

Franco said: 'I know.'

'Open it.'

Franco released two brass clips and swung back the lid. There was no explosion, no release of gas.

Carlos said: 'Why didn't *you* open it?'

'Because the world is full of untrustworthy people. Lots of these boxes of tricks around. If an unauthorized opener doesn't know where a secret switch or button is he's going to inhale a very nasty gas. Most of the latest safes incorporate some such device.' He took the box from Franco. The interior was shaped and lined with velvet and contained glass ampoules, two round boxes and two small hypodermic syringes. Petersen took out one of the round boxes and shook it: it rattled. Petersen handed the box to Carlos.

'Should interest a medical man. At a guess, a variety of liquids and tablets to render the victim temporarily or permanently unconscious, by which I mean dead. Seven ampoules, you observe. One green, three blue, three pink. At a guess, the green is scopolamine, an aid to flagging memories.

As for the difference in colour in the other six ampoules, there can be only one reason. Three are lethal, three non-lethal. Wouldn't you agree, Captain?'

'It's possible.' It was Carlos' night for being unhappy and Petersen was no longer as surprised by his unhappiness as he had been earlier, nor at the obvious apprehension in which he held Alessandro. 'There's no means of telling one from the other, of course.'

'I wouldn't bet on that,' Petersen said. He turned round as George came through the doorway. 'All is well?'

'A little trouble with the young lady,' George said. 'She put up a surprisingly spirited resistance to the confiscation of her radio.'

'Nothing surprising about that. Fortunately, you're bigger than she is.'

'I'm hardly proud of that. The radios are in the captain's cabin.' George looked around the cabin which looked as if a small tornado had lately passed by. 'Untidy lot, aren't they?'

'I helped a little.' Petersen took the box from Carlos and handed it to George. 'What do you make of that?'

It is difficult to conceive of a beaming, plump and cherubic face changing in an instant to one of graven stone but that was what happened to George's.

'Those are death capsules.'

'I know.'

'Alessandro's?'

'Yes.'

George looked at Alessandro for some seconds, nodded, and turned back to Petersen. 'I think perhaps we should have a talk with our friend.'

'You're making a mistake.' Carlos' voice was not quite as steady as it could have been. 'I'm a doctor. You don't know human nature. Alessandro will never talk.'

George faced him. His expression hadn't changed and Carlos visibly recoiled.

'Be quiet, little man. Five minutes alone with me, ten at the most, and any man in the world will talk. Alessandro is a five minute man.'

'It may come to that,' Petersen said. 'It probably will. But first things first. Apart from the capsules, we picked up one or two other interesting objects. This silenced gun, for instance.' He showed George the Walther. 'Two gas-grenades and a spirit burner and kettle and about two hundred rounds of ammunition. What do you think the kettle was for?'

'One thing only. He was going to gas us, steal some real or imagined document, steam open the envelope – odd, that he should be convinced that there was an envelope around – study the contents, reseal the envelope, return it to our cabin, gas us again, wait a few seconds, replace the envelope, remove the gas-canister and leave. When we woke up in the morning we almost certainly wouldn't be aware that anything had happened.'

'That's the only way it could have happened or was intended to happen. There are three questions. Why was Alessandro so interested in us? What were his future plans? And who sent him?'

'We'll find all that out easily enough,' George said.

'Of course we will.'

'Not aboard this ship,' Carlos said.

George studied him with mild interest. 'Why not?'

'There will be no torture aboard any vessel I command.' The words sounded more resolute than the tone of the voice.

'Carlos,' Petersen said. 'Don't make things any more difficult for yourself – or us – than you can help. Nothing easier than to lock you up with this bunch of villains: you're not the only person who can find his way to Ploče. We don't want to nor do we intend to. We realize you find yourself in an invidious situation through no fault of your own. No torture. We promise.'

'You've just said you'll find out.'

'Psychology.'

'Drugs?' Carlos was immediately suspicious. 'Injections?'

'Neither. Subject closed. I had another question but the answer is obvious – why did Alessandro choose to surround himself with such a bunch of incompetents? Camouflage. A dangerous man might well be tempted to surround himself with other dangerous men. Alessandro's too smart.'

Petersen looked around. 'No heavy metal objects and only a cat could get out of that port-hole. Carlos, would you have one of your men bring us a sledge-hammer or as near to it as you have aboard.'

The suspicion returned. 'What do you want a sledge-hammer for?'

'To beat out Alessandro's brains,' George said patiently. 'Before we start asking questions.'

'To close this door from the outside,' Petersen said. 'The clips, you understand.'

'Ah!' Carlos stepped into the passage-way, gave an order and returned. 'I'll go and have a look at the fallen hero. Not much I can do for him, I'm afraid.'

'A favour, Carlos. When we leave, may we go up to your cabin or whatever you call the place we met you first?'

'Certainly. May one ask why?'

'If you'd been standing frozen in that damned passage-way for an hour and a half you'd understand why.'

'Of course. Restoratives. Help yourselves, gentlemen. I'll step by and let you know how Cola is.' He paused then added drily: 'That should give you plenty of time to prepare your intensive interrogation of me.'

He left almost immediately to be replaced by Pietro, bearing a small sledge-hammer. They closed the door and secured one of the eight water-tight clips. One was enough. George struck it with one blow of the hammer. That, too, was enough – not even a gorilla could now have opened that clip from the inside. They left the sledge-hammer in the passage-way and went directly to the engine-room, which was unmanned, as they had known it would be: all controls were operated from the wheel-house. It took them less than a minute to find what they were looking for. They made a brief excursion to the upper deck then repaired to Carlos' cabin.

'A thirsty night's work,' George said. He was on his second, or it could have been third, glass of grappa. He looked at the von Karajans' radios on the deck beside him. 'These would have been safer in our cabins. Why have them here?'

'They'd have been too safe in our cabins. Young Michael would never have dared to try to get at them there.'

'Don't try to tell me that he might try to get at them here.'

'Unlikely, I admit. Michael, it is clear, is not cast in the heroic mould. He might, of course, be a consummate actor, but I don't see him as an actor any more than a hero. However, if he's desperate enough – and he must have been desperate to try to get off a message at the time and place he did – he might try.'

'But the radios will be in the safe as soon as Carlos returns. And Carlos has the only key.'

'Carlos might give him that key.'

'Oh! So that's the way our devious mind works. So we keep an eye on our Michael for the remainder of the night? Not that there's all that much left of it. And if he does try to recover the radios, what does that prove except that there is a connection between him and Carlos?'

'That's all I want to prove. I don't expect either would say or admit to anything. They don't have to. At least, Michael doesn't have to. I can have him detained in Ploče for disobedience of orders and suspicion of trying to communicate with the enemy.'

'You really suspect him of that?'

'Good Lord, no. But, no question, he's been trying to communicate with someone and that someone might as well be a spy. It'll look better on a charge sheet. All I want to see is if there's any connection between him and Carlos.'

'And if there is you're prepared to clap him into durance vile?'

'Sure.'

'And his sister?'

'She's done nothing. She can come along with us, hang around Ploče or join him in, as you say, durance vile. Up to her.'

'The very flower of chivalry.' George shook his head and reached for the grappa. 'So we may or may not suspect a connection between Carlos and Michael but we do suspect one between Carlos and Alessandro.'

'I don't. I do think that Carlos knows a great deal more about Alessandro than we do but I don't think he knows what Alessandro is up to on this passage. A very simple point. If Carlos were privy to Alessandro's plans then he, Alessandro, wouldn't have bothered to bring along a kettle and burner: he'd just have gone to the galley and steamed the envelope open.' He turned round as Carlos entered. 'How's Cola?'

'He'll be all right. Well, no danger. His shoulder is a mess. Even if it were a flat calm I wouldn't touch it. It needs a surgeon or an osteologist and I'm neither.' He unlocked a safe, put the radio gear inside then relocked the door. 'Well, no hurry for you, gentlemen, but I must return to the wheelhouse.'

'A moment, please.'

'Yes, Peter?' Carlos smiled. 'The interrogation?'

'No. A few questions. You could save us a lot of time and trouble.'

'What? In interrogating Alessandro? You promised me no torture.'

'I still promise. Alessandro tried to assault us and steal some papers tonight. Did you, do you know about this?'

'No.'

'I believe you.' Carlos raised his eyebrows a little but said nothing. 'You don't seem unduly concerned that your fellow-Italian has been made a prisoner by a bunch of uncivilized Yugoslavs, do you?'

'If you mean does he mean anything personally to me, no.'

'But his reputation does.'

91

Carlos said nothing.

'You know something about his background, his associations, the nature of his business that we don't. Is that not so?'

'That could be. You can't expect me to divulge anything of that nature.'

'Not expect. Hope.'

'No hope. You wouldn't break the Geneva Conventions to extract that information from me.'

Petersen rose. 'Certainly not. Thank you for your hospitality.'

Petersen was carrying a canvas chair and the metal box of capsules when he entered the cabin in which Alessandro and his three men were imprisoned. George was carrying two lengths of heaving line and the sledge-hammer with which he had just released the outside clip. Alex was carrying only his machine-pistol. Petersen unfolded the chair, sat on it and watched with apparent interest as George hammered home a clip.

'We'd rather not have any interruptions, you see,' Petersen said. He looked at Franco, Sepp and Guido. 'Get into that corner there. If anyone moves Alex will kill him. Take your jacket off, Alessandro.'

Alessandro spat on the floor.

'Take your jacket off,' George said pleasantly, 'or I'll knock you out of it.'

Alessandro, not a man of a very original turn of mind, spat again. George hit him somewhere in the region of the solar plexus, not a very hard blow, it seemed, but enough to make Alessandro double up, whooshing in agony. George removed the jacket.

'Tie him up.'

George set about tying him up. When Alessandro had recovered a little from his initial bout of gasping, he tried to offer some resistance, but an absentminded cuff from George to the side of the jaw convinced him of the unwisdom of this. George tied him in such a fashion that both arms were lashed immovably to his sides. His knees and ankles were bound together and then, for good measure, George used the second heaving line to lash Alessandro to the cot. No chicken was ever so securely trussed, so immobile, as Alessandro was then.

George surveyed his handiwork with some satisfaction then turned to Petersen: 'Isn't there something in the Geneva Conventions about this?'

'Could be, could be. Truth is, I've never read them.' He opened the metal box and looked at Alessandro. 'In the interests of science, you understand. This shouldn't take any time at all.' The words were light enough but Alessandro wasn't listening to the words, he was looking at the implacable face above and not liking at all what he saw. 'Here we have three blue ampoules and three pink. We think, and Captain Tremino who is also a doctor agrees with us, that three of these are lethal and three non-lethal. Unfortunately, we don't know which is which and there's only one simple, logical way to find out. I'm going to inject you with one of these. If you survive it, then we'll know it's a non-lethal ampoule. If you don't, we'll know it's the other ones that are non-lethal.' Petersen held up two ampoules, one blue, one pink. 'Which would you suggest, George?'

George rubbed his chin thoughtfully. 'A big responsibility. A man's life could hang on my decision. Well, it's not all that big a responsibility. No loss to mankind, anyway. The blue one.'

'Blue it shall be.' Petersen broke the ampoule into a test tube, inserted the needle of the hypodermic and began to withdraw the plunger. Alessandro stared in terrified fascination as the blue liquid seeped up into the hypodermic.

'I'm afraid I'm not very good at this job.' Petersen's conversational calm was more terrifying than any sibilant threats could ever have hoped to be. 'If you're careless an air bubble can get in and an air bubble in the blood stream can be very unpleasant. I mean, it can kill you. However, in your case, I don't think it's going to make very much difference one way or another.'

Alessandro's eyes were staring, his whitened lips drawn back in a rictus of terror. Petersen touched the inside of Alessandro's right elbow. 'Seems a suitable vein to me.' He pinched the vein and advanced the syringe.

'No! No! No!' Alessandro's voice was an inhuman scream torn from his throat. 'God, no! No!'

'You've nothing to worry about,' Petersen said soothingly. 'If it's a non-lethal dose you'll just slip away from us and come back in a few minutes. If it's a lethal dose, you'll just slip away.' He paused. 'Just a minute, though. He just might die in screaming agony.' He brought out a pad of white linen cloth and handed it to George. 'Just in case. But watch your hand, though. When a dying man's teeth clench they stay clenched. Worse, if he draws blood you'll get infected too.'

Petersen pinched the vein between fingers and thumb. Alessandro screamed. George applied the pad to his mouth. After a few seconds, at a nod from Petersen, he withdrew the pad. Alessandro had stopped screaming now and a weird moaning noise came from deep in his throat. He was struggling insanely against his bonds, his face was a mask of madness and a seizure, a heart attack, seemed imminent Petersen looked at George: the big man's face was masked in sweat.

Petersen said in a quiet voice: 'This is the killer dose, isn't it?' Alessandro didn't hear him. Petersen had to repeat the questions twice before the question penetrated the fear crazed mind.

'It's the killer dose! It's the killer dose.' He repeated the words several times, the words a babble of near-incoherent terror.

'And you die in agony?'

'Yes, yes! Yes, yes!' He was gasping for breath like a man in the final stages of suffocation. 'Agony! Agony!'

'Which means you have administered this your-self. There can be no pity, Alessandro, no mercy. Besides, you could still be telling a lie.' He touched the tip of the needle against the skin. Alessandro screamed again and again. George applied the clamp.

'Who sent you?' Twice Petersen repeated the question before Alessandro rolled his eyes. George removed the pad.

'Cipriano.' The voice was a barely distinguishable croak. 'Major Cipriano.'

'That's a lie. No major could authorize this.' Careful not to touch the plunger Petersen inserted the tip of the needle just outside the vein. Alessandro opened his mouth to scream again but George cut him off before he could make a sound. 'Who authorized this? The needle's inside the vein now, Alessandro. All I have to do is press the plunger. Who authorized this?'

George removed the pad. For a moment it seemed that Alessandro had lost consciousness. Then his eyes rolled again.

'Granelli.' The voice was a faint whisper. 'General Granelli.' Granelli was the much-feared, much-hated Chief of Italian Intelligence.

'The needle is still inside the vein, my hand is still on the plunger. Does Colonel Lunz know of this?'

'No. I swear it. No!'

'General von Löhr?'

'No.'

'Then how did Granelli know I was on board?'

'Colonel Lunz told him.'

'Well, well. The usual trusting faith between the loyal allies. What did you want from my cabin tonight?'

'A paper. A message.'

'Perhaps you'd better withdraw that syringe,' George said. 'I think he's going to faint. Or die. Or something.'

'What were you going to do with it, Alessandro?' The tip of the needle had remained where it was.

'Compare it with a message.' Alessandro really did look very ill indeed. 'My jacket.'

Petersen found the message in the inside pocket of the jacket. It was the duplicate of the one he had in his cabin. He refolded the paper and put it in his own inside pocket.

'Odd,' George said. 'I do believe he's fainted.'

'I'll bet his victims never had a chance to faint. I wish,' Petersen said with genuine regret, 'that I had pressed that plunger. No question our friend here is – was – a one-man extermination squad.' Petersen sniffed at the test-tube, dropped it and the ampoule to the deck, crushed them both beneath his heel and then squirted the contents of the hypodermic on the deck.

'Spirit-based,' Petersen said. 'It will evaporate quickly enough. Well, that's it.'

In the passage-way, George mopped his forehead. 'I wouldn't care to go through that again. Neither, I'm sure, would Alessandro.'

'Me neither,' Petersen said. 'How do you feel about it, Alex?'

'I wish,' Alex said morosely, 'that you had pushed that plunger. I could have shot him as easy as a wink.'

'That would have been an idea. At least he'd have gone without the agony. In any event, he's all washed up as an operative of any kind or will be as soon as he gets back to Termoli. Or even to Ploče. Let's fix this door.'

All eight water-tight clips were engaged and with each clip in turn, to muffle sound, Alex held in position the pad that had been so lately used for another purpose, while George hammered home the clip. When the eighth had been so dealt with, George said: 'That should hold it for a while. Especially if we throw this hammer overboard.'

'Let's make sure,' Petersen said. He left and returned within a minute with a gas cylinder, a welder's rod and a face-mask. Petersen was, at best, but an amateur welder but what he lacked in expertise he made up in enthusiasm. The completed result would have won him no prizes for finesse but that was unimportant. What was important was that for all practical purposes that door was sealed for life.

'What I'd like to do now,' Petersen said, 'is to have a word with Carlos and Michael. But first, I think, a pause for reflection.'

*   *   *

'How does this sound,' Petersen said. He was seated at Carlos' desk, a scotch in front of him and, beside it, a message he had just drafted. 'We'll have Michael send it off by and by. Plain language, of course. COLONEL LUNZ. Then his code number. YOUR WOULD-BE ASSASSINS AND/OR EXTERMINATORS A BUNCH OF INCOMPETENTS STOP ALESSANDRO AND OTHER BUNGLERS NOW CONFINED FORE CABIN *COLOMBO* BEHIND WELDED STEEL DOOR STOP SORRY CANNOT CONGRATULATE YOU GENERAL VON LOHR GENERAL GRANELLI MAJOR CIPRIANO ON CHOICE OF OPERATIVES REGARDS ZEPPO. "Zeppo", you may recall, is my code name.'

George steepled his fingers. 'Fair,' he said judicially, 'fair. Not entirely accurate, though. We don't *know* that they are assassins and/or etc.'

'How are they to know that we don't know? Should cause quite a stirring in the dovecote. Not too much billing and cooing, wouldn't you think?'

George smiled broadly. 'Colonel Lunz and General von Löhr are going to be fearfully upset. Alessandro said they knew nothing of this set-up.'

'How are they to know that we didn't know,' Petersen said reasonably. 'They'll be fit to be tied and ready to assume anything. I'd love to be listening in to the heated telephone calls among the named parties later on today. Nothing like spreading confusion, dissension, suspicion and mistrust among the loyal allies. Not a bad night's work, gentlemen. I think we're entitled to a small night-cap before going to have a word with Carlos.'

The wheelhouse was lit only by the dim light from the binnacle and it had taken Petersen and his two companions some time to adjust their eyes to the gloom. Carlos himself was at the wheel – at a discreet word from Petersen the helmsman had taken temporary leave of absence.

Petersen coughed, again discreetly, and said: 'I am surprised, Carlos – I would almost say acutely distressed – to find a simple honest sailorman like yourself associating with such notorious and unscrupulous characters as General Granelli and Major Cipriano.'

Carlos, hands on the wheel, continued to gaze straight ahead and when he spoke his voice was surprisingly calm. 'I have never met either. After tonight, I shall take care that I never shall. Orders are orders but I will never again carry one of Granelli's murderous poisoners. They may threaten court-martial but threats are as far as they will go. I take it that Alessandro has talked?'

'Yes.'

'He is alive?' From the tone of his voice Carlos didn't particularly care whether he were or not.

'Alive and well. No torture, as promised. Simple psychology.'

'You wouldn't and couldn't say so unless it were true. I'll talk to him. By and by.' There was no hint of urgency in his voice.

'Yes. Well. I'm afraid that to talk to him you'll have to have yourself lowered in a bo'sun's chair to his cabin porthole. Door's locked, you see.'

'What's locked can be unlocked.'

'Not in this case. We apologize for having taken liberties with an Italian naval vessel but we thought it prudent to weld the door to the bulk-head.'

'Ah, so.' For the first time Carlos looked at Petersen his expression registering, if anything, no more than a polite interest. 'Welded? Unusual.'

'I doubt whether you'll find an oxyacetylene lance in Ploče.'

'I doubt it.'

'You might have to go all the way back to Ancona to have them freed. One would hope you are not sunk before you get there. It would be a terrible thing if Alessandro and his friends were to go to a watery grave.'

'Terrible.'

'We've taken another liberty. You did have an oxyacetylene flame. It's at the bottom of the Adriatic.'

Although he could see no gleam of white teeth, Petersen could have sworn that he was smiling.

FOUR

As the seas had remained rough throughout the crossing and had hardly moderated when they reached what should have been the comparative shelter of the Neretva Channel between the island of Pelješac and the Yugoslav mainland, the seven passengers who were in a position to sit down to have breakfast did not in fact do so until they had actually tied up to the quay in Ploče. True to Carlos' prediction, because they had arrived after dawn and were flying a ludicrously large Italian flag, the harbour garrison had refrained from firing at them as they made their approach towards the port that not even the most uninhibited of travel brochure writers would have described as the gem of the Adriatic.

Breakfast was unquestionably the handiwork of Giovanni, the engineer: the indescribable mush of eggs and cheese seemed to have been cooked in diesel oil, and the coffee made of it, but the bread was palatable and the sea air lent an edge to the appetite, more especially for those who had suffered during the passage.

Giacomo pushed his half-finished plate to one side. He was freshly shaven and, despite the ghastly meal, as cheerful as ever. 'Where are Alessandro and his cut-throats? They don't know what they're missing.'

'Maybe they've had breakfast aboard the *Colombo* before,' Petersen said. 'Or already gone ashore.'

'Nobody's gone ashore. I've been on deck.'

'Prefer their own company, then. A secretive lot.'

Giacomo smiled. 'You have no secrets?'

'Having secrets and being secretive are two different things. But no, no secrets. Too much trouble trying to remember who you are supposed to be and what you are supposed to be saying. Especially, if like me, you have difficulty in remembering. Start a life of deception and you end up by being trapped in it. I believe in the simple, direct fife.'

'I could believe that,' Giacomo said. 'Especially if last night's performance was anything to go by.'

'Last night's performance?' Sarina, her face still pale from what had obviously been an unpleasant night, looked at him in puzzlement. 'What does that mean?'

'Didn't you hear the shot last night?'

Sarina nodded towards the other girl. 'Lorraine and I both heard a shot.' She smiled faintly.

103

'When two people think they are dying they don't pay much attention to a trifle like a shot. What happened?'

'Petersen shot one of Alessandro's men. An unfortunate lad by the name of Cola.'

Sarina looked at Petersen in astonishment. 'Why on earth did you do that?'

'Credit where credit is due. Alex shot him – with, of course, my full approval. Why? He was being secretive, that's why.'

She didn't seem to have heard. 'Is he – is he dead?'

'Goodness me no. Alex doesn't kill people.' Quite a number of ghosts would have testified to the contrary. 'A damaged shoulder.'

'Damaged!' Lorraine's dark eyes were cold, the lips compressed. 'Do you mean shattered?'

'Could be.' Petersen lifted his shoulders in a very small shrug indeed. 'I'm not a doctor.'

'Has Carlos seen him?' It was less a question than a demand.

Petersen looked at her thoughtfully. 'What good would that do?'

'Carlos, well – ' She broke off as if in confusion.

'Well, what? Why? What could he do?'

'What could he – he's the Captain, isn't he?'

'Both a stupid answer and a stupid question. Why should he see him? I've seen him and I'm certain I've seen many more gunshot wounds than Carlos has.'

'You're not a doctor?'

'Is Carlos?'

'Carlos? How should I know?'

'Because you do,' Petersen said pleasantly. 'Every time you speak you tread deeper water. You are not a born liar, Lorraine, but you are a lousy one. When first we practise to deceive – you know. Deception again – and it's not your forte, I'm afraid. Sure he's a doctor. He told me. He didn't tell you. How did you know?'

She clenched her fists and her eyes were stormy. 'How dare you cross-examine me like this.'

'Odd,' Petersen said contemplatively. 'You look even more beautiful when you're angry. Well, some women are like that. And why are you angry? Because you've been caught out, that's why.'

'You're smug! You're infuriating! So calm, so reasonable, so sure, so self-satisfied, Mr Clever know-all!'

'My, my. Am I all those things? This must be another Lorraine talking. Why have you taken such offence?'

'But you're not so clever. I *do* know he is a doctor.' She smiled thinly. 'If you were clever you'd remember the conversation in the café last night. You'd remember that it came up that I, too, was born in Pescara. Why should I *not* know him?'

'Lorraine, Lorraine. You're not only treading deep water, you're in over your head. You were not born in Pescara. You weren't born in Italy. You're not even Italian.'

There was silence. Petersen's quiet statement carried complete conviction. Then Sarina, as angry as Lorraine had been a few moments earlier, said: 'Lorraine! Don't listen to him. Don't even talk to him. Can't you see what he's trying to do? To needle you? To trap you? To make you say things you don't mean to say, just to satisfy his great big ego.'

'I *am* making friends this morning,' Petersen said sadly. 'My great big ego notices that Lorraine hasn't contradicted me. That's because she knows that I know. She also knows that I know she's a friend of Carlos. But not from Pescara. Tell me if I'm wrong, Lorraine.'

Lorraine didn't tell him anything. She just caught her lower Lip and looked down at the table.

Sarina said: 'I think you're *horrible*.'

'If you equate honesty with horror then, sure, I'm horrible.'

Giacomo was smiling. 'You certainly do know a lot, don't you, Peter?'

'Not really. I've just learned to learn enough to stay alive.'

Giacomo was still smiling. 'You'll be telling me next that *I'm* not Italian.'

'Not if you don't want me to.'

'You mean I'm not Italian?'

'How can you be if you were born in Yugoslavia? Montenegro, to be precise.'

'Jesus!' Giacomo was no longer smiling, but there was neither rancour nor offence in face or tone. Then he started smiling again.

Sarina looked bleakly at Petersen then turned to Giacomo. 'And what else did this – this –'

'Monster?' Petersen said helpfully.

'This monster. Oh, do be quiet. What other outrage did this man commit last night?'

'Well, now.' Giacomo linked his fingers behind his head and seemed prepared to enjoy himself. 'It all depends upon what you call an outrage. To start with, after he had Cola shot he gassed Alessandro and three other men.'

'Gassed them?' She stared at Giacomo in disbelief.

'Gassed. It was their own gas he used. They deserved it.'

'You mean he killed them? Murdered them?'

'No, no. They recovered. I know. I was there. Simply,' he added hastily, 'you understand, as an observer. Then he took away their guns, and ammunition, and grenades and a few. other nasty things. Then he locked them up. That's all.'

'That's all.' Sarina breathed deeply, twice. 'When you say it quickly it sounds like nothing, doesn't it? Why did he lock them up?'

'Maybe he didn't want them to have breakfast. How should I know. Ask him.' He looked at Petersen. 'A pretty fair old job of locking up, if I may say so. I just happened along that way as we were coming into port.'

'Ah!'

'Ah, indeed.' Giacomo looked at Sarina. 'You didn't smell any smoke during the night, did you?'

'Smoke? Yes, we did.' She shuddered, remembering. 'We were sick enough already when we smelled it. That was really the end. Why?'

'That was your friend Peter and *his* friends at work. They were welding up the door of Alessandro's cabin.'

'Welding up the door?' A faint note of hysteria had crept into her voice. 'With Alessandro and his men inside! Why on earth – ' She was suddenly at a loss for words.

'I guess he didn't want them to get out.'

The two girls looked at each other in silence. There was nothing more to say. Petersen cleared his throat in a brisk fashion.

'Well, now that's everything satisfactorily explained.' The two girls turned their heads in slow unison and looked at him in total incredulity. 'The past, as they say, is prologue. We'll be leaving in about half an hour or whatever time it takes to obtain some transport. Time to brush your teeth and pack your gear.' He looked at Giacomo. 'You and your friend coming with us?'

'Lorraine, you mean?'

'Got any other friends aboard? Don't stall.'

'All depends where you're going.'

'Same place as you. Don't be cagey.'

'Where are you going?'

'Up the Neretva.'

'We'll come.'

Petersen made to rise when Carlos entered, a piece of paper in his hand. Like Giacomo, he was shaven, brisk and apparently cheerful. He didn't look like a man who hadn't slept all night but then, in his business, he probably slept enough during the day.

'Good morning. You've had breakfast?'

'Our compliments to the chef. That paper for me?'

'It is. Radio signal just come in. Code, so it doesn't make any sense to me.'

Petersen glanced at it. 'Doesn't make any sense to me either. Not until I get the code book.' He folded the paper and put it in an inside pocket.

'Might it not be urgent?' Carlos said.

'It's from Rome. I've invariably found that whenever Rome thinks something is urgent it's never urgent to me.'

Lorraine said: 'We've just heard that a man has been shot. Is he badly hurt?'

'Cola?' Carlos didn't sound very concerned about Cola's health. 'He thinks he is. I don't. Anyway, I've sent for an ambulance. Should have been here by now.' He looked out of the small window. 'No ambulance. But a couple of soldiers approaching the gangway. If, that is, you could call them soldiers. One's about ninety, the other ten. Probably for you.'

'We'll see.'

Carlos had exaggerated the age disparity between the two soldiers but not by much: the younger was indeed a beardless youth, the older well stricken in years. The latter saluted as smartly as his arthritic bones would permit.

'Captain Tremino. You have a Yugoslav army officer among your passengers?'

Carlos waved a hand. 'Major Petersen.'

'That's the name.' The ancient saluted again. 'Commandant's compliments, sir, and would you be so kind as to see him in his office. You and your two men.'

'Do you know why?'

'The Commandant does not confide in me, sir.'

'How far is it?'

'A few hundred metres. Five minutes.'

'Right away.' Petersen stood and picked up his machine-pistol. George and Alex did the same. The older soldier coughed politely.

'The commandant doesn't like guns in his office.'

'No guns? There is a war in progress, this is a military post, and the commandant doesn't like guns.' He looked at George and Alex, then slipped off his machine-pistol. 'He's probably in his dotage. Let's humour him.'

They left. Carlos watched through the window as they descended the gangway to the quayside. He sighed.

'I can't bear it. I can't. As an Italian, I can't bear it. It's like sending a toothless old hound and a frisky puppy to round up three timber wolves. Sabre-toothed tigers, more like.' He raised his voice. 'Giovanni!'

Sarina said hesitatingly: 'Are they really like that? I mean, I heard a man in Rome yesterday call them that.'

'Ah! My old friend Colonel Lunz, no doubt.'

'You know the Colonel?' There was surprise in her voice. 'I thought – well, everybody seems to know everything around here. Except me.'

'Of course I know him.' He turned as the lean, dyspeptic looking engineer-chef appeared in the doorway. 'Breakfast, Giovanni, if you would.'

Giacomo said wonderingly: 'You can really eat that stuff?'

'Atrophied taste-buds, a zinc-lined stomach, a little imagination and you could be in Maxim's. Sarina, one does not approach me at the quayside at Termoli, jerk a thumb towards the east and ask for a lift to Yugoslavia. Do you think you'd be aboard the *Colombo* if I didn't know the Colonel? Do you have to be suspicious about everyone?'

'I'm suspicious about our Major Petersen. I don't trust him an inch.'

'That's a fine thing to say about a fellow-countryman.' Carlos sat and buttered bread. 'Honest and straightforward sort of fellow, one would have thought.'

'One would have – look, we've got to go up into the mountains with that man!'

'He seems to know his way around. In fact, I know he does. You should reach your destination all right.'

'Oh, I'm sure. Whose destination – his or ours?'

111

Carlos looked at her in mild exasperation. 'Do you have any option?'

'No.'

'Then why don't you stop wasting your breath?'

'Carlos! How can you talk to her like that?' Lorraine's voice was sharp enough to bring a slightly thoughtful look to Giacomo's face. 'She's worried. Of course she's worried. I'm worried, too. We're both going up into the mountains with that man. You're not.' She was either nervous or had a low temper flash-point. 'It's all very well for you sitting safe and sound here aboard the *Colombo*.'

'Oh, come now,' Giacomo said easily. 'I don't think that's being too fair. I'm quite sure, Carlos, that she didn't mean what she implied.' He looked at Lorraine in mock-reproval. 'I'm sure Carlos would willingly leave his safe and sound ship and accompany you into the mountains. But there are two inhibiting factors. Duty and a tin leg.'

'I *am* sorry.' She was genuinely contrite and put her hand on Carlos' shoulder to show it: Carlos, who was addressing himself to the confection that Giovanni had just brought, looked up at her and smiled amiably. 'Giacomo's right' she said. 'Of course I didn't mean it. It's just that – well, Sarina and I feel so helpless.'

'Giacomo is in the same position. He doesn't look in the slightest bit helpless to me.'

She shook his shoulder in exasperation. 'Please. You don't understand. We don't know what's going on. We don't know *anything*. He seems to know everything.'

'He? Peter?'

'Who else would I be talking about?' For so patrician-looking a lady she could be very snappish. 'Perhaps I can shake you out of your complacency. Do you know that he knows where Giacomo and I are going? Do you know that he seems to know about my background? Do you know that he knows I'm not Italian? That he knows that you and I knew each other in the past, but not in Pescara?'

If Carlos was shaken he concealed it masterfully. 'Peter knows a great number of things that you wouldn't expect him to. Or so Colonel Lunz tells me. For all I know Colonel Lunz told him about you and Giacomo, although that wouldn't be like the Colonel. He may have expected you aboard. He didn't seem annoyed by your presence.'

'He was annoyed enough by Alessandro's presence.'

'He wouldn't know about Alessandro. Alessandro is controlled by another agency.'

She said quickly: 'How do you know that?'

'He – Peter – told me.'

She removed her hand and straightened. 'So. You and Peter have your little secrets too.' She turned to Sarina. 'We can trust everybody, can't we?'

Giacomo said: 'Carlos, you're beginning to look like a hen-pecked husband.'

'I'm beginning to feel like one, too. My dear girl, I only learnt this during the night. What did you expect me to do? Come hammering on your cabin door at four in the morning to announce this earth-shaking news to you and Sarina?' He looked up as the dyspeptic engineer-chef appeared again in the doorway.

'Breakfast has been served, Carlos.'

'Thank you, Giovanni.' He looked at Lorraine. 'And before you start getting suspicious of Giovanni he only means that he's given food to our friends in the fore cabin.'

'I thought the door was locked.'

'Oh dear, oh dear.' Carlos laid down knife and fork. 'Suspicious again. The door *is* locked. Breakfast was lowered in a bucket to their cabin porthole.'

'When are you going to see them?'

'When I'm ready. When I've had breakfast.' Carlos picked up his knife and fork again. 'If I get peace to eat it, that is.'

George said: 'Took a bit of a risk back there, didn't you? Chanced your arm, as they say, pretending you knew all about their plans and backgrounds when you knew nothing.'

'Credit's all yours, George. Just based on a couple of remarks of yours about ethnic background. Couldn't very well tell them that, though. Besides, Lorraine gave away more than I extracted. I don't think she'd make a very good espionage agent.'

They were threading their way through cranes, trucks, both army and civilian, and scattered dock buildings, a few yards behind the two Italian soldiers. The snow had stopped now, the Rilić hills were sheltering them from the north-east wind but the temperature was still below freezing point. There were few enough people around, the early hour and the cold were not such as to encourage outdoor activity. The soldiers, as Carlos had said, were either reservists or youths. The few civilians around were in the same age categories. There didn't seem to be a young or middle-aged man in the port.

'At least,' George said, 'you've established a kind of moral ascendancy over them. Well, over the young ladies, anyway. Giacomo doesn't lend himself to that sort of thing. That paper Carlos gave you – a message from our Roman allies?'

'Yes. We are requested to remain in Ploče and await further orders.'

'Ridiculous.'

'Isn't it?'

'You think sending that cablegram was wise? We might have expected this.'

'I did. I hoped to precipitate exactly this. We know what to expect and we've got the initiative. If we'd got clear of the port without trouble and then were stopped by a couple of tanks up the valley road we'd have lost the initiative. Our two guards in front there – they're not very bright, are they?'

'You mean they didn't search us for hand-guns? One's too old to care, the other's too inexperienced to know. Besides, look at our honest faces.'

The two guards led the way to a low wooden hut, obviously a temporary affair, up some steps and, after knocking, into a small room about as spartan and primitive as the exterior of the hut – cracked linoleum on the floor, two metal filing cabinets, a radio transceiver, a telephone, a table and some chairs. The officer behind the table rose at their entrance. He was a tall thin man, middle-aged, with pebble glasses which explained clearly enough why he wasn't at the front. He peered at them myopically over the tops of his glasses.

'Major Petersen?'

'Yes. Glad to meet you, Commandant.'

'Oh. I see. I wonder.' He cleared his throat. 'I have just received a detention order –'

'Ssh!' Petersen had a finger to his lips. He lowered his voice. 'Are we alone?'

'We are.'

'Quite sure?'

'Quite sure.'

'In that case put your hands up.'

Carlos pushed his chair back and rose. 'Excuse me. I must have a look at that cabin door.'

Lorraine said: 'You mean you haven't seen it yet?'

'No. If Peter says it's welded, then it is. I should imagine one welded door looks very much like another. Curiosity, really.'

He was back in just over a minute.

'A welded door is a welded door and the only way to open it is with an oxyacetylene flame-cutter. I've sent Pietro ashore to try and find one. I don't have much hope. We had one but Peter and his friends dropped it over the side.'

Lorraine said: 'You don't seem worried about it.'

'I don't get worried about trifles.'

'And if you can't get them out?'

'They'll have to stay there till we get back to Termoli. Plenty of facilities there.'

'You could be sunk before you get there. Have you thought of that?'

'Yes. That would upset me.'

'Well, that's better. A little compassion, at least.'

'It would upset me because I've really grown quite fond of this old boat. I would hate to think it would be Alessandro's tomb.' Carlos' face and voice were cold. 'Compassion? Compassion for that monster? Compassion for a murderer, a hired assassin, a poisoner who travels with hypodermics and ampoules of lethal liquids? Compassion for a psychopath who would just love to inject you or Sarina there and giggle his evil head off as you screamed your way to death? Peter spared him: I wish he'd killed him. Compassion!' He turned and walked out.

'And now you've upset him,' Giacomo said. 'Nag, nag, nag. It's bloody marvellous. People – well, Peter and Carlos – tried, judged and condemned when you don't have the faintest idea what you're talking about.'

'I didn't mean anything.' She seemed bewildered.

'It's not what you mean. It's what you say. You could always try watching your tongue.' He rose and left.

Lorraine stared at the empty doorway, her face woebegone. Two large tears trickled slowly down her cheeks. Sarina put her arm around her shoulders.

'It's all right,' she said. 'It really is. They don't understand. I do.'

Ten minutes later Petersen and his two companions arrived. Petersen was driving an elderly truck, civilian not army, with a hooped canvas roof and canvas flaps at the rear. Petersen jumped down from the driving seat and looked at the five on the deck of the *Colombo* – Carlos, Giacomo, Lorraine, Michael and Sarina, the last four with their rucksacks and radios beside them.

'Well, we're ready when you are,' Petersen said. He seemed in excellent spirits. 'We'll just come aboard for our gear.'

'No need,' Carlos said. 'The two Pietros are bringing that.'

'And our guns?'

'I wouldn't want you to feel undressed.' Carlos led the way down the gangway. 'How did things go?'

'Couldn't have been better. Very friendly, cooperative and helpful.' He produced two papers. 'A military pass and a permit for me to drive this vehicle. Only as far as Metković but it will at least get us on the way. Both signed by Major Massamo. Would you two young ladies come up front with me? It's much more comfortable and the cab is heated. The back is not.'

'Thank you,' Lorraine said. 'I'd rather sit in the back.'

'Oh, no, she wouldn't,' Sarina said. 'I'm not putting up with this walking inquisition all by myself.' She took Lorraine's arm and whispered in her ear while Petersen lifted patient eyes to heaven. At first Lorraine shook her head vigorously, then reluctantly nodded.

They shook hands with Carlos, thanked him and said goodbye. All except Lorraine – she just stood there, her eyes on the dockside. Carlos looked at her in exasperation then said: 'All right. You upset me and I, forgetting that I'm supposed to be an officer and a gentleman, upset you.' He put his arm round her shoulders, gave her a brief hug and kissed her none too lightly on the cheek. 'That's by way of apology and goodbye.'

Petersen started up the rather asthmatic engine and drove off. The elderly guard at the gate ignored Petersen's proffered papers and lackadaisically waved them on: he probably didn't want to leave the brazier in his sentry-box. As he drove on, Petersen glanced to his right. Lorraine, at the far end of the seat was staring straight ahead: her face was masked in tears. Petersen, frowning, leaned forward and sideways but was brought up short by a far from gentle elbow in the ribs. Sarina, too, was frowning and giving an almost imperceptible shake of the head. Petersen looked at her questioningly, got a stony glance in return and sat back to concentrate on his driving.

In the back of the truck, already heavily polluted by George's cigars, Giacomo kept glancing towards the tarpaulin-covered heap in the front. Eventually, he tapped George on the arm.

'George?'

'Yes.'

'Have you ever seen a tarpaulin moving of its own accord?'

'Can't say that I have.'

'Well, I can see one now.'

George followed the direction of the pointing finger. 'I see what you mean. My goodness, I hope they're not suffocating under that lot.' He pulled back the tarpaulin to reveal three figures lying on their sides, securely bound at wrists and ankles and very effectively gagged. 'They're not suffocating at all. Just getting restless.'

The light inside the back of the truck was dim but sufficient to let Giacomo recognize the elderly soldier and his very junior partner who had come aboard earlier in the morning to collect Petersen and the other two. 'And who's the other person?'

'Major Massamo. Commandant – Deputy Commandant, I believe – of the port.'

Michael, seated with Alex on the opposite side of the truck, said: 'Who are those people? What are they doing here? Why are they tied up?' The questions didn't betray any real interest: the voice was dull as befitted one still in a state of dazed incomprehension. They were the first words he had spoken that day: sea-sickness and the traumatic experience he had undergone during the night had wrought their toll to the extent that he had not even been able to face breakfast.

'The Port Commandant and two of his soldiers,' George said. 'They are here because we couldn't very well leave them behind to raise the alarm the moment we were gone, and we couldn't very well shoot them, could we? And they're bound and gagged because we couldn't very well have them raising a song and dance on the way out of the harbour. You do ask stupid questions, Michael.'

'This is the Major Massamo that Major Petersen mentioned? How did you manage to get him to sign those permits you have?'

'You, Michael, have a suspicious mind. It doesn't become you. He didn't sign them. I did. There were lots of notices in his room all signed by him. You don't have to be a skilled forger to copy a signature.'

'What's going to happen to them?'

'We will dispose of them at a convenient time and place.'

'Dispose of them?'

'They'll be back in Ploče, safe and unharmed, this evening. Good heavens, Michael, you don't go around shooting your allies.'

Michael looked at three bound and gagged men. 'Yes. I see. Allies.'

They were stopped at roadblocks at the next two villages but the questioning was very perfunctory and routine. At the third village, Bagalović, Petersen pulled up by a temporary army filling station, descended, gave some papers to the corporal in attendance, waited until the truck had been fuelled, gave the corporal some money for which he was rewarded by a surprised salute, then drove off again.

Sarina said: 'They don't look like soldiers to me. They don't behave like soldiers. They seem so – so – what is the word? – apathetic.'

'A marked lack of enthusiasm, agreed. Their behaviour doesn't show them up in the best of light, does it? The Italians can, in fact, be very very good soldiers, but not in this war. They have no heart for it, in spite of Mussolini's stirring, martial speeches. The people didn't want this war in the first place and they want it less and less as time goes by. Their front-line troops fight well enough, but not from patriotism, just professional pride. But it's convenient for us.'

'What were those papers you gave to that soldier?'

'Diesel coupons. Major Massamo gave them to me.'

'Major Massamo gave them to you. Free fuel, of course. That tip you handed to the soldier. I suppose Major Massamo gave you the money as well?'

'Of course not. We don't steal.'

'Just trucks and fuel coupons. Or have you just borrowed those?'

'Temporarily. The truck, anyway.'

'Which, of course, you will return to Major Massamo?'

Petersen spared her a glance. 'You're supposed to be apprehensive, nervous, not full of nosey questions. I don't much care to be cross-examined. We're supposed to be on the same side, remember? As for the truck, I'm afraid the Major won't be seeing it again.'

They drove on in silence and after another fifteen minutes ran into the town of Metković. Petersen parked the truck in the main street and stepped down to the roadway. Sarina said: 'Forgotten something, haven't you?'

'What?'

'Your keys. You've left them in the ignition.'

'Please don't be silly.' Petersen crossed the street and disappeared into a store.

Lorraine spoke for the first time since leaving Ploče. 'What did he mean by that?'

'What he says. He knows so much that he probably knows I can't drive anyway. Certainly not this rackety old monster. Even if I could, what place would I have to drive to?' She touched the back of the cab. 'Wood. I couldn't get five yards – that fearful Alex could shoot through that.' She looked and sounded doleful in the extreme.

Lorraine said: 'Wouldn't it be nice to see him, just once, make a mistake, do something wrong?'

'I'd love it. But I don't think we should want it. I have the feeling that what is good for Major Petersen is good for us. And vice versa.'

Twenty minutes elapsed before Petersen returned. For a man who might have been regarded as being on the run, he was in no hurry. He was carrying a large wicker basket, its contents covered with brown paper. This he took round to the back of the truck. Moments later he was back in the driving seat. He seemed in good humour.

'Well, go on,' he said. 'Ask away.'

Sarina made a moue, but curiosity won. 'The basket.'

'An army marches on its stomach. Stretch a point and you might regard us as part of an army. Provisions. What else would I have been buying in a food store? Bread, cheese, hams, various meats, goulash, fruits, vegetables, tea, coffee, sugar, a spirit stove, kettle and stewpan. I promised Colonel Lunz to deliver you in fairly good condition.'

In spite of herself, she smiled faintly. 'You sound as if you wanted to deliver us in prime condition at a slave market. Overlooked your fat friend, didn't you?'

'My first purchase. George had the top off a litre flask of beer within five seconds. Wine, too.'

They cleared the outskirts of the town. Sarina said: 'I thought the permit took you only as far as Metković?'

'I have two permits. I showed only one to Carlos.'

Half an hour later Petersen recrossed the Neretva and pulled up at a fairly large garage on the outskirts of Čapljina. Petersen went inside and returned in a few minutes.

'Just saying "hallo" to an old friend.'

They passed through the village of Trebižat and not long afterwards Petersen pulled off the highway and turned up a secondary road, climbing fairly steeply as they went. From this they turned on to yet another road which was no more than a grass track, still climbing, until they finally rounded and came to a halt about fifty yards from a low stone building. They could approach no further because the road ended where they were.

They dismounted from the cab and went round to the back of the truck. Petersen tweaked back one of the canvas flaps. 'Lunch,' he said.

Perhaps a minute passed without any signs of activity. Sarina and Lorraine looked at each other in a puzzled apprehension which was in no way lessened by Petersen's air of relaxed calm.

'When George ties a knot,' Petersen said cryptically, 'it takes a fair deal of untying.'

Suddenly the flaps were parted and Major Massamo and his two soldiers, untied and ungagged, were lowered from the tailboard. Massamo and the older soldier collapsed dramatically immediately on touching the ground.

' "Who have we here and what have the wicked Petersen and his evil friends done to those poor men",' Petersen said. The young soldier had now joined the two others in a sitting position on the ground. 'Well, the officer is Major Massamo, the Port Commandant, and the other two you have already seen. We have not broken their legs or anything like that. They're just suffering from a temporary loss of circulation.' The other four men in the back of the truck had now jumped to the ground. 'Walk them around a bit, will you?' Petersen said.

George lifted the Major, Giacomo the young soldier, and Michael the elderly soldier. But the last was not only old but fat and didn't seem at all keen to get to his feet. Sarina gave Petersen what was probably intended to be a withering glance and moved to help her brother. Petersen looked at Lorraine and then at George.

'What shall we do?' His voice was low. 'Stab her or club her?'

Not a muscle flickered in George's face. He appeared to ponder. 'Either. Plenty of ravines hereabouts.'

Lorraine looked at them in perplexity: Serbo-Croat, evidently, was not her language.

Petersen said: 'I can understand now why the boyfriend is along. Bodyguard *and* interpeter. I know who she is.'

'So do I.'

Lorraine could be irritated and imperious at the same time and she was good at being both.

'What are you two talking about? It *is* bad manners, you know.' In another day and age she would have stamped her foot.

'It is our native language. No offence. My dear Lorraine, you would make life so much easier for yourself if you stopped being suspicious of everyone. And yes, we were talking about you.'

'I thought as much.' But her voice was a shade less assertive.

'Just try to trust people occasionally.' Petersen smiled to rob his words of any offence. 'We're as much looker-afterers as your Giacomo is. Will you please understand that we want to take care of you. If anything were to happen to you, Jamie Harrison would never forgive us.'

'Jamie Harrison! You know Jamie Harrison.' Her eyes had widened and a half-smile touched her lips. 'I don't believe it. You know Captain Harrison!'

' "Jamie" to you.'

'Jamie.' She looked at George. 'Do you know him?'

'Tush, tush! Suspicions again. If Peter says he knows him then I must know him. Isn't that so?' He smiled as colour touched her cheeks. 'My dear, I don't blame you. Of course I know him. Tall, very tall. Lean. Brown beard.'

'He didn't have a brown beard when I knew him.'

'He has now. And a moustache. Brown hair, anyway. And, as they say in English, he's terribly terribly English. Wears a monocle. Sports it, I should say. Claims he needs it, but he doesn't. Just English.'

She smiled. 'It couldn't be anyone else.'

Major Massamo and his two men, their grimaces bespeaking their still returning circulation, were now at least partially mobile. Petersen retrieved the heavy wicker basket from the back of the truck and led the way up grass-cut steps to the stone hut and produced a key. Sarina looked at the key, then at Petersen but said nothing.

Petersen caught her glance. 'I told you. Friends.' The combination of the creaking hinges as the door swung open and the musty smell from within was indication enough that the place hadn't been used for months. The single room, which made up the entire hut, was icy, bleak and sparsely furnished: a deal table, two benches, a few rickety wooden chairs, a stove and a pile of cordwood.

'Be it ever so humble,' Petersen said briskly. 'First things first.' He looked at George who had just extracted a bottle of beer from the basket. 'You have your priorities right?'

'I have a savage thirst,' George said with dignity. 'I can slake that and light a stove at the same time.'

'You'll look after our guests? I have a call to make.'

'Half an hour. I hope.'

It was an hour later when Petersen returned. George was no believer in doing things by half and by that time the hut was a great deal more than pleasantly warm. The top of the stove glowed a bright cherry red and the room was stiflingly hot. Petersen pointedly left the door open and set on the table a second wicker basket he had brought with him.

'More provisions. Sorry I'm late.'

'We weren't worried,' George said. 'Food's ready when you are. We've eaten.' He peered inside the basket Petersen had brought. 'Took you all that time to get that?'

'I met some friends.'

Sarina said from the doorway. 'Where's the truck?'

'Round the corner. Among trees. Can't be seen from the air.'

'You think they're carrying out an air search for us?'

'No. One doesn't take chances.' He sat at the table and made himself a cheese and salami sandwich. 'Anyone who needs some sleep had better have it now. I'm going to have some myself. We didn't have any last night. Two or three hours. Besides, I prefer to travel at night.'

'And I prefer to sleep at night,' George said. He reached out for another bottle. 'Let me be your trusty guard. Enjoy yourself. We did.'

'After Giovanni's cooking anyone would be ravenous.'

Petersen set about proving that he was no exception. After a few minutes he looked up, looked around and said to George: 'Where have those pesky girls gone to?'

'Just left. For a walk, I suppose.'

Petersen shook his head. 'My fault. I didn't tell you.' He rose and went outside. The two girls were about forty yards away.

'Come back!' he called. They stopped and turned around. He waved a peremptory arm. 'Come back.' They looked at each other and slowly began to retrace their steps.

George was puzzled. 'What's wrong with a harmless walk?'

Petersen lowered his voice so that he couldn't be heard inside the hut. 'I'll tell you what's wrong with a harmless walk.' He told him briefly and George nodded. He stopped talking as the girls approached.

Sarina said: 'What is it? What's wrong?'

Petersen nodded to a small outhouse some yards from the cabin. 'If that's what you're looking for –'

'No. Just a walk. What's the harm?'

'Get inside.'

'If you say so.' Sarina smiled at him sweetly. 'Would it kill you to tell us why?'

'Other ranks don't talk to officers in that tone. The fact that you're females doesn't alter a thing.' Sarina had stopped smiling, Petersen's own tone was not such as to encourage levity. 'I'll tell you why. Because I say so. Because you can't do anything without my permission. Because you're babes in the woods. And because I'll trust you when you trust me.' The two girls looked at each other in incomprehension then went inside without a word.

'A bit harsh, I would have thought,' George said.

'You and your middle-aged susceptibility. Sure, it was a bit harsh. I just wanted them to get the message that they don't wander without permission. They could have made it damned awkward for us.'

'I suppose so. Of course I know they could. But they don't know they could have. For them, you're just a big, bad, bullying wolf and a nasty one to boot. Irrational, they think you are. Orders for orders' sake. Never mind, Peter, when they come to appreciate your sterling qualities, they may yet come to love you.'

Inside the hut, Petersen said: 'Nobody is to go outside, please. George and Alex of course. And, yes, Giacomo.'

131

Giacomo, seated on a bench by the table, lifted a drowsy head from his folded arms. 'Giacomo's not going anywhere.'

Michael said: 'Not me?'

'No.'

'Then why Giacomo?

Petersen was curt. 'You're not Giacomo.'

Petersen woke two hours later and shook his head to clear it. As far as he could tell only the indefatigable George, a beaker of beer to hand, and the three captives were awake. Petersen got up and shook the others.

'We're going shortly. Time for tea, coffee, wine or what you will and then we're off.' He started to feed cordwood into the stove.

Major Massamo, who had kept remarkably quiet since his gag had been taken off, said: 'We're going with you?'

'You're staying here. Bound, but not gagged – you can shout your heads off but no-one will hear you.' He raised a hand to forestall a protest. 'No, you won't perish of cold during the long watches of the night. You'll be more than warm enough until help comes. About an hour after we leave I'll phone the nearest army post – it's only about five kilometres from here – and tell them where you are. They should be here within fifteen minutes of getting the call.'

'You're very kind, I'm sure.' Massamo smiled wanly. 'It's better than being shot out of hand.'

'The Royal Yugoslav Army takes orders from no-one, and that includes Germans and Italians. When our allies prove to be obstructive we're forced to take some action to protect ourselves. But we don't shoot them. We're not barbarians.'

A short time later Petersen looked at the three freshly-bound captives. 'The stove is stoked, there's no possibility of sparks, so you won't burn to death. You'll certainly be freed inside an hour and a half. Goodbye.'

None of the three prisoners said 'goodbye' to him.

Petersen led the way down the grassy steps and round the first corner. The truck was standing in a small clearing without a tree near it. Sarina said: 'Ooh! A *new* truck.'

' "Ooh! A *new* truck",' Petersen mimicked. 'Which is exactly what you would have said when you'd come back to the hut after finding it. It's as I say, you can't trust babes in the woods. Major Massamo would just have loved to hear you say that. He would then have known that we had ditched the old truck and would have called off the hunt for the old truck – there must be a search under way by now – and, when freed, ask for a search for another missing truck and broadcast its details. It's most unlikely, but it could have happened and then I'd have been forced to lumber myself with Massamo again.'

Giacomo said: 'Someone might stumble across the old one?'

'Not unless someone takes it into his head to go diving into the freezing Neretva River. And why on earth should anyone be daft enough to do that? I drove it off only a very small cliff but the water is deep there. A local fisherman told me.'

'Can it be seen underwater?'

'No. At this time of year the waters of the Neretva are brown and turgid. In a few months' time, when the snow in the mountains melts, then the river runs green and clear. Who worries about what happens in a few months' time?'

George said: 'What kindly soul gave you this nice new model? Not, I take it, the Italian army?'

'Hardly. My fisherman friend, who also happens to be the proprietor of the garage I stopped at on the way up here. The army has no local repair facilities here and he does the occasional repair job for them. He had a few civilian trucks he could have offered me but we both thought this was much more suitable and official.'

'Won't your friend be held answerable for this?'

'Not at all. We've already wrenched off the padlock at the rear of the garage just in case some soldier happens by tomorrow, which is most unlikely, as it is Sunday. Come Monday morning, as a good collaborator should, he'll go to the Italian army authorities and report a case of breaking, entering and theft of one army motor vehicle. No blame will attach to him. The culprits are obvious. Who else could it be but us?'

Sarina said, 'And come Monday morning? When the search starts?'

'Come Monday morning this truck will probably have joined the old one. Whatever happens, we'll be a long way away from it by then.'

'You *are* devious.'

'You're being silly again. This is what you call forward planning. Get inside.'

The new truck was rather more comfortable and much quieter than the old one. As they drove off, Sarina said: 'I'm not carping or criticizing but – well, you do have rather a cavalier attitude towards the property of your allies.'

Petersen glanced at her then returned his attention to the road. '*Our* allies.'

'What? Oh! Yes, of course. Our allies.'

Petersen kept looking ahead. He could have become suddenly thoughtful but it was impossible to tell. Petersen's expression did what he told it to do. He said: 'That mountain inn yesterday. Lunchtime. Remember what George said?'

'Remember – how could I? He says so much – all the time. Said about what?'

'Our allies.'

'Vaguely.'

'Vaguely.' He clucked his tongue in disapproval. 'This augurs ill. A radio operator – any operative – should remember everything that is said. Our alliance is simply a temporary measure of convenience and expediency. We are fighting *with* the Italians – George said "Germans" but it's the same thing – not *for* them. We are fighting for ourselves. When they have served their purpose it will be time for them to be gone. In the meantime, a conflict of interests has arisen between the Italians and the Germans on the one hand and us on the other. Our interests come first. Pity about the trucks but the loss of one or two isn't going to win or lose the war.'

There was a short silence then Lorraine said: 'Who *is* going to win this dreadful war, Major Petersen?'

'We are. I'd rather you'd just call me Peter. As long as you're otherwise civil, that is.'

The two girls exchanged glances. If Petersen saw the exchange he gave no signs.

In Čapljina, in the deepening dusk, they were halted at an army roadblock. A young officer approached, shone his torch at a piece of paper in his hand, switched it to the truck's plates, then played it across the windscreen. Petersen leaned out of the window.

'Don't shine that damned light in our eyes!' he shouted angrily.

The light beam dipped immediately.

'Sorry, sir. Routine check. Wrong truck.' He stepped back, saluted and waved them on. Petersen drove off.

'I didn't like that,' Sarina said. 'What happens when your luck runs out? And why did he let us through so easily?'

'A young man with taste, sensibility and discretion,' Petersen said. 'Who is he, he said to himself, to interfere with an army officer carrying on a torrid affair with two beautiful young ladies. The hunt, however, is on. The paper he held had the number of the old truck. Then he checked driver and passengers, a most unusual thing. He had been warned to look out for three desperadoes. Anyone can see that I'm perfectly respectable and neither of you could be confused with a fat and thin desperado.'

'But they must know we're with you.'

'No "must" about it. They will, soon enough, but not yet. The only two people who knew that you were aboard the ship were the two who are still tied up in the hut back there.'

'Somebody may have asked questions at the *Colombo.*'

'Possibly. I doubt it. Even if they had, no member of the crew would divulge anything without Carlos' okay. He has that kind of relationship with them.'

Sarina said doubtfully: 'Carlos might tell them.'

'Carlos wouldn't volunteer anything. He might have a struggle with his conscience but it would be a brief one and duty would lose out: he's not going to sell his old girlfriend down the river, especially, as is like enough, there would be shooting.'

Lorraine leaned forward and looked at him. 'Who's supposed to be the girlfriend? Me?'

'A flight of fancy. You know how I ramble on.'

Twice more they were stopped at roadblocks, both times without incident. Some minutes after the last check, Petersen pulled into a lay-by.

'I'd like you to get in the back, now, please. It's colder there but my fisherman friend did give me some blankets.'

Sarina said: 'Why?'

'Because from now on you might be recognized. I don't think it likely but let's cater for the unlikely. Your descriptions will be out any minute now.'

'How can they be out until Major Massamo – ' She broke off and looked at her watch. 'You said you'd phone the army post at Čapljina in an hour. That was an hour and twenty minutes ago. Those men will freeze. Why did you lie –'

'If you can't think, and you obviously can't, at least shut up. Just a little, white, necessary lie. What would have happened if I phoned now or had done in the past twenty minutes?'

'They'd have sent out a rescue party.'

'That all?'

'What else?'

'Heaven help Yugoslavia. They'd have traced the call and know roughly where I am. The call *was* sent on the hour by my friend. From Gruda, on the Čapljina – Imotski road away to the north-west of here. What more natural than we should be making for Imotski – an Italian division is head-quartered there. So they'll concentrate their search on the Imotski area. There's an awful lot of places – buildings, store-houses, trucks – where a person can hide in a divisional headquarters, and as the Italians like the Germans about as much as they like the Yugoslavs – and the order for my detention comes from the German HQ in Rome – I don't suppose they'll conduct the search with any great enthusiasm. They *may* have double-guessed – I don't think they'd even bother trying – but go in the back anyway.'

Petersen descended, saw them safely hoisted aboard the rear of the track, returned to the cab and drove off.

He passed two more roadblocks – in both cases he was waved on without stopping – before arriving at the town of Mostar. He drove into the middle of the town, crossed the river, turned right by the Hotel Bristol and two minutes later pulled up and stopped the engine. He went round to the back of the track.

'Please remain inside,' he said. 'I should be back in fifteen minutes.'

Giacomo said: 'Are we permitted to know where we are?'

'Certainly. In a public car park in Mostar.'

'Isn't that rather a public place?' It was, inevitably, Sarina.

'The more public the better. If you really want to hide, there's no place like hiding in the open.'

George said: 'You won't forget to tell Josip that I've had nothing to eat or drink for days?'

'I don't have to tell him. He's always known that.'

When Petersen returned it was in a small fourteen-seater Fiat bus which had seen its heyday in the middle twenties. The driver was a small, lean man with a swarthy complexion, a ferocious black moustache, glittering eyes and a seemingly boundless source of energy.

'This is Josip,' Petersen said. Josip greeted George and Alex with great enthusiasm, they were obviously acquaintances of old standing. Petersen didn't bother to introduce him to the others. 'Get your stuff into the bus. We're using the bus because Josip doesn't care too much to have an Italian army lorry parked outside the front door of his hotel.'

'Hotel?' Sarina said. 'We're going to stay in a *hotel*?'

'When you travel with us,' George said expansively, 'you may expect nothing but the best.'

The hotel, when they arrived there, didn't look like the best. The approach to it could not have been more uninviting. Josip parked the bus in a garage and led the way along a narrow winding lane that was not even wide enough to accommodate a car, fetching up at a heavy wooden door.

'Back entrance,' Petersen said. 'Josip runs a perfectly respectable hotel but he doesn't care to attract too much attention by bringing so many people in at once.'

They passed through a short passage into the reception area, small but bright and clean.

'Now then.' Josip rubbed his hands briskly, he was that kind of man. 'If you'll just bring your luggage, I'll show you to your rooms. Wash and brush up, then dinner.' He spread his hands. 'No Ritz, but at least you won't go to bed hungry.'

'I can't face the stairs, yet,' George said. He nodded towards an archway. 'I think I'll just go and rest quietly in there.'

'Barman's off tonight, Professor. You'll have to help yourself.'

'I can take the rough with the smooth.'

'This way, ladies.'

In the corridor upstairs Sarina turned to Petersen and said in a low voice: 'Why did your friend call George "Professor"?'

'Lots of people call him that. A nickname. You can see why. He's always pontificating.'

Dinner was rather more than Josip had promised it would be but, then, Bosnian innkeepers are renowned for their inventiveness and resourcefulness, not to mention acquisitiveness. Considering the ravaged and war-stricken state of the country, the meal was a near miracle: Dalmatian ham, grey mullet with an excellent Pošip white wine and, astonishingly, venison accompanied by one of the renowned Neretva red wines. George, after

141

remarking, darkly, that one never knew what the uncertain future held for them, thereafter remained silent for an unprecedented fifteen minutes: no mean trencherman at the best of times, his current exercise in gastronomy bordered on the awesome.

Apart from George, his two companions and their host, Marija, Josip's wife, was also at the table. Small, dark and energetic like her husband, she was in other ways in marked contrast to him: he was intense, she was vivacious: he was taciturn, she was talkative to the point of garrulity. She looked at Michael and Sarina, seated some distance away at one small table, and at Giacomo and Lorraine, seated about the same distance away, at another, and lowered her voice.

'Your friends are very quiet.'

George swallowed some venison. 'It's the food.'

'They're talking, all right,' Petersen said. 'You just can't hear them over the champing noise George is making. But you're right, they are talking very softly.'

Josip said: 'Why? Why do they have to murmur or whisper? There's nothing to be afraid of here. Nobody can hear them except us.'

'You heard what George said. They don't know what the future holds for them. This is a whole new experience for them – not, of course, for Giacomo, but for the other three. They're apprehensive and from their point of view they have every right to be. For all they know, tomorrow may be their last day on earth.'

'It could be yours, too,' Josip said. 'The word in the market-place – we hoteliers spend a lot of time in the market-place – is that groups of Partisans have by-passed the Italian garrison at Prozor, moved down the Rama valley and are in the hills overlooking the road between here and Jablanica. They may even be astride the road: they're crazy enough for anything. What are your plans for tomorrow? If, I may add hastily, one may ask.'

'Why ever not? We'll have to take to the mountains by and by of course, but those three young people don't look much like mountain goats to me so we'll stick as long as possible to the truck and the road. The road to Jablanica, that is.'

'And if you run into the Partisans?'

'Tomorrow can look after itself.'

At the end of the meal, Giacomo and Lorraine rose and crossed to the main table. Lorraine said: 'I tried to have a walk, stretch my legs, this afternoon, but you stopped me. I'd like to have one now. Do you mind?'

'Yes. I mean, I do mind. At the moment, this is very much a frontier town. You're young, beautiful and the streets, as the saying goes, are full of licentious soldiery. Even if a patrol stops you, you don't speak a word of the language. Besides, it's bitterly cold.'

'Since when did you begin to worry about my health?' She was back to being her imperious self again. 'Giacomo will look after me. What you mean is, you still don't trust me.'

'Well, yes, there's that to it also.'

'What do you expect me to do? Run away? Report you to – to the authorities? What authorities? There *is* nothing I can do.'

'I know that. I'm concerned solely with your own welfare.'

Beautiful girls are not much given to snorting in disbelief but she came close. 'Thank you.'

'I'll come along with you.'

'No, thank you. I don't want you.'

'You see,' George said, 'she doesn't even like you.' He pushed back his chair. 'But everyone likes George. Big, cheerful, likeable George. I'll come along with you.'

'I don't want you either.'

Petersen coughed. Josip said: 'The Major is right, you know, young lady. This *is* a dangerous town after dark. Your Giacomo looks perfectly capable of protecting anyone, but there are streets in this town where even the army police patrols won't venture. I know where it's safe to go and where it isn't.'

She smiled. 'You are very kind.'

Sarina said: 'Mind if we come, too?'

'Of course not.'

All five, Michael included, buttoned up in their heavy coats and went out, leaving Petersen and his two companions behind. George shrugged his shoulders and sighed.

'To think I used to be the most popular person in Yugoslavia. That was before I met you, of course. Shall we retire?'

'So soon?'

'Through the archway, I meant.' George led the way and ensconced himself behind the bar counter. 'Strange young lady. Lorraine, that is. I muse aloud. Why did she sally forth into the dark and dangerous night. She hardly strikes one as a fresh-air fiend or fitness fanatic.'

'Neither does Sarina. Two strange young ladies.'

George reached for a bottle of red wine. 'Let us concede that the vagaries of womankind, especially young womankind, are beyond us and concentrate more profitably on this vintage '38.'

Alex said suddenly: 'I don't think they're all that strange.'

Petersen and George gave him their attention. Alex spoke so seldom, far less ventured an opinion, that he was invariably listened to when he did speak.

George said: 'Can it be, Alex, that you have observed something that has escaped our attention?'

'Yes. You see, I don't talk as much as you do.' The words sounded offensive but weren't meant to be, they were simply by way of explanation. 'When you're talking I look and listen and learn, while you're listening to yourselves talking. The two young ladies seem to have become very friendly. I think they've become too friendly too quickly. Maybe they really like each other, I don't know. What I do know is that they don't trust each other. I am sure that Lorraine went out to

145

learn something. I don't know what. I think Sarina thought the same thing and wanted to find out, so she's gone to watch.'

George nodded a judicious head. 'A closely reasoned argument. What do you think they both went out to learn?'

'How should I know?' Alex sounded mildly irritable. 'I just watch. You're the ones who are supposed to think.'

The two girls and their escorts were back even before the three men had finished their bottle of wine, which meant that they had returned in very short order indeed. The two girls and Michael were already slightly bluish with cold and Lorraine's teeth were positively chattering.

'Pleasant stroll?' Petersen said politely.

'Very pleasant,' Lorraine said. Clearly, she hadn't forgiven him for whatever sin he was supposed to have committed. 'I've just come to say goodnight. What time do we leave in the morning?'

'Six o'clock.'

'Six o'clock!'

'If that's too late –'

She ignored him and turned to Sarina. 'Coming?'

'In a moment.'

Lorraine left and George said, 'For a nightcap, Sarina, I can recommend this Maraschino from Zadar. After a lifetime –'

She ignored him as Lorraine had ignored Petersen, to whom she now turned and said: 'You lied to me.'

'Dear me. What a thing to say.'

'George here. His "nickname". The Professor. Because, you said, he was loquacious –'

'I did not. "Pontificated" was the word I used.'

'Don't quibble! Nickname! Dean of the Faculty of Languages and Professor of Occidental Languages at Belgrade University!'

'My word!' Petersen said admiringly. 'You *are* clever. How did you find out?'

She smiled. 'I just asked Josip.'

'Well done for you. Must have come as a shock. I mean, you had him down as the janitor, didn't you?'

She stopped smiling and a faint colour touched her cheeks. 'I did not. And why did you lie?'

'No lie, really. It's quite unimportant. It's just that George doesn't like to boast of his modest academic qualifications. He's never reached the dizzying heights of a degree in economics and politics in Cairo University.'

She coloured again, more deeply, then smiled, a faint smile, but a smile. 'I didn't even qualify. I didn't deserve that.'

'That's true. Sorry.'

She turned to George. 'But what are you doing – I mean, a common soldier –'

Behind the bar, George drew himself up with dignity. 'I'm a very uncommon soldier.'

'Yes. But I mean – a dean, a professor –'

George shook his head sadly. 'Hurling pluperfect subjunctives at the enemy trenches never won a battle yet.'

Sarina stared at him then turned to Petersen. 'What on earth does he mean?'

'He's back in the groves of academe.'

'Wherever we're going,' she said with conviction, 'I don't think we're going to get there. You're mad. Both of you. Quite mad.'

FIVE

It was three-thirty in the morning when Petersen
woke. His watch said so. He should not have been
able to see his watch because he had switched the
light off before going to sleep. It was no longer off
but it wasn't the light that had wakened him, it
was something cold and hard pressed against his
right cheek-bone. Careful not to move his head.
Petersen swivelled his eyes to take in the man
who held the gun and was sitting on a chair
beside the bed. Dressed in a well-cut grey suit, he
was in his early thirties, had a neatly trimmed
black moustache of the type made famous by
Ronald Colman before the war, a smooth clear
complexion, an engaging smile and very pale
blue, very cold eyes. Petersen reached across a
slow hand and gently deflected the barrel of the
pistol.

'You need to point that thing at my head?
With three of your fellow-thugs armed to the
teeth?'

There were indeed three other men in the bedroom. Unlike their leader they were a scruffy and villainous looking lot, dressed in vaguely paramilitary uniforms but their appearance counted little against the fact that each carried a machine-pistol.

'Fellow thugs?' The man on the chair looked pained. 'That makes me a thug too?'

'Only thugs hold pistols against the heads of sleeping men.'

'Oh, come now, Major Petersen. You have the reputation of being a highly dangerous and very violent man. How are we to know that you are not holding a loaded pistol in your hand under that blanket?'

Petersen slowly withdrew his right hand from under the blanket and turned up his empty palm. 'It's under my pillow.'

'Ah, so.' The man withdrew the gun. 'One respects a professional.'

'How did you get in? My door was locked.'

'Signor Pijade was most cooperative.' "Pijade" was Josip's surname.

'Was he now?'

'You can't trust anyone these days.'

'I've found that out, too.'

'I begin to believe what people say of you. You're not worried, are you? You're not even concerned about who I might be.'

'Why should I be. You're no friend. That's all that matters to me.'

'I may be no friend. Or I may. I don't honestly know yet. I'm Major Cipriano. You may have heard of me.'

'I have. Yesterday, for the first time. I feel sorry for you, Major, I really do, but I wish I were elsewhere. I'm one of those sensitive souls who feel uncomfortable in hospital wards. In the presence of the sick, I mean.'

'Sick?' Cipriano looked mildly astonished but the smile remained. 'Me? I'm as fit as a fiddle.'

'Physically, no doubt. Otherwise a cracked fiddle and one sadly out of tune. Anyone who works as a hatchet-man for that evil and sadistic bastard, General Granelli, has to be sick in the mind: and anyone who employs as *his* hatchet-man the psychopathic poisoner, Alessandro, has to be himself a sadist, a candidate for a maximum-security lunatic asylum.'

'Ah, so! Alessandro.' Cipriano was either not a man easily to take offence or, if he did, too clever to show it. 'He gave a message for you.'

'You surprise me. I thought your poisoner – and poisonous – friend was in no position to give messages. You have seen him, then?'

'Unfortunately, no. He's still welded up in the fore cabin of the *Colombo*. One has to admit, Major Petersen, that you are not a man to do things by half-measures. But I spoke to him. He says that when he meets you again you'll take a long time to die.'

'He won't. I'll gun him down as I would a mad dog with rabies. I don't want to talk any more about your psycho friend. What do you want of me?'

'I'm not quite sure yet. Tell me, why do you keep referring to Alessandro as a poisoner?'

'You don't know?'

'I might. If I knew what you were talking about.'

'You know that he carried knockout gas-grenades with him?'

'Yes.'

'You knew that he carried a nice little surgical kit with him along with hypodermics and liquids in capsules that caused unconsciousness – some form of scopolamine, I believe?'

'Yes.'

'Do you know that he also carried capsules which, when injected, led to the victims dying in screaming agony?'

Cipriano had stopped smiling. 'That's a lie.'

'May I get out of bed?' Cipriano nodded. Petersen crossed to his rucksack, extracted the metal box he had taken from Alessandro, handed it to Cipriano and said: 'Take that back to Rome or wherever and have the contents of those capsules analyzed. I would not drink or self-inject any of them if I were you. I threatened to inject your friend with the contents of the missing capsule and he fainted in terror.'

'I know nothing about this.'

'That I believe. Where would Alessandro get hold of such lethal poison?'

'I don't know that either.'

'That I don't believe. Well, what do you want of me?'

'Just come along with us.' Cipriano led the way to the dining-room where Petersen's six companions were already assembled under the watchful eye of a young Italian officer and four armed soldiers. Cipriano said: 'Remain here. I know you're too professional to try anything foolish. We won't be long.'

George, inevitably, was relaxed in a carver chair, a tankard of beer in his hand. Alex was looking quietly murderous. Giacomo just looked thoughtful. Sarina was tight-lipped and pale while the mercurial Lorraine, oddly enough, was expressionless.

Petersen shook his head. 'Well, well, we're a fine lot. Major Cipriano has just said I was a professional. If –'

'That was Major Cipriano?' George said.

'That's what he says.'

'A fast mover. He doesn't *look* like a Major Cipriano.'

'He doesn't talk like one either. As I was about to say, George, if I were a professional, I'd have posted a guard, a patrolling sentry. Mea culpa. I thought we were safe here.'

'Safe!' Sarina spoke with a wealth of contempt.

'Well, no harm done, let's hope.'

'No harm done!'

Petersen spread his hands. 'There are always compensations. You – and Lorraine – wanted to

153

see me in, what shall we say, a disadvantaged position. Well, you see it now. How do you like it?' There was no reply. 'Two things. I'm surprised they got you, Alex. You can hear a leaf fall.'

'They had a gun at Sarina's head.'

'Ah! And where is our good friend Josip?'

'*Your* good friend,' Sarina said acidly, 'will be helping Cipriano and his men to find whatever they're looking for.'

'My goodness! What a low opinion – what an immediate low opinion – of my friend.'

'Who tipped them off that we were here? Who let them in? Who gave them the keys – or the master key – to the bedrooms?'

'One of these days,' Petersen said mildly, 'someone's going to clobber you, young lady. You've a waspish tongue and you're far too ready to judge and condemn. If that soldier with the gun at your head had taken the second necessary to pull the trigger he'd be dead now. So, of course, would you. But Alex didn't want you to die. Nobody let them in – Josip never locks his front door. Once in, getting the keys would be no trouble. I don't know who tipped them off. I'll find out. It could even have been you.'

'Me!' She stared at him, at first stunned and then furious.

'No-one's above suspicion. You've said more than once that I don't trust you. If you said that, you must have had reasons to think that I have reservations about you. What reasons?'

154

'You must be out of your mind.' She wasn't mad any more, just bewildered.

'You've turned pale very suddenly. Why have you turned pale?'

'Leave my sister alone!' Michael's voice was an angry shout. 'She's done nothing! Leave her alone. Sarina? A criminal? A traitor? She's right, you must be out of your mind. Stop tormenting her. Who the hell do you think you are?'

'An army officer who wouldn't hesitate to instruct a very raw enlisted man – boy, I should say – in the elements of discipline. Mind you, a show of spirit at last, but I'm afraid it's mistimed and misplaced. Meantime, you should rest content with the knowledge that *you* are not under suspicion.'

'I'm supposed to be pleased with that while Sarina is under suspicion?'

'I don't care whether you're pleased or not.'

'Look here, Petersen –'

'Petersen? Who's Petersen? "Major Petersen" to a ranker. Or "Sir".' Michael made no reply. 'You're not under suspicion because after you'd transmitted this message to Rome yesterday morning I rendered your radio inoperable. You could have used your sister's tonight, but you wouldn't have had the guts, not after being caught out the previous night. I know you're not very bright but the inference is obvious. Alex, a word with you.'

As brother and sister looked at each other in mingled apprehension, incomprehension and dismay, Alex crossed the room and listened as Petersen began talking to him.

'Stop!' The young Italian officer's voice was sharp.

Petersen looked at him patiently. 'Stop what?'

'Stop talking.'

'Why ever should I? You just let me talk to that young man and girl.'

'I understood that. I don't understand Serbo-Croat.'

'Your lack of education doesn't concern me. To compound your ignorance, we're not talking Serbo-Croat but a Slavonic dialect understood only by this soldier here, the fat gentleman with the beer glass and myself. You think, perhaps, that we are planning a suicidal attack on you, three unarmed men against four machine-guns and a pistol? You can't possibly be so crazy as to think we're so crazy. What rank are you?'

'Lieutenant.' He was a very stiff, very correct and very young, lieutenant.

'Lieutenants don't give orders to majors.'

'You're my prisoner.'

'I have yet to be informed of that. Even if I were, which legally I'm not, I'd be Major Cipriano's prisoner and he would regard me as a very important one and one not to be molested or harmed in any way, so don't bother looking at your men. If any of them comes over to try to stop or separate us I'll take his gun from him and break it over his head and then you might shoot me.

You'd be court-martialled, cashiered and then, by the stipulations of the Geneva Conventions, face a firing squad. But you know that, of course.' Petersen hoped the lieutenant didn't, for he himself had no idea, but apparently the young man didn't either for he made no further attempt to pursue the matter.

Petersen talked to Alex for no more than a minute, went behind the bar, picked up a wine bottle and glass – this without even a raised eyebrow from the young lieutenant who might have been wondering how many men it took to constitute a firing squad and sat down at the table with George. They talked in low and seemingly earnest tones and were still talking when Cipriano returned with his three soldiers, Josip and his wife, Marija. Cipriano not only looked less buoyant and confident than he had done when he had left the dining-room: he was still smiling, because he was an habitual smiler, but the smile was of such a diminished quality that he looked positively morose.

'I am glad to see that you are enjoying yourselves.'

'We might be just a little justifiably annoyed at having our sleep disturbed.' Petersen replenished his glass. 'But we are of a forgiving nature, happy and relaxed in our carefree conscience. You will join us in a nightcap? I'm sure it would help you to frame a more graceful apology.'

'No nightcap, thank you, but you are correct in saying that an apology is in order. I have just made a telephone call.'

'To the wise men of your intelligence HQ, of course.'

'Yes. How did you know?'

'Where else does all the misinformation come from? We, as you know, are in the same line of business and it happens to us all the time.'

'I am genuinely sorry to have inconvenienced you all over a stupid false alarm.'

'What false alarm?'

'Papers missing from our Rome HQ. Some misguided genius on General Granelli's staff – I don't know, yet, who it was but I'll find out before the day is over – decided that they had fallen, if that's the word, into the hands of either yourself or one of your group. Very important papers, very top-secret.'

'All missing papers are top-secret. I have some papers with me myself, but I assure you they're not stolen and how top-secret or important they may be I don't know.'

'I know about those papers.' Cipriano waved a dismissive hand and smiled. 'As you're probably well aware. Those other, and much more important papers have never left their safe in Rome. A top-secret filing clerk careless about filing top-secret documents.'

'May one ask what they are about?'

'You may and that's all the answer you'd get. I don't know and even if I did I couldn't tell you.

I wish you an undisturbed night – or what's left of it. Again, my apologies. Goodbye, Major Petersen.'

'Goodbye.' Petersen took the extended hand. 'My regards to Colonel Lunz.'

'I will.' Cipriano frowned. 'I hardly know the man.'

'In that case, my regards to Alessandro.'

'I'll give him more than that.' He turned to Josip and took his hand. 'Many thanks, Signor Pijade. You have been most helpful. We will not forget.'

It was Sarina, nothing if not resilient, who broke the conversational hiatus that followed the departure of Cipriano and his men. '"Thank you, Signor Pijade. Most helpful, Signor Pijade. We won't forget, Signor Pijade."'

Josip looked at her in puzzlement then turned to Petersen. 'Is the young lady talking to me?'

'I think she's addressing the company.'

'I don't understand.'

'I don't think she does either. The young lady, as you call her, is under the ridiculous impression that you notified Major Cipriano – one assumes she thinks it was by telephone – of our presence and then took him and his men on a guided tour of the premises, distributing keys where necessary. She may, of course, be trying to divert from herself the suspicion that she is the guilty party.'

Sarina made to speak but an outraged Marija gave her no chance. Three quick steps and she was before the suddenly apprehensive Sarina. The ivory-knuckled fists and arms held rigidly by her sides spoke eloquently of her outrage: her eyes were stormy and her clenched teeth remained that way even when she spoke.

'Such a beautiful face, my dear.' It is difficult not to hiss when one's teeth are clenched. 'Such a delicate complexion. And I have long nails. Should I tear your face because you insult the honour of my husband? Or would a few slaps – hard slaps – be enough for a creature like you?' In the technique of expressing contempt, Marija Pijade had nothing to learn from anyone.

Sarina said nothing. The apprehensive expression on her face had given way to one of near shock.

'A soldier – not the Major, he's a civilized man and was not there – pointed a gun at me. Like this.' Dramatically, she swung up her right arm and pressed her forefinger against her neck. 'Not pointed. Pushed. Pushed hard. Three seconds, he said, for my husband to hand over the master key. I am sure he would not have fired but Josip handed over the key at once. Do you blame him for that?'

Slowly, dumbly, Sarina shook her head.

'But do you still think Josip betrayed you?'

'No. I don't know what to think, but I don't think that any more. I just don't know what to think. I'm sorry, Marija, I'm truly sorry.' She smiled wanly. 'A soldier threatened me with a gun, too. He pressed it in my ear. Maybe that doesn't make for very clear thinking.'

The cold fury in Marija's face gave way to speculation then softened into concern. She took an impulsive step forward, put her arms round the girl and began to stroke her hair.

'I don't think any of us is thinking very clearly. George!' This over Sarina's shoulder. 'What are you thinking of?'

'Šljivovica,' George said decisively. 'The universal specific. If you read the label on a Pellegrino bottle –'

'George!'

'Right away.'

Josip rubbed a blue and unshaven chin. 'If Sarina and I are not the culprits, then we're no nearer to an answer. Who did talk? Have you no suspicions, Peter?'

'None. I don't need any. I know who it is.'

'You know – ' Josip turned to the bar, picked up a bottle of Šljivovica from a tray George was preparing, filled a small glass, drained it in two gulps and when he'd finished coughing and spluttering said: 'Who?'

'I'm not prepared to say at the moment. That's not because I'm intending to prolong anxiety, increase tension, give the villain enough rope to hang him – or herself – or anything stupid like that. It's because I can't prove it – yet. I'm not even sure I want to prove it. Perhaps the person I have in mind was misguided, or the action may have been unintentional, accidental, inadvertent or even done from the best motives – from, of course, the viewpoint of the person concerned. Unlike Sarina here, I don't go in much for premature judgments and condemnation.'

'Peter!' Marija's voice held a warning, almost peremptory, note. She still had an arm around Sarina's shoulders.

'Sorry, Marija. Sorry, Sarina. Just my natural nastiness surfacing. By the way, if you people want to go to bed, well of course, go. But no hurry now. Change of plan. We won't be leaving until the late forenoon tomorrow. Certainly not before. Giacomo, could I have a quiet word with you?'

'Have I any option?'

'Certainly. You can always say "no".'

Giacomo smiled his broad smile, stood up and put his hand in his pocket. 'Josip, if I could buy a bottle of that excellent red wine –'

Josip was mildly affronted. 'Peter Petersen's friends pay for nothing in my hotel.'

'Maybe I'm not his friend. I mean, maybe he's not my friend.' Giacomo seemed to find the thought highly amusing. 'Thanks all the same.' He picked up a bottle and two glasses from the bar, led the way to a distant table, poured wine and said admiringly: 'That Marija. Quite a girl. Not quite a tartar but no shrinking violet. Changes her mind a bit quick, doesn't she?'

'Mercurial, you'd say?'

'That's the word. Seems to know you pretty well. Has she known you long?'

'She does and she has.' Petersen spoke with some feeling. 'Twenty-six years, three months and some days. The day she was born. My cousin. Why do you ask?'

'Curiosity. I was beginning to wonder if you knew everyone in the valley. Well, on with the inquisition. Incidentally, I would like to say that I'm honoured to be the prime suspect and/or the chosen villain.'

'You're neither a suspect nor villain. Wrong casting. If you wanted, say, to dispose of George or Alex or myself, or get your hands on something you thought we had, you'd use a heavy instrument. Surreptitious phone calls or secret tip-offs are not in your nature. Deviousness is not part of your stock-in-trade.'

'Well, thank you. It's a disappointment, though. I take it you want to ask some questions?

'If I may.'

'About myself, of course. Fire away. No, don't fire away. Let *me* give you my curriculum vitae. Behind me lies a blameless existence. My life is an open book.

'You're right, I'm Montenegrin. Vladimir was my given name. I prefer Giacomo. In England they called me "Johnny". I still prefer Giacomo.'

'You lived in England?'

'I am English. Sounds confusing, but not really. Before the war I was a second officer in the

163

Merchant Navy – the Yugoslav one, I mean. I met a beautiful Canadian girl in Southampton so I left the ship.' He said it as if if had been the most natural thing in the world to do and Petersen could readily understand that for him it had been. 'There was a little difficulty at first at staying on in England but I'd found an excellent and very understanding boss who was working on a diving contract for the Government and who was one experienced diver short. I'd qualified as a diver before joining the merchant marine. By and by I got married –'

'Same girl?'

'Same girl. I became naturalized in August 1939 and joined the services on the outbreak of war the following month. Because I had a master's ocean-going ticket and was a qualified diver who could have been handy at things like sticking limpet mines on to warships in enemy harbours and was a natural for the Navy, it was inevitable, I suppose, that they put me into the infantry. I went to Europe, came back by Dunkirk, then went out to the Middle East.'

'And you've been in those parts ever since. No home leave?'

'No home leave.'

'So you haven't seen your wife in two years. Family?'

'Twin girls. One still-born. The other died at six months. Polio.' Giacomo's tone was matter-of-fact, almost casual. 'In the early summer of '41, my wife was killed in a Luftwaffe attack on Portsmouth.'

Petersen nodded and said nothing. There was nothing to say. One wondered why a man like Giacomo smiled so much but one did not wonder long.

'I was with the Eighth Army. Long-Range Desert Group. Then some genius finally discovered that I was really a sailor and not a soldier and I joined Jellicoe's Special Boat Service in the Aegean.' Both those hazardous services called for volunteers, Petersen knew: it was pointless to ask Giacomo why he had volunteered. 'Then the same genius found out some more about me, that I was a Yugoslav, and I was called back to Cairo to escort Lorraine to her destination.'

'And what happens when you've delivered her to her destination?'

'When *you've* delivered her, you mean. Responsibility over, from here on I just sit back and relax and go along for the ride. They thought I was the best man for the job but they weren't to know I was going to have the good luck to meet up with you.' Giacomo poured some more wine, leaned back in his chair and smiled broadly. 'I haven't a single cousin in the whole of Bosnia.'

'If it's luck, I hope it holds. My question, Giacomo.'

'Of course. Afterwards. I'd happily turn back now, conscience clear, but I've got to get a receipt or something from this fellow Mihajlović. I think they want me to take up diving again. Not hard to guess why – must have been the same genius who found out that I was an ex-sailor. As Michael said in that mountain inn, it's a funny old world. I spent over three years fighting the Germans and in a couple of weeks I'll be doing the same thing. This interlude, where I'm more or less fighting with the Germans – although I don't expect I'll ever see a German in Yugoslavia – I don't like one little bit.'

'You heard what George said to Michael. No point in rehashing it. A very brief interlude, Giacomo. You bid your charge a tearful farewell, trying not to smile, then heigh-ho for the Aegean.'

'Trying not to smile?' He considered the contents of his glass. 'Well, perhaps. Yes and no. If this is a funny old world, she's a funny young girl in a funny old war. Mercurial – like your cousin. Temperamental. Patrician-looking young lady but sadly deficient in patrician sang-froid. Cool, aloof, even remote at one moment, she can be friendly, even affectionate, the next.'

'The affectionate bit has escaped me so far.'

'A certain lack of rapport between you two has not escaped me either. She can be sweet and bad-tempered at the same time which is no small achievement. Most un-English. I suppose you know she's English. You seem to know quite a bit about her.'

'I know she's English because George told me so. He also told me you were from Montenegro.'

'Ah! Our professor of languages.'

'Remarkable linguist with a remarkable ear. He could probably give you your home address.'

'She tells me you know this Captain Harrison she's going to work for?'

'I know him well.'

'So does she. Used to work for him before. Peacetime. Rome. He was the manager of the Italian branch of an English ball-bearing company. She was his secretary. That's where she learned to speak Italian. She seems to like him a lot.'

'She seems to like men a lot. Period. You haven't fallen into her clutches yet, Giacomo?'

'No.' Again the broad smile. 'But I'm working on it.'

'Well, thanks.' Petersen stood. 'If you'll excuse me.' He crossed to where Sarina was sitting. 'I'd like to talk to you. Alone. I know that sounds ominous, but it isn't, really.'

'What about?'

'That's a silly question. If I want to talk to you privately I don't talk publicly.'

She rose and Michael did the same. He said: 'You're not going to talk to her without me.'

George sighed, rose wearily to his feet, crossed to where Michael was standing, put his two ham-like hands on the young man's shoulders and sat him in his chair as easily as he would have done a little child.

'Michael, you're only a private soldier. If you were in the American army you'd be a private

167

soldier, second class. I'm a Regimental Sergeant-Major. Temporary, mind you, but effective. I don't see why the Major should have to be bothered with you. I don't see why *I* should have to be bothered with you. Why should you bother us? You're not a boy any more.' He reached behind him, picked up a glass of Maraschino from the table and handed it to Michael, who took it sulkily but did not drink. 'If Sarina's kidnapped, we'll all know who did it.'

Petersen took the girl up to her room. He left the door ajar, looked around but not with the air of one expecting to find anything and sniffed the air. Sarina looked at him coldly and spoke the same way.

'What are you looking for? What are you sniffing for? Everything you do, everything you say is unpleasant, nasty, overbearing, superior, humiliating –'

'Oh, come on. I'm your guardian angel. You don't talk to your guardian angel that way.'

'Guardian angel! You also tell lies. You were telling lies in the dining-room. You still think I sent a radio message.'

'I don't and didn't. You're far too nice for anything underhand like that.' She looked at him warily then almost in startlement as he put his hands lightly on her shoulders, but did not try to flinch away. 'You're quick, you're intelligent-unlike your brother but that's not his fault – and I've no doubt you can or could be devious because

168

your face doesn't show much. Except for the one thing that would disqualify you from espionage. You're too transparently honest.'

'That's a kind of left-handed compliment,' she said doubtfully.

'Left or right, it's true.' He dropped to his knees, felt under the foot of the rather ill-fitting door, stood, extracted the key from the inside of the lock and examined it. 'You locked your door last night?'

'Of course.'

'What did you do with the key?'

'I left it in the lock. Half-turned. That way a person with a duplicate key or a master can't push your key through or on to a paper that's been pushed under the door. They taught us that in Cairo.'

'Spare me. Your instructor was probably a ten-year-old schoolboy. See those two tiny bright indentations on either side of the stem of the key?' She nodded. 'Made by an instrument much prized by the better-class burglar who's too sophisticated to batter doors open with a sledge-hammer. A pair of very slender pincers with tips of either Carbo-rundum or titanium stainless steel. Turn any key in a lock. You had a visitor during the night.'

'Somebody took my radio?'

'Somebody sure enough used it. Could have been here.'

'That's impossible. Certainly, I was tired last night but I'm not a heavy sleeper.'

'Maybe you were last night. How did you feel when you woke up this morning – when you were woken, I mean?'

'Well.' She hesitated. 'I felt a bit sick, really. But I thought I was perhaps over-tired and hadn't had enough sleep or I was scared – I'm not a great big coward but I'm not all that brave either and it was the first time anyone had ever pointed a gun at me – or perhaps I just wasn't used to the strange food.'

'You felt dopey, in other words.'

'Yes.'

'You probably were doped. I don't suggest flannel-foot crept stealthily in and applied a chloroform pad or anything of the kind, for the smell of that lingers for hours. Some gas that was injected through the keyhole from a nozzled canister that may well have come from the chemist's joker shop where Alessandro buys his toys. In any event, I can promise you that you won't be disturbed again tonight. And you rest easy in the knowledge that you're not on anyone's black list. Not judged, not condemned, not even suspected. You might at least have the grace to say that I'm not such an awful monster as you thought.'

She smiled faintly. 'Maybe you're not even a monster at all.'

'You're going to sleep, now?' She nodded so he said goodnight and closed the door behind him.

*   *   *

Almost an hour elapsed before Petersen, George and Josip were left together in the dining-room. The others had been in no hurry to depart. The night's events had not been conducive to an immediately renewed slumber and, besides, they were secure in the knowledge that there would be no early morning start.

George, who had returned to his red wine, was making steady inroads on his current uncounted bottle, looked and spoke as if he had been on mineral water all the time. There was, unfortunately, not the same lack of evidence about his cigar-smoking: an evil-smelling blue haze filled the upper half of the room.

'Your friend, Major Cipriano, didn't over-stay his welcome,' Josip said.

'He's no friend of mine,' Petersen said. 'Never seen him before. Appearances mean nothing but he seems a reasonable enough character. For an intelligence agent, that is. Have *you* known him long?'

'He has been here twice. As a bona-fide traveller. He's no friend. Thanking me for my help was just an attempt to divert suspicion from whoever tipped him off. A feeble attempt, he must have known it would fail but probably the best he could think up at the time. What was his object in coming here?'

'No mystery about that. Both the Germans and Italians are suspicious of me. I have a message to deliver to the leader of the Četniks. On the boat coming across from Italy one of his agents, an unpleasant character called Alessandro, tried to get this message from me. He wanted to see if it was the same as a copy he was carrying. He failed, so Cipriano got worried and came across to Ploče. He was tipped off as to our whereabouts, came up here – almost certainly by light plane – and, when we were herded down here, went through our possessions, steamed open the envelope containing my message, found that it was unchanged and resealed it. Exit Cipriano, baffled but satisfied – for the moment anyway.'

George said: 'Sarina?'

'Someone got into her room in the early hours of this morning. That was after she had been doped. Her radio was used to call up Cipriano. Sarina says she trusts me now. I don't believe her.'

'It is as always,' George said mournfully. 'Every man's – and woman's – hands are against us.'

'Doped?' Josip was incredulous. 'In my hotel? How can anyone be doped in my hotel?'

'How can anyone be doped anywhere?'

'Who was this villain?'

'Villainess. Lorraine.'

'Lorraine! That beautiful girl?'

'Maybe her mind is not as beautiful as the rest of her.'

'Sarina. Now Lorraine.' George shook his head sadly. 'The monstrous regiment of women.'

Josip said: 'But how do you know?'

'Simple arithmetic. Elimination. Lorraine went for a walk tonight and returned very hurriedly. She didn't go for the walk's sake. She went for something else. Information. You went with her, Josip. Do you recall her doing or saying anything odd?'

'She didn't do anything. Just walked. And she said very little.'

'That should make it easy to remember.'

'Well, she said it was odd that I didn't have the name of the hotel outside. I told her I hadn't yet got around to putting it up and that it was the Hotel Eden. She also said it was funny that there were no streets signs up, so I gave her the name of the street. Ah! So she got the name and address, no?'

'Yes.' Petersen rose. 'Bed. I trust you're not going to stay here for the remainder of the night, George.'

'Certainly not.' George fetched a fresh bottle from behind the bar. 'But we academics must have our moments for meditation.'

At noon that day, Petersen and his six companions had still not left the Hotel Eden. Instead, they were just sitting down to a lunch which Josip had insisted they have, a meal that was to prove to be on a par with the dinner they had had the previous evening. But there was one vacant seat.

Josip said: 'Where is the Professor?'

'George,' Petersen said, 'is indisposed. In bed. Acute stomach pains. He thinks it must have been something he had to eat last night.'

'Something he had to eat!' Josip was indignant. 'He had exactly the same to eat as anyone else last night – except, of course, a great deal more of it – and nobody else is stricken. My food, indeed! *I* know what ails the Professor. When I came down early this morning, just about two hours after you went to bed, the Professor was still here, still, as he said, meditating.'

'That might help to account for it.'

That might have accounted for it but it didn't account for George's appearance some ten minutes after the meal had commenced. He tried to smile wanly but he didn't look wan.

'Sorry to be late. The Major will have told you I was unwell. However, the cramps have eased a little and I thought I might try a little something. To settle the stomach, you understand.'

By one o'clock George's stomach seemed to have settled in a most remarkable fashion. In the fifty minutes that had intervened since his joining the company he had consumed twice as much as anyone else and effortlessly disposed of two large bottles of wine.

'Congratulations are in order, George,' Giacomo said. 'One moment at death's door and now – well, an incredible performance.'

'It was nothing,' George said modestly. 'In many ways, I am an incredible man.'

Petersen sat on the bed in George's room. 'Well?'

'Satisfactory. In one way, not well. There were two items that one would not have looked for in such an aristocratic young lady's luggage. One was a very small leather case with a few highly professional burglarious tools. The other was a small metal box with some sachets inside, the sachets containing a liquid. When squeezed, the liquid turned into a gas. I sniffed only a very tiny amount. An anaesthetic of some kind, that's certain. The interesting thing is that this little box, though smaller than Alessandro's, was made of and lined with the same materials. What do we do with this young charmer?'

'Leave her be. She's not dangerous. If she were, she wouldn't have made so amateurish a mistake.'

'You said you knew the identity of the miscreant. She's going to wonder why you haven't disclosed it.'

'Let her wonder. What's she going to do about it?'

'There's that,' George said. 'There's that.'

SIX

It was snowing heavily and the temperature was below freezing when Petersen drove the stolen Italian truck out of Mostar shortly after two o'clock that afternoon. The two girls beside him were silent and withdrawn, a circumstance that affected Petersen not at all. Relaxed and untroubled, he drove as unhurriedly as a man with all the time in the world and, after passing unhindered through a check-point at Potoci, slowed down even more, an action dictated not by any change of mood but by the nature of the road. It was narrow, twisting and broken-surfaced and urgently in need of the attentions of road repair gangs who had not passed that way for a long time: more importantly, they had begun to climb, and climb quite steeply, as the Neretva valley narrowed precipitously on either side of the river which sank further and further below the tortuous road until there was an almost sheer drop of several hundred feet to the foaming river that lay beneath them. Given the unstable nature of the road, the fact that there were no crash-barriers or restraining walls to prevent their sliding off the slippery road and the fact that the river itself increasingly disappeared in the thickening snowsqualls, it was not a route to lighten the hearts of those of an imaginative or nervous disposition. Judging by the hand-clenching and highly apprehensive expression of Petersen's two front-seat companions, they clearly came well within that category. Petersen had neither comfort nor cheer to offer them, not through any callous indifference but because on the evidence of their own eyes they wouldn't have believed a word he said anyway.

Their relief was almost palpable when Petersen abruptly turned off the road into a narrow gully which suddenly – and to the two girls, miraculously – appeared in the vertical cliff-side to their right. The road was no road at all, just a convoluted, rutted track that offered only minimal traction for the almost constantly spinning rear wheels, but at least there was no way they could fall off it: high walls of rock pressed in closely on both sides. Perhaps five minutes after leaving the main road, Petersen stopped, cut the engine and dropped down.

'This is as far as we go,' he said. 'As far as we can go in this truck, anyway. Stay here.' He walked round to the back of the truck, parted the curtains, repeated his words and disappeared into the swirling snow.

He was back within a few minutes, sitting beside the driver of a peculiar open vehicle which looked as if it might once have been a small truck that had had both its top and rear sliced off. The driver, clad in British warm – a thick, khaki, woollen overcoat – could have been of any nationality: with a fur cap pulled down to eyebrow level, a luxuriant black beard and moustache and a pair of horn-rimmed sunglasses, there wasn't a single distinguishable feature of his face to be seen except for a nose that could have belonged to anyone. Petersen stepped down as the vehicle came to a halt.

'This is Dominic,' he said. 'He's come to help us along a bit. That's a four-wheel-drive vehicle he's got there. It can go places where this truck can't, but even then it can't go very far, perhaps a couple of kilometres. Dominic will take the two young ladies, all our gear and all our blankets – I can assure you we're going to need those tonight – as far as he can, then come back for the rest of us. We'll start walking.'

Sarina said: 'You mean to tell us you expected this friend of yours to meet us here? And at just this time?'

'Give or take a few minutes. I wouldn't be much of a tour guide, would I, if I got all my connections wrong?'

'This truck,' Giacomo said. 'You're surely not going to leave it here?'

'Why ever not?'

'I thought it was your custom to park unwanted Italian trucks in the Neretva. I saw some lovely parking spots in the god-awful ravine we just came through.'

'A sinful waste. Besides, we might even want it again. What matters, of course, is that our friend Major Cipriano already knows we have it.'

'How would he know that?'

'How would he not know it, you mean. Has it not occurred to you that the informer who tipped him off to our presence in the Hotel Eden would also have given him all the details of our trip from the torpedo boat, including those of this vehicle? Either by radio or before being apparently dragged from an hotel bedroom, it doesn't matter. We passed through a check-point at Potoci about an hour ago and the guard didn't even bother to slow us down. Odd, one might think, except that he had already been given details of our vehicle, recognized it at once and obeyed orders to let us through. Let's get that stuff out quickly. It's turned even colder than I thought it would be.'

It had indeed. A south-east wind had sprung up, a wind from which they would have been sheltered in the Neretva valley, and was steadily strengthening. This would not normally have been a cold wind but this was a wind that paid no attention to meteorological norms: it could have been blowing straight from Siberia. The four-wheel-drive vehicle was loaded with passengers and gear and drove off in a remarkably short time:

there could be no doubt that Dominic's sunglasses were, in effect, snow-glasses.

The five men set out on foot and were picked up some fifteen minutes later by the returning Dominic. The ride along an even more bumpy and deteriorating track was, because of the increase in snowdepth and incline, uncomfortable and haphazard to a degree, and only marginally better and faster than walking. None of the passengers was sorry when the truck pulled up at the track's end outside a ramshackle wooden hut which proved to be its garage. Inside, the two girls were sheltering from the snow. They were not alone. There were three men – boys, rather – in vaguely paramilitary uniforms and five ponies.

Sarina said: 'Where on earth are we?'

'Home, sweet home,' Petersen said. 'Well, an hour and a half's gentle ride and we'll be there. This is the mountain of Prenj, more of a massif, really. The Neretva river makes a big U-turn here and runs around three sides of it, which makes Prenj, in defensive terms, an ideal place to be. Only two bridges cross the river, one to the northwest at Jablanica, the other to the north-east at Konjik, and both of those are easily guarded and defended. It's open to the south-east but no danger threatens from that direction.'

'Gentle ride, you said. Do those horses canter or gallop? I don't like horses.'

'They're ponies, not horses, and, no, they don't canter or gallop. Not on this occasion anyway.

They wouldn't be stupid enough to try. It's all uphill and pretty steeply uphill.'

'I don't think I'm going to enjoy this climb.'

'You'll enjoy the view.'

It was half an hour later and she was enjoying neither the climb nor the view. The climb, though not impossibly steep, was a difficult enough one and the view, remarkable though it was, engendered in her only a feeling that lay halfway between fascinated horror and paralysed terror. The path, barely two metres in width and sometimes noticeably less, had been gouged out of the side of a slope so steep as to be virtually a cliff-side, and ascended it by a series, a seemingly endless series, of hairpin twists and turns. With every step the pony took, the floor of the narrow valley, when it could be seen at all through the driving snow, seemed more remotely and vertically distant. Only she and Lorraine had been mounted: the other three ponies carried all their securely strapped gear and blankets. Lorraine was on foot now, clutching Giacomo's arm as if he was her last faint hope on earth.

Petersen, walking beside Sarina's pony, said: 'I'm afraid you're not enjoying this as much as I would like you to.'

'Enjoying it!' She shuddered uncontrollably, not with cold. 'Back in the hotel I told you I wasn't a great big coward. Well, I am, I am! I'm terrified. I keep on telling myself it's silly, it's stupid, but I can't help it.'

Petersen said matter-of-factly: 'You're not a coward. It's been like this since you were a child.'

'Like what? What do you mean?'

'Vertigo is what I mean. Anyone can suffer from it. Some of the bravest men I know, some of the most fearsome fighters I've ever met, won't climb a step-ladder or set foot in a plane.'

'Yes, yes. Always. Do you know about it?'

'I don't get it, but I've seen it too often not to know about it. Dizziness, loss of equilibrium, an almost uncontrollable desire to throw yourself over the edge and, in the present case, a conviction on your part that your pony is about to jump out into space at any moment. That's about it, isn't it?'

She nodded, dumbly. Petersen refrained from saying that if she'd known about her condition and the Yugoslav mountains, she should have stayed in Cairo. Instead he moved round the head of the horse and took her stirrup-leather in his hand.

'These ponies are more sure-footed than we are and by a long way. Even if it should suffer from a bout of vertigo now, and ponies never do, I would be the first over the edge. And even if you felt like throwing yourself over, you can't because I'm between you and the cliff edge and I'd stop you and catch you. And I'll change sides at every corner. That way we'll be sure to make it to the top. I won't be so silly as to tell you to sit back and relax: all I can say is that you'll be feeling a lot better in fifteen minutes or so.'

'We'll be away from this cliff by that time?' The tremor was still in her voice.

'We will, we will.' They wouldn't be, but by that time it would be so dark that she would be unable to see the valley below.

It was quite some time after dark when they passed through the perimeter of what seemed to be a permanent camp of sorts. There were a large number of huts and tents, all close together and nearly all illuminated: not brightly illuminated, for at that remote altitude there was no central power grid and the only small generator available was reserved for the headquarters area: for the rest, the great majority of the guerrilla soldiers and the inevitable camp-followers, there was only the light to be had from oil, tallow or coke braziers. Then there came a quite uninhabited and gently rising slope of perhaps three hundred metres before their small cavalcade fetched up at a large hut with a metal roof and two windows which gave out a surprising amount of light.

'Well, here we are,' Petersen said. 'Home or what you'd better call home until you find a better word for it.' He reached up his hands and swung the shivering girl to the ground. She clung to him as if she were trying to prevent herself from falling to the ground which was what she was indeed trying to do.

'My legs feel all funny.' Her voice was low and husky but at least the tremor had gone.

'Sure they do. I'll bet you've never been on a horse before.'

'You'd win your bet but it's not that. The way I hung on to that horse, clung to it –' She tried to laugh but it was a poor enough attempt. 'I'll be surprised if that poor pony doesn't have bruised ribs for days to come.'

'You did very well.'

'Very well! I'm ashamed of myself. I hope you won't go around telling everyone that you've met up with the most cowardly radio operator in the Balkans.'

'I won't. I won't because I don't go around telling lies. I think you may be the bravest girl I ever met.'

'After that performance!'

'Especially after that performance.'

She was still clinging to him, clearly still not trusting her balance, was silent for a few moments, then said: 'I think you may be the kindest man I've ever met.'

'Good God!' He was genuinely astonished. 'The strain has been too much. After all you've said about me!'

'Especially after everything I said about you.'

She was still holding him, although now only tentatively, when they heard the sound of a heavy fist banging on a wooden door and George's booming voice saying: 'Open up, in the name of the law or common humanity or whatever. We have crossed the burning sands and are dying of thirst.'

The door opened almost immediately and a tall, thin figure appeared, framed in the rectangle of light. He came down the two steps and thrust out a hand.

'It cannot be . . .' He had an excruciatingly languid Oxbridge accent.

'It is.' George took his hand. 'Enough of the formalities. At stake there is nothing less than the sacred name of British hospitality.'

'Goodness gracious!' The man screwed a monocle, an oddly-shaped oval one, into his right eye, advanced towards Lorraine, took her hand, swept it up in a gesture of exquisite gallantry and kissed it. 'Goodness gracious me. Lorraine Chamberlain!' He seemed about to embark upon a speech of some length, caught sight of Petersen and went to meet him. 'Peter, my boy. Once again all those dreadful trials and tribulations lie behind you. My word, I can't tell you how dull and depressing it's been here during the two weeks you've been gone. Dreadful, I tell you. Utterly dreadful.'

Petersen smiled. 'Hello, Jamie. Good to see you again. Things should improve now. George, quite illicitly, of course, has brought you some presents – quite a lot of presents, they almost broke the back of one of the ponies coming up here. Presents that go clink.' He turned to Sarina. 'May I introduce Captain Harrison. Captain Harrison,' he added with a straight face, 'is English. Jamie, this is Sarina von Karajan.'

Harrison shook her hand enthusiastically. 'Delighted, delighted. If only you knew how we miss even the commonest amenities of civilization in these benighted parts. Not, of course,' he added hastily, 'that there's anything common about you. My goodness, I should say not.' He looked at Petersen. 'The Harrisons' ill luck runs true to form again. We were born under an evil and accursed star. Do you mean to tell me that you have had the great fortune, the honour, the pleasure of escorting those two lovely ladies all the way from Italy?'

'Neither of them think there was any fortune, honour or pleasure about it. I didn't know you had the pleasure of knowing Lorraine before.' Giacomo had a sudden but very brief paroxysm of coughing which Petersen ignored.

'Oh, my goodness, yes, indeed. Old friends, very old. Worked together once, don't you know? Tell you some time. Your other new friends?' Petersen introduced Giacomo and Michael whom Harrison welcomed in what was his clearly customary effusive fashion, then said: 'Well, inside, inside. Can't have you all freezing to death in this abominable weather. I'll have your goods and chattels taken in. Inside, inside.'

'Inside' was surprisingly roomy, warm, well-lit and, by guerrilla standards, almost comfortable. There were three bunks running the length of each side of the room, some tall articles of furniture that could have been either cupboards or wardrobes, a deal table, half a dozen pine chairs, the unheard luxury of a couple of rather scruffy arm-chairs and even two strips of worn and faded carpet. At either end of the room were two doors that led, presumably, to further accommodation. Harrison closed the outside door behind him.

'Have a seat, have a seat.' The Captain was much given to repeating himself. 'George, if I may suggest – ah, foolish of me, I might have known that any such suggestion was superfluous.' George had, indeed, lost no time in doubling in his spare-time role of barman. Harrison looked around him with an air of proprietorial pride. 'Not bad, although I say it myself, not bad at all. You won't find many such havens in this strife-torn land. I regret to say that we live in accommodation such as this all too infrequently, but when we do we make the best of it. Electric light, if you please – you can't hear it but we have the only generator in the base apart from the commander. Need it for our big radios.' He pointed to two six-inch diameter pipes angling diagonally upwards along either wall to disappear through the roof. 'Central heating, of course. Actually, they're only the stove-pipes from our coke and wood stove outside. Would have it inside but we'd all be asphyxiated in minutes. And what do we have here, George?' He inspected the contents of a glass George had just handed him.

George shrugged and said diffidently: 'Nothing really. Highland malt whisky.'

'Highland malt whisky.' Harrison reverently surveyed the amber liquid, sipped it delicately and smiled in rapture. 'Where on earth did you get this, George?'

'Friend of mine in Rome.'

'God bless your Roman friends.' This time assuming his beatific expression in advance, Harrison sipped again. 'Well, that's about all the mod cons. That door to the left leads to my radio room. Some nice stuff in there but unfortunately we can't take most of it with us when we travel which, again unfortunately, is most of the time. The other door leads to what I rather splendidly call my sleeping quarters. It's about the size of a couple of telephone boxes but it does have two cots.' Harrison took another sip from his glass and went on gallantly: 'Those quarters, naturally, I will gladly vacate for the night for the two young ladies.'

'You are very kind,' Sarina said doubtfully. 'But I – we – were supposed to report to the Colonel.'

'Nonsense. Not to be thought of. You are exhausted by your travels, your sufferings, your privations. One has only to look at you. I am sure the Colonel will gladly wait until the morning. Is that not so, Peter?'

'Tomorrow will be time enough.'

'Of course. Well, we castaways marooned on a mountain top are always eager for news of the outside world. What of the past fortnight, my friend?'

Petersen put down his untouched glass and rose. 'George will tell you. He's a much better raconteur than I am.'

'Well, yes, you do rather lack his gift for dramatic embellishment. Duty calls?' Petersen nodded.

'Ah! The Colonel?'

'Who else. I won't be long.'

When Petersen returned, he was not alone. The two men accompanying him were, like himself, covered in a heavy coating of snow. While they were brushing this off, Harrison rose courteously and introduced them.

'Good evening, gentlemen. We are honoured.' He turned to the newcomers. 'Let me introduce Major Ranković, Major Metrović, two of the Colonel's senior commanders. You venture forth on a wild night, gentlemen.'

'You mean, of course, why have we come?' The speaker, Major Metrović, was a man of medium height, dark, thickset and cheerful. 'Curiosity, of course. Peter's movements are always shrouded in mystery and heaven knows we see little enough of new faces from the outer world.'

'Peter didn't also mention that two of those new faces were young, female and – I speak as a detached observer, of course – rather extraordinarily good-looking?'

'He may have done, he may have done.' Metrović smiled again. 'You know how it is with my colleague and myself. Our minds are invariably preoccupied with military matters. Isn't that so, Marino?'

Marino – Major Ranković – a tall, thin, dark-bearded and rather gloomy character, who looked as if he let Metrović do all the smiling for both of them, didn't say whether it was so or not. He seemed preoccupied and the source of his preoccupation was unquestionably Giacomo.

'I asked them along,' Petersen said. 'I felt it was the least I could do to bring some relief into their cheerless lives.'

'Well, welcome, welcome.' Harrison looked at his watch. 'Won't be long, you said. What do you call short?'

'I wanted to give George a chance to finish his story. Besides, I was detained. Much questioning. And I stopped by at my radio hut to see if you'd made off with anything during my absence. It seems not. Perhaps you mislaid the key.'

'The radio hut?' Sarina glanced at the door at the end of the room. 'But we heard nothing. I mean –'

'My radio hut is fifty metres away. No mystery. There are three radios in the camp. One for the Colonel. One for Captain Harrison. One for me. You will be assigned to the Colonel. Lorraine comes here.'

'You arranged that?'

'I arranged nothing. I take orders, just like anyone else. The Colonel arranged it, Lorraine's assignation here was arranged weeks ago. There's no secret about it. The Colonel, for reasons that may seem obscure to you but which I understand very well, prefers that Captain Harrison's radio operator, like Captain Harrison himself, should not speak or understand Serbo-Croat. The basis of the Colonel's security beliefs is that one should trust nobody.'

'You must have a lot in common with the Colonel.'

'I think that's rather unfair, young lady.' It was Metrović again and he was still smiling. 'I can confirm what the Major has said. I'm the go-between, the translator, if you like, for the Colonel and Captain Harrison. Like the major, I was partly educated in England.'

'Enough,' Harrison said. 'Let us put unworthy thoughts to one side and concentrate on more important things.'

'Such as hospitality?' George said.

'Such as hospitality, as you say. Be seated, please. What is your choice, gentlemen – and ladies, of course?'

They all told him what they wanted, all, that is, except Major Ranković. He crossed to where Giacomo was seated and said: 'May I ask what your name is?'

Giacomo lifted his eyebrows in slight puzzlement, smiled and said: 'Giacomo.'

'That's an Italian name, isn't it?'

'Yes.'

'Giacomo what?'

'Just Giacomo.'

'Just Giacomo.' Ranković's voice was deep and gravelly. 'It suits you to be mysterious?'

'It suits me to mind my own business.'

'What's your rank?'

'That's my business, too.'

'I've seen you before. Not in the army, though. Rijeka, Split, Kotor, some place like that.'

'It's possible.' Giacomo was still smiling but the smile no longer extended to his eyes. 'It's a small enough world. I used to be a sailor.'

'You're a Yugoslav.'

Giacomo, Petersen was aware, could easily have conceded the fact but he knew he wouldn't. Ranković was an able soldier but no psychologist.

'I'm English.'

'You're a liar.'

Petersen stepped forward and tapped Ranković on the shoulder. 'If I were you, Marino, I'd quit while I was ahead. Not, mind you, that I think you are ahead.'

Ranković turned. 'What do you mean?'

'I mean that you're still intact and in one piece. Keep on like this and you'll wake up in hospital wondering if you fell under a train. I can vouch for Giacomo. He is English. He's got so long and so distinguished a war record that he puts any man in this room to shame. While you've been pottering around the mountains he's been fighting in France and Belgium and North Africa and the

192

Aegean and usually on assignments so dangerous that you couldn't even begin to wonder what they were like. Look at his face, Marino. Look at it and you'll look into the face of war.'

Ranković studied Giacomo closely. 'I'm not a fool. I never questioned his qualities as a soldier. I was curious, that is all, and maybe, like the Colonel and yourself, I am not much given to trusting anyone. I did not intend to give offence.'

'And I didn't intend to take any,' Giacomo said. His good humour had returned. 'You're suspicious, I'm touchy. A bad mix. Let me suggest a good mix or rather no mix at all. You never mix malt whisky with anything, do you, George? Not even water?'

'Sacrilege.'

'You were right on one count, Major. I am English but I was born in Yugoslavia. Let us drink to Yugoslavia.'

'A toast no man could quarrel with,' Ranković said. There were no handshakes, no protestations of eternal friendship. It was, at best, a truce. Ranković, no actor, still had his reservations about Giacomo.

Petersen, for his part, had none.

Considerably later in the evening an understandably much more relaxed and mellowed atmosphere had descended upon the company. Some of them had paid a brief visit to a mess four hundred metres distant for an evening meal. Sarina and

Lorraine had point-blank – and as it turned out, wisely – refused to brave the near blizzard that was now sweeping by outside. Michael, inevitably, had elected to remain with them and Giacomo, after a quick exchange of glances with Petersen, had announced that he was not hungry. Giacomo did not have to have it spelt out to him that, even among his own people, Petersen was suspicious of practically everybody in sight.

Compared to Josip Pijade's midday offerings, the meal was a gastronomic disaster. It was no fault of the Četnik cooks – as elsewhere through that ravaged country, food was at a premium and fine food almost wholly unobtainable. Still, it was a sad come-down from the flesh-pots of Italy and Mostar and even George could manage no more than two platefuls of the fatty mutton and beans which constituted the main and only course of the evening. They had left as soon as decency permitted.

Back in Harrison's radio hut their relative sufferings were soon forgotten.

'There's no place like home,' Harrison announced to nobody in particular. Although it would have been unfair to call him inebriated, it would have been fair to pass the opinion that he wasn't stone cold sober either.

He bent an appreciative gaze on the glass in his hand. 'Nectar emboldens me. George has given me a very comprehensive account of your activities over the past two weeks. He has not, however, told me *why* you went to Rome in the first place. Nor did you seek to enlighten me on your return.'

'That's because I didn't know myself.'

Harrison nodded sagely. 'That makes sense. You go all the way to Rome and back and you don't know why.'

'I was just carrying a message. I didn't know the contents.'

'Is one permitted to ask if you know the contents now?'

'One is permitted. I do.'

'Ah! Is one further permitted to know the contents?'

'In your own language, Jamie, I don't know whether I'm permitted or not. All I can say is that this is purely a military matter. Strictly, I am not a military man, a commander of troops. I'm an espionage agent. Espionage agents don't wage battles. We're far too clever for that. Or cowardly.'

Harrison looked at Metrović and Ranković in turn. 'You're military men. If I'm to believe half you tell me, you wage battles.'

Metrović smiled. 'We're not as clever as Peter.'

'You know the contents of the message?'

'Of course. Peter's discretion does him credit but it's not really necessary. Within a couple of days the news will be common knowledge throughout the camp. We – the Germans, Italians, ourselves and the Ustaša – are to launch an all-out offensive against the Partisans. We shall annihilate Titoland. The Germans have given the name of the attack "Operation Weiss": the Partisans will doubtless call it the Fourth Offensive.'

Harrison seemed unimpressed. He said, doubtfully: 'That means, of course, that you've made three other offensives already. Those didn't get you very far, did they?'

Metrović was unruffled. 'I know it's easy to say, but this time really will be different. They're cornered. They're trapped. They've no way out, no place left to go. They haven't a single plane, fighter or bomber. We have squadrons upon squadrons. They haven't a tank, not even a single effective anti-aircraft gun. At the most, they have fifteen thousand men, most of them starving, weak, sick and untrained. We have almost a hundred thousand men, well-trained and fit. And Tito's final weakness, his Achilles' heel, you might say, is his lack of mobility: he is known to have at least three thousand wounded men on his hands. It will be no contest. I don't say I look forward to it, but it will be a massacre. Are you a betting man, James?'

'Not against odds like that, I'm not. Like Peter here, I lay no claim to being a military man – I never even *saw* a uniform until three years ago – but if the action is so imminent why are you drinking wine at your leisured ease instead of being hunched over your war maps, sticking flags in here, flags in there, drawing up your battle plans or whatever you're supposed to be doing in cases like this?'

Metrović laughed. 'Three excellent reasons. First, the offensive is not imminent – it's two weeks away yet. Second, all the plans have already been drawn up and all the troops are already in position or will be in a few days. Third, the main assault takes place at Bihać, where the Partisan forces are at present centred, and that's over two hundred kilometres north-west of here. We're not taking part in that: we're staying just where we are in case the Partisans are so foolish, or optimistic or suicidal to try to break out to the south-east: stopping them from crossing the Neretva, in the remote possibility of a few stragglers getting as far as here, would be only a formality.' He paused and gazed at a darkened window. 'There may well be a fourth possibility. If the weather worsens, or even continues like this, the best laid plans of the High Command could well go wrong. A postponement would be inevitable. Nobody's going to be moving around the mountains in those impossible weather conditions for days to come, that's for sure. Days might well become weeks.'

'Well, yes,' Harrison said. 'One sees why you face the future with a certain resigned fortitude. On the basis of what you say the chances are good that you won't even become involved at all. For myself, I hope your prognosis is correct – as I've said I'm no man of war and I've become quite attached to these rather comfortable quarters. And do you, Peter, expect to hibernate along with us?'

'No. If the Colonel has nothing for me in the morning – and he gave no indication tonight that he would have – then I shall be on my way the following morning. Provided, of course, that we're not up to our ears in snowdrifts.'

'Whither away, if one is –'

'Permitted to ask? Yes. A certain Italian intelligence officer is taking an undue amount of interest in me. He's trying either to discredit me or hamper me in my operations. Has tried, I should say. I would like to find out why.'

Metrović said: 'In what way has he tried, Peter?'

'He and a gang of his thugs held us up in a Mostar hotel in the early hours of this morning. Looking for something, I suppose. Whether they found it or not I don't know. Shortly before that, on the boat coming from Italy, some of his minions tried to carry out a night attack on us. They failed, but not for the want of trying, for they were carrying syringes and lethal drugs which they were more than prepared to use.'

'Goodness me.' Harrison looked suitably appalled. 'What happened?'

'It was all quite painless, really,' George said with satisfaction. 'We welded them up in a cabin on the boat. Last heard of they were still there.'

Harrison looked reproachfully at George. 'Missed this out in your stirring account of your activities, didn't you?'

'Discretion, discretion.'

'This Italian intelligence officer,' Metrović said, 'is, of course an ally. With some allies, as we know, you don't need enemies. When you meet up with this ally what are you going to do? Question him or kill him?' The Major seemed to regard that as a very natural query.

'Kill him?' Sarina looked and was shocked. 'That nice man. Kill him! I thought you rather liked him.'

'Liked him? He's reasonable, personable, smiling, open-faced, has a firm handshake and looks you straight in the eye – anyone can tell at once that he's a member of the criminal classes. He was prepared to kill me, by proxy, mind you, through his hatchet-man Alessandro – which, if anything, makes it an even more heinous intention on his part – so why shouldn't I be prepared to pre-empt him? But I won't, at least not right away. I just want to ask him a few questions.'

'But – but you might not even be able to find him.'

'I'll find him.'

'And if he refuses to answer?'

'He'll answer.' There was the same chilling certainty in the voice.

She touched her lips with the back of her hand and fell silent. Metrović, his face thoughtful, said: 'You're not the man to ask questions unless you're pretty certain of the answers in advance. You're after confirmation of something. Could you not have obtained this confirmation at the hotel you mentioned?'

'Certainly. But I didn't want the place littered with corpses, not all of which might have been theirs. I'd promised to deliver this lot intact first. Everything in its due turn. Confirmation? I want confirmation of why Italy is planning to pull out of this war. That they want out I don't for a moment doubt. Their people never wanted this war. Their army, navy and air force never wanted it. Remember when Wavell's army in North Africa overwhelmed the Italians? There was a picture taken just after the last battle, a picture that was to become world-famous. It showed about a thousand Italian prisoners being marched off to their barbed wire cages escorted by three British soldiers. The sun was so hot that the soldiers had given their rifles to three of the prisoners to carry. That about sums up the Italian attitude to the war.

'Given a cause that is close to their hearts, the Italians can fight as gallantly as any people on earth. This cause is not close to their hearts – it couldn't be further away from it. This is Germany's war and they don't like fighting Germany's war because, basically, they don't like the Germans. It has been repeatedly claimed, both by the Italians and the British that the Italians are, at bottom, pro-British. The truth is, of course, that they're just pro-Italian.

'No-one is more acutely aware of this than the Italian high command. But there's more to it of course than just patriotism. There's no lack of first-class minds in the Italian high command and it's my belief that they are convinced, even at this early stage, that the Germans are going to lose the war.' Petersen looked round the room. 'It may not be your belief, it may not be my belief, but that's irrelevant. What matters is that I'm convinced it is their belief and that they are even now figuring out a way to arrive at an accommodation – for want of a better word – with the British and Americans. This accommodation, of course, would take the form of a full-scale surrender but, of course, it would be nothing of the sort. It would involve full-scale cooperation upon the part of the Italians with every aspect of the British and American forces just short of the front-line engagement of their troops in the front line.'

'You seem very sure about this, Peter,' Metrović said. 'How can you be so sure?'

'Because I have access to sources and information that none of you has. I am in constant touch with both Italian and German forces in this country and, as you know, I'm a frequent visitor to Italy and have talked to literally hundreds of Italians there, both military men and civilians. I am neither literally deaf nor figuratively dumb. I know, for instance, that Italian Intelligence and German Intelligence are barely on civil speaking terms with each other and most certainly do not trust each other round the nearest corner in the street.

'General Granelli, Head of Italian Intelligence and Cipriano's boss – Cipriano is this Intelligence Major I was talking about – is an evil and warped character but out-and-out brilliant. He knows the situation and the options as well as anyone and is in no doubt that the Germans are going to go down in dust and flames and has no intention of joining them there. He's also pretty certain that I know quite well what the true situation is and that if I start voicing my doubts – my convictions, rather – out loud I could be a positive danger to him. I think he's been twice on the point of having me eliminated and has twice changed his mind at the last minute. I know there's going to be a third time which is one reason why I want to get out of here – before Cipriano or some other comes, in the guise of a loyal ally, naturally, and arranges for an accident to happen to me. But the main reason, of course, for my departure is to get to their link-man before he gets to me.'

'Link-man? Link-man?' Harrison shook his head in bafflement. 'You speak in riddles, Peter.'

'A riddle with a childishly easy answer. If the Germans go down who else is going to go down with them?'

'Ah-ha!'

'As you've just said, ah-ha. All those who have fought with them, that's who. Including us. If you were General Granelli and with Granelli's keen eye to the future, which of the opposing forces in Yugoslavia would you back?'

'Good Lord!' Harrison sounded slightly stunned. He looked around the room. The others, if not quite stunned, looked for the most part deeply pensive, not least Ranković and Metrović. 'What you are saying is that Granelli and this Major Cipriano are working hand-in-hand with the Partisans and that Cipriano is the master double-agent?'

Petersen rubbed his chin with his hand, glanced briefly at Harrison, sighed, poured himself some more red wine and did not deign to answer.

Petersen's radio shack did not begin to compare in magnificence with Harrison's, which they had left only a few moments previously, a premature departure arising directly from the conversational hiatus that had ensued immediately after Harrison's last words, a lacuna that went on and on and on. Harrison and the two Četnik officers were sunk in profound reverie, Sarina and Lorraine, by their expressions not by words, had made it clear that their aversion to Petersen had not only returned but was in fuller flood than ever and Alex and Michael, as ever, had nothing to say. Those two master conversationalists, George and Giacomo, had battled bravely but only briefly on. It was a lost cause.

The hut would have been big enough to serve as a one-car garage, if the car were small enough. Three beds, a table, three chairs, a cooking stove and that was all: the radio room was a tiny office next door.

'I am sad and disturbed,' George said. 'Profoundly disturbed.' He poured himself a large glass of wine and drank half of it in one apparently endless gulp just to show how profoundly disturbed he was. 'Sad, perhaps, is a better word. The realization that one's life and one's lifework has been a failure is a bitter pill to swallow. The damage to one's pride and self-esteem is irreparable. The effect, overall, is crushing.'

'I know what you mean,' Petersen said sympathetically. 'I've felt that myself.'

George might not have heard him. 'You will not have forgotten the days when you were my student in Belgrade?'

'Who could, ever? As you said yourself, not more than a hundred times, a walk with you through the rose-arboured groves of academe was an experience to remain with one always.'

'Remember the precepts I preached, the eternal verities I cherished? Honour, honesty, straightforwardness, the pure in mind, the open heart, the outright contempt for deceit, deception, dishonesty: we were, remember, to go through the darkness of this world guided solely by the light of the everlasting flame of truth?'

'Yes, George.'

'I am a broken man.'

'I'm sorry, George.'

SEVEN

There were six of them in all, and six tougher looking and more villainous characters it would have been almost impossible to imagine, far less find. There was a curious likeness about them. They were all just over medium height, all lean and broad-shouldered, all clad exactly alike: khaki trousers tucked into high boots, belted khaki canvas jacket over a khaki tunic, and khaki forage caps. They carried no badges, no identification marks. All were armed in precisely the same fashion: machine-pistols in hands, a revolver at waist level and hunting knives stuck into a sheath on the right boot. Their faces were dark and still, their eyes quiet and watchful. They were dangerous men.

Surprise had been complete, resistance – even the thought of a token resistance – unthinkable. The same company as had been in Harrison's hut the previous evening, had been there just a few minutes before eight that evening when the outside door had burst open and three men had been inside the door with levelled guns before anyone could even react. Now there were six inside, and the door was closed. One of the intruders, a little shorter and a little broader than the others, took a pace forward.

'My name is Crni.' It was the Serbo-Croat word for black. 'You will take off your weapons, one by one, and place them on the floor.' He nodded at Metrović. 'You begin.'

Within a minute every gun in the room – at least every visible gun – was lying on the floor. Crni beckoned Lorraine. 'Pick up those guns and put them on that table there. You will not, of course, be so stupid as to even think of firing any of them.'

Lorraine had no thought of firing any of them, her hands were shaking so much that she had some difficulty in picking them up. When they were on the table Crni said: 'Are either of you two young ladies armed?'

'They're not,' Petersen said. 'I guarantee it. If you find a weapon on their persons or in their bags you can shoot me.'

Crni looked at him almost quizzically, reached under his canvas jacket and produced a piece of paper from his tunic. 'What's your name?'

'Petersen.'

'Ah! Major Peter Petersen. At the very top of the list. One can see they're not carrying a weapon on their persons. But their bags?'

'I've searched them.'

The two girls momentarily stopped being apprehenisve and exchanged indignant glances. Crni smiled slightly.

'You should have told them. I believe you. If any man here is carrying a gun on his person and conceals the fact, then if I find it I'll shoot him. Through the heart.' Crni's matter-of-fact tone carried an unpleasant degree of conviction.

'There's no need to go around making all those ludicrous threats,' George said complainingly. 'If it's cooperation you want, I'm your man.' He produced an automatic from the depths of his clothing and nudged Alex in the ribs. 'Don't be foolish. I don't think this fellow Crni has any sense of humour.' Alex scowled and threw a similar automatic on the table.

'Thank you.' Crni consulted his list. 'You, of course, have to be the learned Professor, number two on our list.' He looked up at Alex. 'And you must be number three. It says here "Alex brackets assassin". Not much of a character reference. We'll bear that in mind.' He turned to one of his men. 'Edvard. Those coats hanging there. Search them.'

'No need,' Petersen said. 'Just the one on the left. That's mine. Right-hand pocket.'

'You are cooperative,' Crni said.

'I'm a professional, too.'

'I know that. I know quite a lot about you. Rather, I've been told quite a lot.' He looked at the gun Edvard had brought him. 'I didn't know they

207

issued silenced Lugers to the Royal Yugoslav Army.'

'They don't. A friend gave it to me.'

'Of course. I have five other names on this list.' He looked at Harrison. 'You must be Captain James Harrison.'

'Why must I?'

'There are two officers in Yugoslavia who wear monocles? And you must be Giacomo. Just the one name. Giacomo.'

'Same question.'

'Description.'

Giacomo smiled. 'Flattering?'

'No. Just accurate.' He looked at Michael. 'And you, by elimination, must be Michael von Karajan. Two ladies.' He looked at Lorraine. 'You're Lorraine Chamberlain.'

'Yes.' She smiled wanly. 'You have my description, too?'

'Sarina von Karajan bears a remarkable resemblance to her twin brother,' Crni said patiently. 'You eight are coming with me.'

George said: 'May I ask a question?'

'No.'

'I think that's downright uncivil,' George said plaintively. 'And unfair. What if I wanted to go to the toilet?'

'I take it you are the resident comedian,' Crni said coldly. 'I hope your sense of humour bears with you in the days to come. Major, I'm going to hold you personally responsible for the conduct of your group.'

Petersen smiled. 'If anyone tries to run away, you'll shoot me?'

'I wouldn't have put it as crudely as that, Major.'

'Major this, Major that. Major Crni? Captain Crni?'

'Captain,' he said briefly. 'I prefer Crni. Do I have to be an officer?'

'They don't send a mess-boy to bring in apparently notorious criminals.'

'Nobody's said you're a criminal. Not yet.' He looked at the two Četnick officers. 'Your names?'

Metrović said: 'I'm Major Metrović. This is Major Ranković.'

'I've heard of you.' He turned to Petersen. 'You eight will be taking your baggage with you.'

'That's nice,' George said.

'What is?'

'Well,' George said reasonably, 'if we're taking our baggage with us it's hardly likely that you're going to shoot us out of hand.'

'To be a comedian is bad enough. To be a buffoon, insufferable.' He turned back to Petersen. 'How many of the eight have their baggage here? Men and women, I mean?'

'Five. Three of us have our baggage in a hut about fifty yards away – myself and those two gentlemen here.'

'Slavko. Sava.' This to two of his men. 'This man Alex will show you where the hut is. Bring the baggage back. Search it very carefully first. And be just as careful in watching this man. He has an appalling record.' For a fleeting moment the expression on Alex's face made Crni's statement more than credible. 'Hurry nothing, watch everything.' He looked at his watch. 'We have forty minutes left.'

In less than half that time all the luggage had been packed and collected. George said: 'I know I'm not allowed to ask a question so may I make a statement? Oh, that's a question, too. I want to make a statement.'

'What?'

'I'm thirsty.'

'I see no harm.'

'Thank you.' George had opened a bottle and downed a glass of wine in what appeared near-impossible time.

'Try that other bottle,' Crni suggested. George blinked, frowned, but willingly did what he was told. 'Seems satisfactory. My men could do with a specific against the cold.'

'Seems satisfactory?' George stared at him. 'You suggest that I could have doctored some bottles, poisoned bottles, against just such an impossible eventuality? Me? A faculty dean? A learned academic? A – a –'

'Some academics are more learned than others. You'd have done the same.' Three of his men took a glass: the other two held their unwavering guns. There was a discouraging certainty about everything Crni said and did: he seemed to take the minutest precautions against anything untoward, including, as George had said, the impossible eventuality.

Metrović said: 'What happens to Major Ranković and myself?'

'You remain behind.'

'Dead?'

'Alive. Bound and gagged but alive. We are not Četniks. We do not murder helpless soldiers, far less helpless civilians.'

'Nor do we.'

'Of course not. Those thousands of Muslims who perished in south Serbia died by their own hands. Cowards, were they not?'

Metrović made no reply.

'And how many more thousand Serbians – men, women and children – were massacred in Croatia, with the most bestial atrocities ever recorded in the Balkans, just because of their religion?'

'We had no hand in that. The Ustaša are no soldiers, just undisciplined terrorists.'

'The Ustaša are your allies. Just as the Germans are your allies. Remember Kragujevac, Major, where the Partisans killed ten Germans and the Germans rounded up and shot five thousand Yugoslav citizens? Marched the children out of schools and shot them in droves until even the execution squads were sickened and mutinied? Your allies. Remember the retreat from Užice where the German tanks rolled backwards and forwards over the fields until all the wounded Partisans lying there had been crushed to death? Your allies. The guilt of your murderous friends is your guilt too. Much as we would like to treat you in the same fashion we will not. I have my orders and, besides, you are at least technically our allies.' Crni's voice was heavy with contempt.

Metrović said: 'You are Partisans.'

'God forbid!' The revulsion in Crni's face was momentary but unmistakable. 'Do we look like guerrilla rabble? We are paratroopers of the Murge division.' The Murge was the best Italian division then operating in south-east Europe. 'Your allies, as I said.' Crni gestured towards the eight prisoners. 'You harbour a nest of vipers. You can't recognize them as such, far less know what to do with them. We can do both.'

Metrović looked at Petersen. 'I think I owe you an apology, Peter. Last night I didn't know whether to believe your assessment or not. It seemed so fantastic. Not any more. You were right.'

'Much good that's done me. My forecast, I mean. I was twenty-four hours out.'

'Tie them up,' Crni said.

Immediately after leaving the hut, to nobody's surprise, they were joined by two other soldiers:

Crni was not the man to spend almost an hour inside any place without having a guard posted outside. That those were élite troops was beyond question. It was a bitter night, with driving snow, a biting wind and zero visibility but Crni and his men not only put up with the extreme conditions but seemed positively to revel in them.

Metrović had been wrong more than once the previous night. He had said that nobody was going to be moving around the mountains in those impossible weather conditions for days to come: Crni and his men were there to prove him wrong.

Once they were well clear of the camp Crni and his men produced torches. The prisoners were arranged so that they trudged on in single file through the deepening snow – it was already almost knee-high – while four of the guards walked on either side of them. By and by, at a command from Crni, they halted.

Crni said: 'Here, I'm afraid, we have to tie you up. Your wrists. Behind your backs.'

'I'm surprised you haven't done it before,' Petersen said. 'I'm even more surprised that you want to do it now. You have in mind to kill us all, perhaps?'

'Explain yourself.'

'We are at the head of that track leading down the mountain-side to the valley floor?'

'How do you know?'

'Because the wind hasn't changed since yesterday. You have ponies?'

'Two only. For the ladies. That was all you required yesterday.'

'You are very well informed. And the rest of us are to have our hands bound behind our backs just in case we feel tempted to give you or one of your men a brisk shove over the precipice. Mistake, Captain Crni, mistake. Out of character.'

'Indeed?'

'Two reasons. The surface of that rock is broken and slippery with either ice or hard-packed snow. If a man slips on that surface how is he, with his hands tied behind his back, going to grab at the ground to stop himself sliding over the edge – and how's he going to be able to maintain his balance in the first place with his hands tied? To keep your balance you have to be able to stretch both arms wide. You should know that. It's as good as sending people to their deaths. Second reason is that your men don't have to be anywhere near the prisoners. Four of them well in advance, four well behind, the prisoners, maybe with a couple of torches, in the middle. What positive action could the prisoners take then except commit suicide by jumping off the precipice? I can assure you that none of them is in the least suicidally inclined.'

'I am not a mountaineer, Major Petersen. I take your point.'

'Another request, if I may. Let Giacomo and myself walk alongside the young ladies' ponies. I'm afraid the young ladies don't care too much for heights.'

'I don't want you!' Even the prospect of the descent had brought a note of hysteria into Sarina's voice. 'I don't want you!'

'She doesn't want you,' Crni said drily.

'She doesn't know what she's saying. It's just a personal opinion of mine. She suffers severely from vertigo. What have I to gain by saying so?'

'Nothing that I can see.'

As they lined up by the cliff-top, Giacomo, leading a pony, brushed by Petersen and said, sotto voce: 'That, Major, was quite a performance.' He vanished into the snow with Petersen looking thoughtfully after him.

A steep descent, in treacherous conditions, is always more difficult and dangerous than a steep ascent and so it was to prove in this case. It is also slower and it took them all of forty minutes to reach the valley floor but reach it they did without incident. Sarina spoke for the first time since they had left the plateau.

'We are down?'

'Safe and sound as ever was.'

She gave a long quavering sigh. 'Thank you. You don't need to hold my horse any more.'

'Pony. Whatever you say. I was getting quite attached to the old lady.'

'I'm sorry,' she said quickly. 'I didn't mean it that way. It's just that you're so – so awful and so kind. No, *I'm* the person who is awful. *You're* the person they're after.'

'As is only fitting. My rank.'

'They're going to kill you, aren't they?'

'Kill me? What a thought. Why should they? A little discreet questioning perhaps.'

'You said yourself that General Granelli is an evil man.'

'General Granelli is in Rome. Haven't you given any thought as to what is going to happen to you?'

'No, I haven't.' Her voice was dull. 'I don't think I care what's going to happen to me.'

'That,' said Petersen, 'is what is known as a conversation stopper.'

They moved on in silence, the still heavily falling snow now at their backs, until Crni called a halt. He had the beam of his torch directed at the Italian army truck Petersen had stolen two days previously.

'It was thoughtful of you, Major, to leave transport so conveniently at hand.'

'If we can help our allies – you didn't arrive by this.'

'It was thoughtful, but not necessary.' Crni moved the beam of the torch. Another, even larger Italian truck, was parked close by. 'All of you, into that truck. Edvard, come with me.'

The eight prisoners were ushered into the larger truck and made to sit on the floor crowded up against the cab. Five soldiers followed them and sat on side benches towards the rear. Five torch beams were directed forwards and in the light of the beams it was possible to see that an equal number of machine-pistol barrels were pointed in the same direction. The engine started up and the truck jolted off. Five minutes later they turned right on to the main Neretva road.

'Ah!' Harrison said. 'Bound for the bright lights of Jablanica, I see.'

'On this road, where else?' Petersen said. 'After that the road divides. We could be going anywhere. I would guess that Jablanica is as far as we go. It's getting late. Even Crni and his men have to sleep.'

Shortly afterwards the driver stopped both the truck and the engine.

'I don't see any bright lights around here,' Harrison said. 'What are those devils up to now?'

'Nothing that concerns us,' Petersen said. 'Our driver is just waiting for Crni and his friend Edvard to join him up front.'

'Why? They have their own transport.'

'Had. It's in the Neretva now. That lad who met us yesterday – you remember, Dominic, the driver with the sunglasses – would not have failed to note the make and number of the truck. When and if Ranković and Metrović are discovered and freed – which may not be for hours yet – the proverbial hue and cry may be raised. "May", I say. I doubt it. The Colonel is not a man to publicize the security gaps in his forces. But Crni doesn't strike me as a man to take the slightest chance.'

'Objection,' Giacomo said. 'If your friend Cipriano is the man behind this, he already knows the description of the truck. So what's the point in destroying the truck?'

'Giacomo, you sadden me. We don't *know* that Cipriano is the man behind this but if he is he wouldn't want to leave any clue that would point a finger at him in connection with the abduction. Remember that, officially, he and the Colonel are sworn allies, faithful unto death.'

Voices came from up front, a door banged, the engine started again and the truck moved off. 'That must be the way of it,' Giacomo said to no-one in particular. 'Pity about the truck, though.'

They jolted on through the snow-filled night, torch beams and barrels still pointed at them, until suddenly Harrison said: 'At last. Civilization. It's a long time since I've seen city lights.'

Harrison, as was his custom, was exaggerating to a considerable extent. A few dim lights appeared occasionally through the opened back of the truck but hardly enough to lend the impression that they were driving through a metropolis. By and by the truck pulled off on to a side road, climbed briefly, then stopped. The guards apparently knew where they were and did not wait for orders. They jumped down, lined up torches and guns as before and were joined by Crni.

'Down,' he said. 'This is as far as we go tonight.'

They lowered themselves to the ground and looked around them. As far as could be judged from the light of the beams, the building before them appeared to be standing alone and seemed, vaguely, to be shaped like a chalet. But, in the darkness and the snow it could have been just any building.

Crni led the way inside. The hallway presented a pleasant contrast to the swirling cold of the wintry night outside. The furnishings were sparse enough, just a table, a few chairs and a dresser, but it was warm – a small log fire burned in a low hearth – and warmly if not brightly lit: electric power had not yet reached this part of Jablanica and suspended oil lamps were the norm.

'Door to the left is a bathroom,' Crni said. 'Can be used anytime. There will, of course,' he added unnecessarily, 'be a guard in the hall all the time. The other door to the left leads to the main quarters of the house and does not concern you. Neither do those stairs.' He led the way to an opened door on the far right and ushered them inside. 'Your quarters for the night.'

The room was unmistakably such as one would only find in a chalet. It was long, wide and low, with beamed ceiling, knotted pine walls and an oak parquet floor. Cushioned benches ran both sides of the room, there was a table, several armchairs, a very commodious dresser, some cupboards and shelves and, best of all, a rather splendid log fire several times the size of the one in the hallway. The only immediately incongruous note was struck by some canvas cots, blankets and pillows stacked neatly in one corner. It was George, inevitably, who discovered the second and not so immediately incongruous note. He pulled back the curtains covering one of the two windows and examined with interest the massive bars on the outside.

'It is part of the general malaise of our times,' he said sadly. 'With the onset of war, the deterioration of standards is as immediate as it is inevitable. The rules of honour, decency and common law go by default and moral degeneracy rears its ugly head.' He let fall the curtains. 'A wise precaution, very wise. One feels sure that the streets of Jablanica are infested by burglars, house-breakers, footpads and other criminals of that ilk.'

Crni ignored him and looked at Petersen who was inspecting the bedding. 'Yes, Major, I can count, too. Only six cots. We have a room upstairs for the two young ladies.'

'Considerate. You were very sure of yourself, weren't you, Captain Crni?'

'Oh, no, he wasn't,' George said disgustedly. 'A blind man could drive a coach and four with bells on through Mihajlović's perimeter.'

For a second time Crni ignored him. He had probably come to the conclusion that this was the only way to treat him.

'We may or may not move on tomorrow. It certainly won't be early. Depends entirely on the weather. From now on our travel will be mainly on foot. Should you be hungry, there's food in that cupboard there. The contents of that high dresser will be of more interest to the professor.'

'Ah!' George opened the doors and looked appreciatively at what was, in effect, a comprehensively stocked miniature bar. 'The window bars are superfluous, Captain Crni. I shall not be moving on tonight.'

'Even if you could, where would you go? When you ladies want to sleep, let the guard know and I'll show you your room. I may or may not wish to interrogate you later, it depends on a call I have to make.'

'You surprise me,' Petersen said. 'I thought the phone system had ceased to work.'

'Radio, of course. We do have one. In fact, we have four, the other three being yours and those two very modern sets belonging to the von Karajans. I expect the code books will also prove to be useful.'

He left behind him a profound and fairly lengthy silence interrupted only by the sound of a cork being extracted from a bottle. Michael was the first to speak.

'Radios,' he said bitterly. 'Code books.' He looked accusingly at Petersen. 'You know what this means, don't you?'

'Yes. Nothing. Crni was amusing himself. All it means is that we will be put to the trouble of getting ourselves a new code. What else do you think they'll do after they discover the books are missing? They will do this, of course, not to protect themselves against their enemies but against their friends. The Germans have twice broken the code

221

that we use among ourselves.' He looked at Harrison, who had seated himself, cross-legged, in an arm-chair before the fire and was contemplating a glass of wine that George had just handed him. 'For a man who has just been driven from house and home, Jamie, or snatched from it, which comes to the same thing, you don't look all that downcast to me.'

'I'm not,' Harrison said comfortably. 'No reason to be. I never thought I'd find quarters better than my last one but I was wrong, I mean, look, a real log fire. Carpe diem, as the man says. What, Peter, do you think the future holds for us?'

'I wouldn't know how to use a crystal ball.'

'Pity. It would have been nice to think that I might see the white cliffs of Dover again.'

'I don't see why not. No one's after your blood. I mean, you haven't been up to anything, have you, Jamie? Such as sending clandestine radio messages, in codes unknown to us, to parties also unknown to us?'

'Certainly not.' Harrison was unruffled. 'I'm not that kind of person, I don't have any secrets and I'm useless with a radio anyway. So you think I might see the white cliffs again. Do you think I'll be seeing the old homestead on Mount Prenj again?'

'I should think it highly unlikely.'

'Well now. A fairly confident prediction *and* without a crystal ball.'

'For that, I don't need a crystal ball. A person who has occupied the – ah – delicate position you have done will never again be employed in that capacity after he's been captured by the enemy. Torturing, brain-washing, reconversion to a double-agent, that sort of thing. Standard practice. You'd never be trusted again.'

'I say, that's a bit thick, isn't it? A blameless, stainless reputation. It's hardly my fault that I've been captured. It wouldn't have happened if you people had looked after me a bit better. Thank you, George, I will have a little more. Now that I'm happily out of that place, I've no intention of ever returning to it, not unless I'm dragged forcibly back to it, kicking and screaming in the accepted fashion.' He raised his glass. 'Your health, Peter.'

'You have taken an aversion to the people, the Četniks, the Colonel, myself?'

'A profound aversion. Well, not to you, although I must admit I don't care overmuch for what might be called your military politics. You're a total enigma to me, Peter, but I'd rather have you on my side than against me. As for the rest, I despise them. An extraordinary position for an ally to find himself in, is it not?'

'I think I'll have some wine, too, George, if I may. Well, yes, Jamie, it's true, you have made your discontent – I might even say displeasure – rather guardedly evident from time to time but I thought you were doing no more than exercising every soldier's inalienable right to complain loudly and at length about every conceivable aspect of army life.' He sipped his wine thoughtfully. 'One gathers there was something a little more to it than that?'

'A little more? There was a great deal more.' Harrison sipped his wine and gazed at the burning logs, a man relaxed, at peace with himself. 'In spite of the fact that the future looks somewhat uncertain, in some ways I owe our Captain Crni a favour. He's done no more than to pre-empt my decision, my intention, to leave Mount Prenj and its miserable inhabitants at the first convenient opportunity. Had it not been for the unexpected happening of the past couple of hours, you'd have discovered that I'd already made an official request for an official recall. But, of course, as matters stood before the appearance of Captain Crni, I wouldn't have made any such disclosures anyway.'

'I could have misjudged you, Jamie.'

'Indeed you could.' He looked around the room to see if there was anyone else misjudging him, but there was no-one thinking along those lines: a magnet to the iron filings, he had the undivided attention of every person in the room.

'So you didn't – don't – like us?'

'I should have thought that I had made that abundantly clear. I may be no soldier, and the good Lord knows that I'm not, but I'm no clown either, all appearances to the contrary. I'm educated after a fashion: in practically any intellectual field that matters the average soldier is a virtual illiterate.

I'm not educated in the way George is, I don't float around in cloud-cuckoo-land or wander among the groves of academe.' George looked profoundly hurt and reached for the wine bottle. 'I have been educated in a more practical fashion. Wouldn't you agree, Lorraine?'

'I would.' She smiled and said as if by rote: 'B.Sc., M.Sc., A.M.I.E.E., A.M.I.Mech.E. Oh, he's educated, all right. I used to be James's secretary.'

'Well, well, well,' Petersen said. 'The world grows even smaller.' Giacomo covered his face with his hand.

'Bachelor of Science, Master of Science we understand,' George said. 'As for the rest, it sounds as if he was coming down with a terminal illness.'

'Associate Member of the Institute of Electrical Engineers,' Lorraine said. 'Associate Member of the Institute of Mechanical Engineers.'

'It's unimportant.' Harrison was impatient. 'Point is I've been trained to observe, evaluate and analyze. I've been out here less than two months but I can tell you it took only a fraction of that time and a minimum of observation, evaluation and analysis to realize that Britain was backing the wrong horse in the Yugoslav stakes.

'I speak as a British officer. I don't want to sound overly dramatic, but Britain is locked, literally, in mortal combat with Germany. How do we defeat the Germans – by fighting them and killing them. How should we judge our allies or potential allies, what yardstick should we use? One. Only one. Are *they* fighting and killing Germans? Is Mihajlović? Is he hell. He's fighting with the Germans, alongside the Germans. Tito? Every German soldier caught in the sights of a Partisan rifle is a dead man. Yet those fools and dolts and idiots in London keep sending supplies to Mihajlović, a man who is in effect their sworn enemy. I am ashamed for my own people. The only possible reason for this – God knows it's no excuse – is that Britain's war, as far as the Balkans is concerned, is being run by politicians and soldiers, and politicians are almost as naïve and illiterate as soldiers.'

George said: 'You speak harsh words about your own people, James.'

'Shut up! No, sorry, George, I didn't mean that, but in spite or maybe because of your vast education you're just as naïve and illiterate as any of them. Harsh but true. How does this extraordinary situation come about? Mihajlović is a near Machiavellian genius in international diplomacy: Tito is too busy killing Germans to have any time for any such thing.

'As far back as September 1941 Mihajlović and his Četniks, instead of fighting the Germans, were busy establishing contacts with your precious Royalist government in London. Yes, Peter Petersen, precious I said and precious I did not mean. They don't give a damn about the unimaginable sufferings of the Yugoslav people, all they want to do is to regain royal power and if it's over the bodies of one or two millions of their countrymen, so much the worse for their countrymen. And, of course, Mihajlović, when contacting King Peter and his so-called advisers could hardly help contacting the British government as well. What a bonus! And naturally, at the same time, he contacted the British forces in the Middle East. For all I know the dunderheaded brasshats in Cairo may still regard the Colonel as the great white hope for Yugoslavia.' He gestured towards Sarina and Michael. 'In fact, the dunderheads unquestionably still do. Look at this gullible young couple here, specially trained by the British to come to the aid and comfort of the gallant Četniks.'

'We're not gullible!' Sarina's voice was strained, her hands twisted together and she could have been close to either anger or tears. 'We weren't trained by the British, we were trained by the Americans. And we *didn't* come to give aid and comfort to the Četniks.'

'There are no American radio operator schools in Cairo. Only British. If you received American training it was because the British wanted it that way.' Harrison's tone was as cool and discouragingas his face. 'I think you're gullible, I think you tell lies and I believe you came to help the Četniks. I also think you're a fine actress.'

'Good for you, Jamie,' Petersen said approvingly. 'You got one thing right there. She *is* a fine actress. But she's not gullible, she doesn't tell

lies – well, maybe one or two little white ones –
and she didn't come to help us.'

Both Harrison and Sarina stared at him in astonishment. Harrison said: 'How on earth can you
say that?'

'Intuition.'

'Intuition!' Harrison, was, for Harrison, being
heavily sardonic. 'If your intuition is on a par with
your judgment you can mothball the two of them
together. And don't try to side-track me. Hasn't
it struck you as ironic that when you and your
precious Četniks' – Harrison was very fond of the
word 'precious' and used it, always in its most
derogatory sense, with telling effect – 'were
receiving arms and payments from the Germans,
Italians and Nedić's quisling Serb régime, that you
were simultaneously receiving arms and payments from the western allies – this, mark you, at
a time when you were fighting along with the
Germans, Italians and Ustaša in an attempt to
destroy the Partisans, Britain's only real allies in
Yugoslavia?'

'Have some more wine, Jamie.'

'Thank you, George.' Harrison shook his head. 'I
confess myself to being totally baffled and, when I
say that, I mean baffled all round. By you Četniks
and by my own people. Can it really be that there
are none so blind as will not see? Are you so gagged
and blinkered by your all-consuming and wholly
misguided sense of patriotism, by your blind alle-
giance to a discredited royalty that your myopic

eyes are so reduced to a ten-degree field of tunnel vision that you have no concept of the three hundred and fifty degree of peripheral vision that lies beyond? Are my people in London similarly affected? They have to be, they have to be, for what else could explain the inexplicable, the incomprehensible idiocy of keeping on sending supplies to Mihajlović when they have before them incontrovertible evidence that he is actively collaborating with the Germans.'

'I'll bet you couldn't say that again,' Petersen said admiringly. 'All the big words, I mean. As you say, Jamie, it's all probably reduced to a factor of vision, what lies in the eye of the beholder.' He rose, crossed over to the fireplace and sat down beside Sarina. 'This is not really a switch, we're talking about the same thing. How did you enjoy your tête-à-tête with the Colonel this morning?'

'Tête-à-tête? I didn't have any tête-à-tête with him. Michael and I just reported to him. You told us to. Or have you forgotten?'

'I've forgotten nothing. But I think you have. Walls have ears. Not original, but still true.'

She glanced quickly at Michael then back again. 'I don't know what you're talking about.'

'Walls also have eyes.'

'Stop brow-beating my sister!' Michael shouted.

'Brow-beating? Asking a simple question is brow-beating? If that's what you call brow-beating maybe I should start beating you about the brow. You were there, too, of course. You got anything to tell me? You have, you know. I already know what your answer should be. Your truthful answer.'

'I've got nothing to tell you! Nothing! Nothing at all!'

'You're a lousy actor. Also, you're too vehement by half.'

'I've had enough of you, Petersen!' Michael was breathing quickly and shallowly. 'Enough of your bullying my sister and me.' He jumped to his feet. 'If you think I'm going to stand –'

'You're not going to stand, Michael.' George had come up behind Michael and laid his hands on his shoulders. 'You're going to sit.' Michael sat. 'If you can't keep quiet I'll have to tie and gag you. Major Petersen is asking questions.'

'Good Lord!' Harrison was or seemed outraged. 'This *is* a bit thick, George. A bit high-handed, I must say. Peter, I don't think you're any longer in a position to –'

'And if *you* don't keep quiet,' George said with a trace of weariness in his voice, 'I'll do the same thing to you.'

'To me!' No question, this time the outrage was genuine. 'Me? An officer? A Captain in the British Army! By God! Giacomo, you're an Englishman. I appeal to you –'

'Appeal is denied. I wouldn't hurt an officer's feelings by telling him to shut up, but I think the Major is trying to establish something. You may not like his military philosophy but at least you should keep an open mind. And I think Sarina should too. I think you're both being foolish.'

Harrison muttered 'My God' twice and subsided.

Petersen said: 'Thanks, Giacomo. Sarina, if you think I'm trying to hurt you or harm you then you are, as Giacomo says, being foolish. I couldn't and wouldn't. I want to help. Did you and the Colonel have or not have a private conversation?'

'We talked, if that's what you mean.'

'Of *course* you talked. If I sound a bit exasperated, it's pardonable. What did you talk about? Me?'

'No. Yes. I mean, among other things.'

'Among other things,' he mimicked. 'What other things?'

'Just other things. Just generally.'

'That's a lie. You talked just about me and, maybe, a bit about Colonel Lunz. Remember, walls can have both ears and eyes. And you can't remember what you said when you sold me down the river which is where I am now. How many pieces of silver did the good Colonel give you?'

'I never did!' She was breathing quickly now and there were patches of red high up on her cheeks. 'I didn't betray you. I didn't! I didn't!'

'And all for a little piece of paper. I hope you got your due. You earned your thirty pieces. You didn't know that I'd picked up the paper later, did

231

you?' He brought a piece of paper out from his tunic and unfolded it. 'This one.'

She stared at it dully, looked at him equally dully, put her elbows on her knees, her face in her hands. 'I don't know what's going on.' Her voice was muffled. 'I don't know any more. I know you're a bad man, a wicked man, but I didn't betray you.'

'I know you didn't.' He reached out a gentle hand and touched her shoulder. 'But I know what's going on. I have done all along. I'm sorry if I hurt you but I had to get you to say it. Why couldn't you have admitted it in the first place? Or have you forgotten what I said only yesterday morning?'

'Forgotten what?' She took her hands from her face and looked at him. It was difficult to say if the hazel eyes were still dull for there were tears in them.

'That you're far too nice and too transparently honest to do anything underhand. There were three pieces of paper. The one I gave to the Colonel, this one I'd made out before leaving Rome – I never picked anything up after your talk with him – and the one Colonel Lunz had given to you.'

'You *are* clever, aren't you?' She'd wiped the tears from her eyes and they weren't dull any more, just mad.

'Cleverer than you are, anyway,' Petersen said cheerfully. 'For some inexplicable reason Lunz thought that I might be some kind of spy or double agent and change the message, forge a different set of orders. But I didn't, did I? The message I gave the Colonel was the one I received and it checked with the copy Lunz had given you. Paradoxically, of course – you being a woman – this annoyed you. If I had been a spy, a sort of reconverted renegade who had gone over to the other side, you would have been no end pleased, wouldn't you? You might have respected me, even liked me a little. Well, I remained an unreconstructed Četnik. You were aware, of course, that if I *had* changed the orders that Mihajlović would have had me executed?'

A little colour drained from her face and she touched her hand to her lips.

'Of course you were unaware. Not only are you incapable of double-dealing, not only are you incapable of thinking along double-dealing lines, you're not even capable of thinking of the consequences to the double-dealer who has overplayed his hand. How an otherwise intelligent girl – well, never mind. As I've said before, in this nasty espionage world, leave the thinking to those who are capable of it. Why did you do it, Sarina?'

'Why did I do what?' All of a sudden she seemed quite defenceless. She said, almost in a monotone: 'What am I going to be accused of now?'

'Nothing, my dear. I promise you. Nothing. I was just wondering, although I'm sure I know why, how it came about that you went along with this underground deal with Colonel Lunz, something so completely alien to your nature. It was because it was your only way into Yugoslavia. If you had refused, he'd have refused you entrance. So I've answered my own question.' Petersen rose. 'Wine, George, wine. All this talk is thirsty work.'

'What is not common knowledge,' George said, 'is that listening is even thirstier work.'

Petersen lifted his replenished glass and turned towards Harrison. 'To your health, Jamie. As a British officer, of course.'

'Yes, yes, of course.' Clutching his glass Harrison struggled to his feet. 'Of course. Your health. Ah. Well. Extenuating circumstances, old boy. How was I —'

'And a gentleman.'

'Of course, of course.' He was still confused. 'A gentleman.'

'Were you being a gentleman, Jamie, when you called her a gullible liar, and an aider and comforter to us miserable lot? This lovely and charming lady is not only not that, she's something you've been looking for, something to gladden your patriotic heart, a true blue loyalist and not a true blue Royalist, a patriot in your best sense of the word, what you would call a Yugoslav. As dedicated a Partisan as one can be who has never seen a Partisan in her life. That's why she and her brother came back to this country the hard way, to give – as you would put it in your customary stirring language, Jamie – their services to their country, i.e., the Partisans.'

Harrison put down his glass, crossed to where Sarina was sitting, stooped low, lifted the back of her hand and kissed it. 'Your servant, ma'am.'

'That's an apology?' George said.

'For an English officer,' Petersen said, 'that is – as an English officer would say – a jolly handsome apology.'

'He's not the only one who's due to make an apology.' Michael wasn't actually shuffling his feet but he looked as if he would have liked to. 'Major Petersen, I have –'

'No apology, Michael,' Petersen said hastily. 'No apology. If I'd a sister like that, I wouldn't even talk to her tormentor, in this case, me. I'd clobber him over the head with a two by four. So if I don't apologise to your sister for what I've done to her, don't you apologize to me.'

'Thank you very much, sir.' He hesitated. 'May I ask how long you've known that Sarina and I were – well, what you say we are.'

'From the first time I saw you. Rather, let me say I suspected something was far wrong when I met you in that Rome apartment. You were both stiff, awkward, ill at ease, reserved, even truculent. No smile on the lips, no song in the heart, none of the eagerness, the youthful enthusiasm of those marching off into a glorious future. Ultra-cautious, ultra-suspicious. Wrong attitude altogether. If you'd been flying red flags you couldn't have indicated more clearly that something was weighing heavily on your minds. Your pasts were so blameless, so your concern was obviously with future problems such – as became evident quite soon – how you were going to transfer yourselves to the Partisan camp after you had arrived at our HQ. Your sister lost little time in giving you away – it was in the mountain inn when she tried to convince me of her Royalist sympathies. Told me she was a pal of King Peter's – prince, as he was then.'

'I never did!' Her indignation was unconvincing. 'I just met him a few times.'

'Sarina.' The tone was mildly reproving.

She said nothing.

'How often must I tell you –'

'Oh, all right,' she said.

'She's never met him in her life. She sympathized with me about his club foot. Young lad's as fit as a fiddle. Wouldn't know a club foot if he saw one. Well, all this is of interest but I'm afraid only academic interest.'

'Oh, I don't know,' Giacomo said. 'It's of more than academic interest to me.' He was, as always, smiling, but in the circumstances, it was difficult to say what he was smiling about. 'However, as a matter of academic interest, I'm totally in agreement with those kids – sorry, I mean Sarina and Michael. I don't want to fight – I mean I don't want to fight in those damned mountains; the

Aegean and the Royal Navy will do me very nicely, thank you – but if I have to it'll be with the Partisans.'

'You're like Jamie,' Petersen said. 'If you're going to fight anybody it's going to be the Germans?'

'I think I made that pretty clear to you back in the Hotel Eden.'

'You did. It's still only a matter of academic interest. What are you going to do about it? How do you intend going about joining your guerrilla friends?'

Giacomo smiled. 'I'll wait for a break.'

'You could wait for ever.'

'Peter.' There was a note of appeal, almost desperation, in Harrison's voice. 'I know you owe us nothing, that you have no responsibility for us any more. But there must be a way. However different our philosophies, we're all in this together. Come on, Peter. We could settle our differences afterwards. Meantime – well, a man of your infinite resources and –'

'Jamie,' Petersen said gently. 'Can't you see the fence down the middle of this room. George, Alex and I are on one side. You five are on the other. Well, you, the von Karajans and Giacomo are. I don't know about Lorraine. It's a mile high, that fence, Jamie, and not for climbing.'

'I see his point, Captain Harrison,' Giacomo said. 'The fence is not for climbing. Besides, my pride wouldn't let me try it. I must say, Major, it's

237

not like you to leave loose ends lying around. Lorraine, here. Doesn't she fit into a category? For our edification, I mean.'

'Category? I don't know. And not to give you offence, Lorraine, but I don't really care now. It doesn't matter. Not any more.' He sat down, glass in hand, and said no more. As far as anyone could tell, Major Petersen had, for the first time in their experience, lapsed into a brooding silence.

It was a silence, punctuated only by the occasional glug-glug as George topped empty wine-glasses, that stretched on and uncomfortably on, until Lorraine said suddenly and sharply: 'What's wrong? Please, what's wrong?'

'Speaking to me?' Petersen said.

'Yes. You're staring at me. You keep on staring at me.'

'Being on the wrong side of a fence doesn't stop a man from having good taste,' Giacomo said.

'I wasn't aware of it,' Petersen said. He smiled. 'Besides, as Giacomo said, it's no hardship. I'm sorry. I was a long long way away, that's all.'

'And speaking of staring,' Giacomo said cheerfully, 'Sarina's no slouch at it either. Her eyes haven't left your face since you started your Rodin the thinker bit. There are deep currents, hereabouts. Do you know what I think? I think she's thinking.'

'Oh, do be quiet, Giacomo.' She sounded positively cross.

'Well, I suppose we're all thinking one way or another,' Petersen said. 'Heaven knows we've plenty to think about. You, Jamie, you're sunk in a pretty profound gloom. The bright lights? No. The white cliffs? No. Ah! The lights of home.'

Harrison smiled and said nothing.

'What's she like, Jamie?'

'What's she like?' Harrison smiled again, shrugged and looked at Lorraine.

'Jenny's wonderful,' Lorraine said quietly. 'I think she's the most wonderful person in the world. She's my best friend and James doesn't deserve her. She's worth ten of him.'

Harrison smiled like a man who was well-pleased with himself and reached for his wine-glass; if he was wounded, he hid it well.

Petersen looked away until his eyes lighted casually on Giacomo, who nodded almost imperceptibly: Petersen smiled slightly and looked away.

Twenty more minutes passed, partly in desultory conversation but mainly in silence, before the door opened and Edvard entered. 'Major Petersen?'

Petersen rose. Giacomo made to speak but Petersen forestalled him. 'Don't say it. Thumb-screws.'

He was back inside five minutes. Giacomo looked disappointed. 'No thumb-screws?'

'No thumb-screws. I would like to say that they're bringing out a rack and that you're next. No rack. But you're next.'

Giacomo left. Harrison said: 'What was it like. What did they want?'

'Very humane. Very civilized. What you would expect of Crni. Lots of questions, some very personal, but I just gave them name, rank and regiment, which is all you're legally required to give. They didn't press the matter.'

Giacomo was back in even less time than Petersen. 'Disappointing,' he said. 'Very disappointing. They'd never have made the Spanish Inquisition. The courtesy of your presence, Captain Harrison.'

Harrison was away a little longer than either but not much. He returned looking very thoughtful. 'You're next, Lorraine.'

'Me?' She stood and hesitated. 'Well, if I don't go I suppose they'll come for me.'

'It would be most unseemly,' Petersen said. 'We've survived. What's a lion's den to an English girl like you?'

She nodded and left, but left reluctantly. Petersen said: 'How was it, Jamie?'

'An urbane lot, as you say. Seemed to know a surprising amount about me. No questions that had any military bearing that I could see.'

Lorraine was absent for at least fifteen minutes. When she returned she was rather pale and although there were no tears on her cheeks it seemed clear that she had been crying. Sarina looked at Petersen, Harrison and Giacomo, shook her head and put her arm round Lorraine's shoulders.

'They're a gallant lot, aren't they, Lorraine? Chivalrous. Concerned.' She gave them a withering glance. 'Maybe they're just shy. Who's next?'

'They didn't ask to see anyone.'

'What did they do to you, Lorraine?'

'Nothing. Do you mean – no, no, they didn't touch me. It was just some of the questions they asked . . .' Her voice trailed off. 'Please, Sarina, I'd rather not talk about it.'

'Maraschino,' George said authoritatively. He took her by the arm, seated her and proffered a small glass. She took it, smiled gratefully and said nothing.

Crni came in accompanied by Edvard. He was, for the first time anyone had seen, relaxed and smiling.

'I have some news for you. I hope you will find it good news.'

'You're not even armed,' George said. 'How do you know we won't break every bone in your bodies? Better still, use you as hostage to escape? We are desperate men.'

'Would you do that, Professor?'

'No. Some wine?'

'Thank you, Professor. Good news, at least I think it's good news, for the von Karajans, Captain

Harrison and Giacomo. I am sorry that we have been guilty of a small deception but it was necessary in the circumstances. We are not members of the Murge Division. We are, thank heavens, not even Italians. We are just common-or-garden members of a Partisan reconnaissance group.'

'Partisans.' There was no excitement in Sarina's voice, just incomprehension tinged with disbelief.

Crni smiled. 'It's true.'

'Partisans.' Harrison shook his head. 'Pon my soul. Partisans. Well, now. I mean. Yes.' He shook his head then his voice rose an octave. 'Partisans!'

'Is it true?' Sarina had Crni by the arms and was actually shaking him. 'Is it true?'

'Of course it's true.'

She searched his eyes as if searching for the truth, then suddenly put her arm around him and hugged him. She was very still for a moment then released him and stepped back. 'I'm sorry,' she said. 'I shouldn't have done that.'

He smiled. 'There's no regulation that says that a young recruit, female, may not hug an officer. Not, of course, to make a practice of it.'

'There's that, too, of course.' She smiled uncertainly.

'There's something else?'

'No, not really. We're terribly glad to see you.'

'Glad?' Harrison said. 'Glad!' The initial shock absorbed, he was in a state bordering on euphoria. 'Nothing less than a merciful providence has sent you our way!'

'It wasn't a merciful providence, Captain Harrison. It was a radio message. When my commanding officer says "move", I move. That's the "something else" you wouldn't talk about, Miss von Karajan. Your fears are groundless. Military regulations don't allow me to shoot my boss.'

'Your boss?' She looked at him, then Petersen, then back at Crni. 'I don't understand.'

Crni sighed. 'You're quite right, Peter. You, too Giacomo. No espionage material among this lot. If there were they wouldn't have to be hit over the head with the obvious. We're both Partisans. We're both in intelligence. I am the ranking subordinate officer. He is the deputy chief. I'm sure that makes everything clear.'

'Perfectly,' George said. He handed Crni a glass. 'Your wine, Ivan.' He turned to Sarina. 'He doesn't really like being called Crni. And don't clench your fists. All right, all right, this is life in a nutshell. Decisions, decisions. Do you kiss him or do you hit him?' The bantering note left George's voice. 'If you're mad because you've been fooled, then you're a fool. There was no other way. You and your hurt pride. You've got your Partisans and he hasn't to face a firing squad. Don't you know how to be glad, girl? Or is there no room for emotions like relief and gratitude in the minds of you spoilt young aristocrats?'

'George!' She was shocked, less because of the words than the tone she had never heard before. 'George! I am so selfish?'

'Never.' His good humour instantly restored, he squeezed her shoulders. 'It's just that I thought it would rather spoil the flavour of the moment if you were to give Peter a black eye.' He glanced sideways. Harrison, his forehead on his forearms on the table, was softly pounding the table with his fist and muttering to himself. 'You are not well, Captain Harrison?'

'My God, my God, my God!' The pounding with the fist continued.

'A Šljivovica?' George said.

Harrison lifted his head. 'And the awful thing is that I am cursed with total recall. That,' he added irrelevantly, 'was why I was so good at passing exams. I can remember every word I said in that stirring speech about patriotism and duty and loyalty and myopic idiocy and – I can't go on, I can't.'

'You mustn't reproach yourself, Jamie,' Petersen said 'Think what it did for our morale.'

'If there was any justice, any compassion in this world,' Harrison said, 'this floor would open up beneath me at this very moment. A British officer, I called myself, thereby meaning there was no other. A highly skilled observer, evaluator, analyzer. Good God! Total recall, I tell you, total recall. It's hell!'

'I'm sorry I missed that speech,' Crni said.

'Pity,' Petersen said. 'Still, you've heard about Jamie's total recall. He can repeat it to you verbatim any time you want.'

'Spare the vanquished,' Harrison said. 'I heard what you said to Sarina, George, but I remain bitter. Fooled, fooled, fooled. And doubly bitter because Peter didn't trust me. But you trusted Giacomo, didn't you? He knew.'

'I told Giacomo nothing,' Petersen said. 'He guessed – he's a soldier.'

'And I'm not? Well, that's for sure. How did you guess Giacomo?'

'I heard what you heard. I heard the Major telling – suggesting rather, to Captain Crni that his intention to rope us up before descending that cliff path was dangerous. Captain Crni is not the man to take an order or suggestion from anyone. So then I knew.'

'Of course. I missed it. So you didn't trust any of us, did you Peter?'

'I didn't. I had to know where I stood with you all. Lots of odd things have been happening in Rome and ever since we left Rome. I had to know. You'd have done the same.'

'Me? I wouldn't have noticed anything odd in the first place. When did you come to the decision that you were free to talk? And why did you decide to talk? My God, when I come to think of it, when have you ever been free to talk? My word, I can't imagine it, I just can't. Can you, Sarina? Living the life of a lie, surrounded by enemies, one false move, one unconsidered slip, one careless word and pouf! And he spent almost half his time with us!'

'Ah! But I spent the other half with our own people. Holiday, you might say.'

'Oh, God, holiday. I knew – and I haven't known you long – that you were something different, but this – but this – it passes my comprehension. And you, a man like you, you're only the deputy chief. I'd love to meet the man you call chief.'

'I don't call him "chief." I call him lots of other things but not that. As for loving to meet him, you don't have to bother. You've already met him. In fact, you've described him. Big fat clown, naïve and illiterate, who spends his time floating around in cloud-cuckoo-land. Or was it the groves of academe? I don't remember.'

Harrison spilled the contents of his glass on the table. He looked dazed. 'I don't believe it.'

'Nobody does. I'm his right arm, only, in charge of field operations. As you know, he seldom accompanies me. This mission was different but, then, this was an unusually important mission. Couldn't be trusted to bunglers like me.'

Michael approached George, a certain awed incredulity in his face. 'But in Mostar you told me you were a Sergeant Major.'

'A tiny prevarication.' George waved his hand in airy dismissal. 'Inevitable in this line of business. Tiny prevarications, I mean. But I did say it was a temporary not substantive rank. Generalmajor.'

'Good God!' Michael was overcome. 'I mean "Sir".'

'It's too much.' Harrison didn't even notice when George courteously refilled his glass. 'It's really too much. Too much for the reeling mind to encompass. Maybe I haven't such a mind after all. Tell me next that I'm Adolph Hitler and I'd seriously consider the possibility.' He looked at George, shook his head and drained half his glass. 'You see before you a man trying to find his way back to reality. Now, where was I? Ah, yes. I was asking you when you came to the decision you were free to talk.'

'When you told me – or Lorraine did – about your Jenny.'

'Ah, yes, of course. Jenny. I see.' It was plain that Harrison was quite baffled. He suddenly, physically, shook himself. 'What the hell has Jenny got to do with this?'

'Nothing, directly.'

'Ah Jenny. Lorraine. The question that Captain Crni asked me through there.'

Lorraine said in a quiet voice: 'What question, James?'

'He asked me if I knew Giancarlo Tremino – you know, Carlos. Of course I said yes, I knew him very well.' He looked down at his glass. 'Perhaps I shouldn't have answered. I mean, they weren't torturing me or anything. Maybe I don't have such a mind after all.'

'It wasn't your fault, James,' Lorraine said. 'You weren't to know. Besides, there's been no harm done.'

'How do you know there's been no harm done, Lorraine?' Sarina sounded bitter. 'I know it wasn't Captain Harrison's fault. And I know it wasn't really Captain Crni who asked the question. Don't you know that Major Petersen *always* finds out what he wants? Are we still to regard ourselves as prisoners in this room, Captain Crni?'

'Good God, no! As far as I'm concerned the house is yours. Anyway, you don't ask me. Major Petersen is in charge.'

'Or you, George?' She smiled faintly. 'Sorry. I'm not used to the Generalmajor yet.'

'Quite frankly, neither am I. George is fine.' He smiled and wagged a finger at her. 'Don't try to spread dissension in the ranks. Outside my head office, which at the moment is a disused shepherd's hut up near Bihać, Peter is in sole charge. I just point in the general direction and then get out of the way. If you know you're not in his class, as I'm wise enough to know, you don't interfere with the best field operative there is.'

'Could I speak to you, Major? In the hall?'

'Ominous,' he said and picked up his glass. 'Very ominous.' He followed her out and closed the door behind them. 'Well?'

She hesitated. 'I don't know quite how to say this. I think –'

'If you don't know what to say and you're still at the thinking stage, why waste my time in this really melodramatic fashion?'

'It's not silly. It's not dramatic! And you're not going to make me mad. What you've just said sums you up. Superior, cutting, contemptuous, never making allowances for people's faults and weaknesses: and at the same time you can be the most thoughtful and kind person I know. It's not just that you're unbearable. You're unknowable. Jekyll and Hyde. The Dr Jekyll bit I like and admire. You're brave, George thinks you're brilliant, you take incredible risks that would destroy a person like me and, best of all, you're very good at looking after people. Anyway, I knew last night that you couldn't belong to those people.'

Petersen smiled. 'I won't give you the chance of telling me again how nasty I am, so I won't say you're being wise after the event.'

'You're wrong,' she said quietly. 'It was something that Major Metrović said last night about Tito's Achilles' heel, his lack of mobility, his three thousand wounded men. In any civilized war – if there is such a thing – those men would be left to the enemy who would treat them in hospital. This is no civilized war. They would be massacred. You could never be a party to that.'

'I have my points. But you did not bring me out here to point those out.'

'I did not. It's the Mr Hyde side – oh, I *don't* want to lecture but I dislike that side, it hurts me and it baffles me. That a man so physically kind can in other ways be so cold, detached, uncaring to the point of not being quite human.'

'Oh, dear. Or, as Jamie would put it, I say, I say.'

'It's true. In order to gain your own ends, you can be – you are – indifferent to people's feelings to the point of cruelty.'

'Lorraine?'

'Yes. Lorraine.'

'Well, well. I thought it was axiomatic that two lovely ladies automatically disliked each other.'

She seized his upper arms. '*Don't* change the subject.'

'I must tell Alex about this.'

'Tell him what?' she said warily.

'He thinks you detest one another.'

'Tell Alex he's a fool. She's a lovely person. And *you* are tearing her to pieces.'

Petersen nodded. 'She's being torn to pieces all right. But I'm not the person who's doing the tearing.'

She looked closely at him, her eyes moving from one of his to the other, as if hoping that would help her find the truth. 'Then who is?'

'If I told you, you'd just go and tell her.' She said nothing, just kept up her intense scrutiny of his face. 'She knows who is. But I don't want her to think that it's public knowledge.

She looked away. 'Two things. Maybe, deep down, you do have some finer feelings after all.' She looked at his eyes again and half-smiled. 'And you don't trust me.'

'I'd like to.'

'Try.'

'She's a good, honest, patriotic British citizen and she's working for the Italian secret service, specifically for Major Cipriano and she may well be responsible, however indirectly, for the deaths of an untold number of my fellow countrymen.'

'I don't believe it! I don't believe it!' Her eyes were wide and full of horror and her voice shook. 'I don't! I don't! I don't!'

'I know you don't,' he said gently. 'That's because you don't want to believe it. I didn't want to believe it myself. I do now. I can prove it. Do you think I'm so stupid as to say I can prove a thing when I can't. Or don't you believe me either?'

'I don't know what to believe,' she said wildly. 'Yes, I do. I do. I do know what to believe. I don't believe Lorraine could be like that.'

'Too lovely a person, too honest, too good, too true?'

'Yes! Yes! That's what I believe.'

'That's what I believed, too. That's what I still believe.'

Her grip on his arms tightened and she looked at him almost beseechingly. 'Please. Please don't make fun of me.'

'She's being blackmailed.'

'Blackmailed! Blackmailed! How could anyone blackmail Lorraine?' She looked away, was silent for some seconds, then looked back again. 'It's something to do with Carlos, isn't it?'

'Yes. Indirectly.' He looked at her curiously. 'How did you know that?'

'Because she's in love with him,' Sarina said impatiently.

'How do you know *that*?' This time he was openly surprised.

'Because I'm a woman.'

'Ah, well, yes. I suppose that explains it.'

'*And* because you had Captain Crni ask her about Carlos. But I knew before that. Anyone could see it.'

'Here's one who didn't.' He thought. 'Well, hindsight, retrospect, yes. But I said only indirectly. Nobody would be stupid enough to use Carlos as a blackmail weapon. They'd find themselves with a double-edged sword in their hands. But, sure, he's part of it.'

'Well?' She'd actually arrived at the stage where she had started shaking him, no mean feat with a person of Petersen's bulk. 'What's the other part of it?'

'I know, or I think I know, the other part of it. But I haven't any proof.'

'Tell me what you think.'

'You think because she's honest and good and true that she has led a blameless life, that she can't possibly have any guilty secrets?'

'Go on.'

'I don't think she's got any guilty secrets either. Unless you call having an illegitimate child a guilty secret, which I don't.'

She took her right hand away from his arm and touched her lips. She was shocked not by what he had said but because of its implications.

'Carlos is a doctor.' He sounded tired and, for the first time since she had met him, he looked tired. 'He qualified in Rome. Lorraine lived with him during the time she was Jamie Harrison's secretary. They have a son, aged two and a half. It's my belief that he's been kidnapped. I'll find out for sure when I have a knife at Cipriano's throat.'

She stared at him in silence. Two tears trickled slowly down her cheeks.

EIGHT

At nine o'clock the next morning Jablanica looked so much like an idealized Christmas postcard that it was almost unreal, untrue in its breathtaking beauty. The snow had stopped, the clouds were gone, the sun shone from a clear pale blue sky and the air on the windless slopes, where the trees hung heavy with snow, was crisp and pellucid and very cold. It required only the sound of sleigh-bells to complete the illusion. But peace on earth and goodwill to all men were the last considerations in the thoughts of those gathered around the breakfast table that morning.

Petersen, his chin on his hand and his coffee growing cold before him, was obviously lost in contemplation. Harrison, who showed remarkably little after-effects from the considerable amount of wine he had found necessary to drown his chagrin and bring himself once more face to face with reality, said: 'A penny for them, Peter, my boy.'

'My thoughts? They'd be worth a lot more than that to the people I'm thinking about. Not, may I add hastily, that they include any of those sitting around the table.'

'And not only do you look pensive,' Harrison went on, 'but I detect a slight diminution in the usual early morning ebullience, the sparkling cheer. You found sleep hard to come by? The change of beds, perhaps?'

'As I sleep in a different bed practically every night in life that would hardly be a factor, otherwise I'd be dead by this time. Fact is, I was up nearly all night, with either George or Ivan, in the radio room. You couldn't possibly have heard it, but there was a long and violent thunderstorm during the night – that's why we have cloudless skies this morning – and both transmission and reception were close on impossible.'

'Ah! That explains it. Would it be in order to ask who you were talking to during the long watches of the night?'

'Certainly. No secrets, no secrets.' Harrison's expression of disbelief was only fleeting and he made no comment. 'We had, of course, to contact our HQ in Bihać and warn them of the impending attack. That, alone, took almost two hours.'

'You should have used my radio,' Michael said. 'It's got a remarkable range.'

'We did. It was no better than the other.'

'Oh. Then perhaps you should have used me. After all, I do know that equipment.'

'Of course you do. But, then, our people in Bihać don't know Navajo which is the only code you are familiar with.'

Michael looked at him, his mouth fallen slightly open. 'How on earth did you know that? I mean, I've got no code books.' He tapped his head. 'It's all up here.'

'You sent a message just after Colonel Lunz and I had been talking to you. You may be a good radio operator, Michael, but otherwise you shouldn't be allowed out without a minder.'

Sarina said: 'Don't forget I was there also.'

'Two minders. I'll bet you never even checked to see if the room was bugged.'

'Good God!' Michael looked at his sister. 'Bugged! Did you – how could you have known we were going to stay –'

'It could have been bugged. It wasn't. George was listening on the balcony.'

'George!'

'You talked in plain language. George said it wasn't any European language he'd ever heard. You had an American instructor. The Americans labour under the happy delusion that Navajo is unbreakable.'

'Now you tell me,' George said. He seemed in no way upset.

'Sorry. Busy. I forgot.'

'Peter's expertise in espionage is matched only by his expertise in codes. The two go hand-in-glove. Makes up codes all the time. Breaks them, too. Remember he said the Germans had twice broken the Četnik code. *They* didn't. Peter gave them the information. Not that they know that. Nothing like spreading dissension among allies.'

Harrison said: 'How do you know the Germans didn't monitor and break your transmission last night?'

'Impossible. Only two people know my codes – me and the receiver. Never use the same code twice. You can't break a code on a single transmission.'

'That's fine. But – not trying to be awkward, old boy – will this information be of any use to your Partisans? Won't the Germans know that you've been kidnapped or disappeared or whatever and might pass this message on. If they did, surely they would change their plan of attack.'

'Don't you think I have considered this, Jamie? You simply don't even begin to know the Balkans. How could you, after less than a couple of months? What do you know of the deviousness, the plotting and counter-plotting, the rivalries, the jealousies, the self-seeking, the total regard for one's own power base, the distrusts, the obsession for personal gain, the vast gulf between the Occidental and Byzantine minds? I don't think there's even a remote chance of the Germans finding out.

'Consider. Who knows I've got the plans? As far as the Colonel is concerned, there are only two plans, he's got both and I've never seen a copy. Why should he think so? Metrović will have given him the name of Cipriano but I'll bet the Colonel has never heard of him and even if he has what's he going to tell him? Even if he did tell him Cipriano would be too smart to believe it was the Murge division – a commando unit like Ivan's never discloses their true identity. Again, apart from the fact that the Colonel's pride would probably stop him anyway from letting anyone know that his defences have been breached, he could be Machiavellian enough to want the Germans to be taken by surprise, not, of course in order that they should be defeated but that they should suffer severe casualties. Sure, he wants the Partisans destroyed but, when and if it happens, he wants the Germans out of the country. Basically, they're both his natural enemies.

'And even if the Germans did eventually find out, so what? It's too late to change plans and, anyway, there *are* no other plans they could make. There *is* no alternative.'

'I have to agree,' Harrison said. 'They'll go ahead as planned. Forewarned, one takes it, is forearmed. A satisfactory night's work, no?'

'It was unimportant. They would almost certainly have found out in any case. We have a considerable number of reliable contacts throughout the country. In the areas held by the Germans, Italians, Četniks and Ustaša – and that's most of the country – there are reliable solid citizens, or are so regarded by the Germans, Italians, Četniks and Ustaša, who, while cheerfully collaborating with the enemy, send us regular and up-to-date reports of the latest enemy troop movements. In other words, they are Partisan spies. Their reports are far from complete but enough to give Tito and his staff a fair indication of the enemy's intentions.'

'I suppose that happens in every war,' Harrison said, 'But I didn't know the Partisans had spies in the enemy's camp.'

'We have had from the very beginning. We couldn't have survived otherwise. What took up most of our time last night was the distressing discovery – well, we first suspected it about ten weeks ago – that the enemy have spies in *our* camp. Even more distressing was the discovery that they had spies in the Partisan HQ. In retrospect, it was naïve of us, we should have suspected the possibility and taken precautions long ago. In fairness to us, we weren't complacent – we were just under the fond misapprehension that every Partisan was a burning patriot. Some, alas, burn less brightly than others. This, and not acting as message boys for General von Löhr, is what has been occupying George, Alex and myself in Italy in the past two weeks. It was a matter of such vital importance that George was actually sufficiently motivated to drag himself away from his snug retreats in Bihać and Mount Prenj. Those spies in our camp had become a major threat to our security: we were trying to uncover the Italian connection.

'That there was, and is, an Italian connection, is beyond dispute. Not German, not Četnik, not Ustaša – specifically Italian, for it has been the Italian Murge division, first-class mountain troops, that have been causing us all the trouble. Our Partisans are as good, probably even better mountain troops, but hundreds of them have been killed by the Murge division in the past few months. Never in pitched battle. Invariably in isolated, one-off, incidents. A patrol, a localized troop movement, a transfer of wounded to a supposedly safer area, a reconnaissance group behind enemy lines – it came to the stage where none of those was immune to a lightning strike by specialized Murge units who apparently knew, always, exactly where to strike, when to strike, how to strike – they even seemed to know the number and composition of the Partisan groups they would be attacking, even the approximate number of the groups themselves. Our small-scale guerrilla movements were becoming very hampered, almost paralysed: and a partisan's army's survival depends almost exclusively on mobility, flexibility and long-range reconnaissance.

'The Murge, of course, were receiving precise advance information of our movements. The information had to be coming from a person or persons in the neighbourhood of our HQ. Those secret messages, messages which led hundreds of men to their deaths, were not of course written down, addressed to the enemy and dropped in the nearest letterbox: they were sent by radio.' Petersen broke off as if to collect his thoughts, his eyes wandering, unseeingly, as it seemed, round the table. Lorraine, he could see, was unnaturally pale: Sarina had her hands clasped tightly together. Petersen appeared to notice nothing.

'I'll carry on for a moment,' George said. 'At this time, you must understand that Peter has been overcome by his habitual modesty. Peter couldn't believe that the traitors could be any long-serving Partisans. Neither could I. Peter suggested that we check the approximate dates of the first transmissions – the times of the first unexpected swoops by the Murge units – with the time of the arrival of the latest recruits to the Partisans. We did and found that this checked with the arrival of an unusually high number of ex-Četniks – Četniks regularly desert to us and it's quite impossible to check out the credentials and good faith of ail of them or even a fraction of them.

'Peter and some of his men checked on a small number of those and found two who had access to long-range transmitters hidden in a forest on a hill-side. They wouldn't talk and we don't torture. They were executed. Thereafter the number of unexpected attacks by the Murge fell off rapidly: but they still continued at sporadic intervals. Which, of course, could only mean that there were still some traitors around.'

George helped himself liberally to some beer. It was but breakfast time, but George claimed to be allergic to both tea and coffee.

'So we went to Italy, the three of us. Why? Because we – are or were – Četnik intelligence officers and naturally associated with our Italian counterparts. Why? Because we were convinced that the messages were being relayed through Italian Intelligence. Why? Because a fighting division has neither the facilities, the ability, the organization nor the cash to mount such an operation. But Italian Intelligence has all of these in abundance.'

'Amidst the welter of "whys", George,' Harrison said, 'why the cash?'

'It's as Peter said,' George said sadly. 'You haven't got the Balkan mentality. Come to that, I doubt whether you have the universal mentality. The Četnik agents, like agents and double-agents the world over, are not motivated simply by altrusim, patriotism or political conviction. The little gears in their minds only mesh efficiently under the influence of the universal lubricant. Money. They are rather highly paid and, considered dispassionately, deserve to be: look what happened to those two unfortunates unmasked by Peter.'

Petersen rose, walked to the window and stood there, gazing down the gentle valley that sloped away from their chalet. He seemed to have lost interest in the conversation.

'All in all,' Harrison said, 'a fair night's work.'

'That wasn't quite all of it,' George said. 'We have located Cipriano.'

'Cipriano!'

'None other. Lorraine, my dear! You look so pale. Are you not well?'

'I feel – I feel a little faint.'

'Maraschino,' George said unhesitatingly. 'Sava!' This to one of Crni's soldiers who rose at once and crossed to the liquor cupboard. 'Yes, indeed. The worthy Major himself.'

'But how on earth –'

'We have our little methods,' George said complacently. 'We have, as Peter told you, our reliable, solid citizens everywhere. Incidentally, you can now forget all that Peter told you – thank you, my boy, just give it to the lady – all he told you about Cipriano working hand-in-glove with the Partisans. I'm afraid he grossly maligned the poor man but at the moment he deemed it prudent to divert any suspicions that Majors Metrović and Ranković might have been harbouring from himself to an absent person. Cipriano was conveniently absent. Our Peter is a very convincing actor, no?'

'He's a very convincing liar,' Sarina said.

'Oh, tush! Hurt pride again. We're just mad because he fooled you, too. Anyway, Cipriano's in Imotski, doubtless closeted with the Murge brigade commander there and hatching fresh devilish schemes against our poor Partisans. I shouldn't have to explain any of this. You will remember that Peter said in Mount Prenj that he wanted to get to the link-man – Cipriano – because he was aiding and abetting the Partisans. What he meant to say was he wanted to get at the link-man because he was a deadly enemy of the Partisans but he couldn't very well say that, could he, in front of Metrović and Ranković? Come, come, my children, you disappoint me: you had all night long to work out something as simple and obvious as that.'

George yawned behind a massive hand. 'Excuse me. Now that I'm breakfasted and am once more at peace with myself, I intend to retire and rest lightly for two or three hours. We will not be moving out until the afternoon at the earliest. We await an urgent communication from Bihać but it will take some time to collect and collate the information we want. Meantime, how do you people propose to spend the morning?' He raised his voice. 'Peter. Those people are free to come and go as they want, inside and out, aren't they?'

'Of course.'

Captain Crni smiled and said: 'May I suggest that you put on your coats and I'll show you around our little town. There's not much to show so it would be a short walk and hardly exhausting. Apart from the fact that it's a lovely morning I know where we can get the best coffee in Bosnia. Far better than that awful swill we've just had.'

Sarina said, 'That way we can still be watched, can't we?'

Captain Crni bowed gallantly. 'It would always be a pleasure to watch you and Miss Chamberlain. If however, you wish to go alone and report to the nearest Italian command post that we are Partisans and have designs on a certain Italian intelligence major, then you are by all means free to do so. That, Miss von Karajan, is the extent to which we trust you.'

'I *am* sorry.' She reached out an impulsive hand and caught his forearm. 'That was a terrible thing to say. Two or three days in this country and I find I can't trust anyone, not even myself.' She smiled. 'Besides, you're the only one who knows where the coffee shop is.'

They left – without Giacomo who had elected to remain behind – shortly afterwards. Petersen said wearily: 'She doesn't trust anyone. God knows I don't blame her. George, I am a hypocritical liar. Even when I say nothing, I'm a hypocritical liar.'

'I know what you mean, Peter. Sometimes a tiny voice reaches down to my conscience – God knows how it ever finds it – and says exactly the same thing. The clarion call to duty strikes a pretty cracked note at times. Sava?'

'General?'

'Go to the window in the front room and watch the road. If they return unexpectedly, call me. I'll be upstairs. I'll let you know when you can stop

the watch. Shouldn't be more than a few minutes.'

After lunch a very refreshed-looking Petersen –
he'd had four hours' sleep – crossed to where
Lorraine sat with Sarina on a bench seat by a window and said: 'Lorraine, please don't start getting
worried because there is no need to. George and I
would like to talk to you.'

She bit her lip. 'I knew you would. Can – can
Sarina come?'

'Certainly.' He looked at Sarina. 'Provided, of
course, that you don't say "Oh!" and "Ah!" and
"monster" and clench your fists. Promise?'

'Promise.'

Petersen ushered them to an upstairs room
where George was already seated, a large tankard
on the table before him and a crate, presumably
for emergency, on the floor beside him. Petersen
said: 'George?'

George shook his head positively. 'Would you
come between a man and his thirst.'

'I would have thought you slaked that pretty
thoroughly at lunch.'

'This is a post-prandial beer,' George said with
dignity. 'Pray proceed.'

'This will be short and painless,' Petersen said
to Lorraine. 'I'm not a dentist and you don't have
to tell lies. As you must have guessed, we know
everything. I can promise you, and George will
confirm, that neither retribution nor punishment

waits for you. You're a victim and not a villain and acted under extreme duress. Besides, you didn't even know what you were doing. All transmissions were not only in code but in Yugoslav code and you don't understand a word of Serbo-Croat. George's word, of course, carries immense weight in the war councils, almost totally so in cases such as this, and they listen to me a bit, too. No harm will come to you or Carlos or Mario.'

She nodded, almost composedly. 'You know about our son, of course?'

'Yes. When was he kidnapped?'

'Six months ago.'

'You have no idea where he is being held?'

'No. Well, vaguely.' She was no longer composed. 'In this country, I know. Major Cipriano wanted him out of Italy. I don't know why.'

'I can understand. There are certain things that even Cipriano can't do in Italy. How do you know he's in this country?'

'They let Carlos see him twice. That was twice when I said I wasn't going to work for them any more because I was sure he was dead. But I don't know where he is.'

'Yes. I see. It doesn't matter.'

'It doesn't matter!' She was no longer composed and her eyes were masked in tears.

George took his evil-smelling cigar from his mouth. 'What Peter means is that Cipriano will tell him.'

'Cipriano will tell –' She broke off, nodded and shivered involuntarily.

'We have your code books, Lorraine. We searched your room when you were out this morning.'

'You searched her room!' Sarina said indignantly. 'What right –'

Petersen rose and opened the door. 'Out.'

'I'm sorry. I forgot. I –'

'You promised.'

'Don't you ever give anyone a second chance?'

Petersen didn't answer. He closed the door, sat down and said: 'False bottoms to kitbags are really dreadfully passé these days. But, then, I don't suppose either you or Cipriano ever dreamed that you would come under suspicion. No names in your book but we don't need them. There are code numbers, call-up signs and call-up times. It will take us little enough time to trap them.'

'And then?'

George removed his cigar again. 'Don't ask silly questions.'

'Tell me, Lorraine. You had no idea why you had been sent to Mount Prenj? Oh, you knew what you were to do, but not why. Well, Cipriano knew that you knew Jamie Harrison and that he trusted you completely – after all, you *were* his confidential secretary – so that he would never suspect you of double-dealing: transferring messages from our diehard Četnik friends in Bihać to him in Rome or wherever, messages which he

268

could re-transmit to the Murge regiment. But the real reason, of course, is that we had destroyed the only two long-range transmitters they had. With short-range transmitters their contacts with Rome could only be sporadic at best. But Mount Prenj is only two hundred kilometres from Bihać. It would be an awfully short range transmitter that couldn't reach there.' Petersen paused and considered. 'Well, that's all. No, one more thing.' He smiled. 'Yes. One more thing. Purely personal. Where did you first meet Carlos?'

'Isle of Wight, where I was born. He was sailing at Cowes.'

'Of course, of course. He told me that he often went sailing there before the war. Well, I hope you'll both go sailing there again after the war.'

'Will – will Carlos be all right, Major Petersen?'

'If you can refer to a Generalmajor as George you can refer to a Major as Peter. Why shouldn't he be? He's in the clear. Under both Italian military and civilian law he has committed no criminal offence, aided and abetted no-one. With any luck we might see him later on tomorrow.'

'What! Carlos?' Her face was transformed.

Petersen looked at Sarina. 'Yes, you were right, no question.' He didn't say what she had been right about. 'Certainly. Carlos. He hasn't been up to any aiding or abetting yet, but tomorrow he will.'

She didn't seem to hear him or, if she did, her mind was elsewhere.

'He's still in Ploče?'

'Yes.'

'He hasn't gone back to Italy?'

'Alas, no. Some disaffected citizen has put sugar in his diesel oil.'

She looked at him for a long moment then smiled slowly. 'It wouldn't have been one of those solid, reliable citizens you talk about, would it?'

He smiled back at her. 'I am not responsible for the actions of solid, reliable citizens.'

At the foot of the stairs Sarina took Petersen's arm and held him back. 'Thank you,' she said. 'Thank you very much. That was very kind.'

He looked at her in amazement. 'What else did you expect me to do?'

'Nothing, I suppose. But it was wonderful. Especially about Carlos.'

'Today I'm not an ogre? Not a monster?'

She smiled and shook her head.

'And tomorrow? When I have to find out where the little boy is? Do you understand what I mean?'

She stopped smiling.

Petersen shook his head sadly. ' "*Souvent femme varie, bien fol est qui s'y fie*".'

'What is that meant to mean?'

'Picked it up from George. Something King Francis I scratched with a diamond on a pane of glass at Chambord. "Often does woman change, and very foolish is he who trusts her".'

'Pfui!' she said. But she was smiling again.

Towards the middle of the afternoon Petersen and Crni walked into the lounge, carrying several machine-pistols and hand-guns.

'Replacement equipment. Ivan here took ours away so it's only fair that he should replace them. We'll be leaving shortly. Ivan, Edvard and Sava are coming with us.' He glanced at his watch. 'Twenty minutes, shall we say? I want to get through the nasty bit of the Neretva gorge in daylight but not to arrive at our destination until it's dark, for the usual reasons.'

'I'm not looking forward to that,' Sarina said.

'Have no fear. I'm not driving. Sava is. He's a truck driver in civilian life.'

'What destination?' Harrison said.

'Ah! I forgot. A new acquaintance for you, Jamie, but an old friend of ours. The proprietor of the Hotel Eden in Mostar, one Josip Pijade.'

'A solid and reliable citizen,' Lorraine said.

'A very solid, very reliable citizen. You have a faraway look on your face, George. What are you thinking of?'

'Venison.'

NINE

And venison it was. Josip and Marija had excelled themselves and achieved the seemingly impossible – the venison tasted even marginally better than the last time. George excelled himself in a corresponding fashion, but failed to achieve the impossible: halfway through his third massive helping of venison he had to admit defeat. Sleep that night, unlike the last occasion, was undisturbed by unwelcome visitors. Breakfast was a late and leisurely meal.

'I wish we'd had you up in the damned Mount Prenj for the past two months,' Harrison said to Josip after the meal. 'But it's been worth the wait. I wish someone would station me here for the duration. He directed his attention towards Petersen. 'Are we permitted to know our plans – well, your plans – for the day?'

'Of course. They're concerned primarily, though not entirely, with one person – Cipriano, his apprehension and interrogation. The Bihać affair we can consider as being virtually a closed matter. As you know, we failed to make contact yesterday, but Ivan and I had better luck during the small hours – reception, as you know, is always better at night. They've come up with no fewer than sixteen Četnik-turned-Partisan suspects, there can't be more than two, at the most three. We send out a coded message at a certain hour on a certain wavelength and note will be taken as to which of the sixteen is absent at the time. He will not of course be apprehended until the other one or two have been similarly trapped. Routine. Forget it.' That the words were tantamount to a death sentence was evident to everyone, except, apparently, Petersen.

'Cipriano,' Giacomo said. 'Still at Imotski?'

'He is. We have two men up there on a twenty-four hour watch. We're in radio contact. Spoke to them last an hour ago. Cipriano's up and around but shows no sign yet of moving on. He's got quite an entourage with him.' He looked at Alex. 'You might be interested in hearing the description of one of them.'

'Alessandro?' Alex said hopefully.

'No other.'

'Ah.' Just for once Alex registered a trace of expression: it was as near to a happy smile as Alex would ever come.

'Plus, I'm almost certain from the description, Alessandro's three henchmen. Seems that Carlos must have found a flame-cutter somewhere. We

273

don't, of course, know which way the fox is going to jump – there are several different exit routes he can take from Imotski – but we'll be told immediately that is known. He could, of course, be taking a back road to Ploče and hitch-hiking a lift home with Carlos – if the *Colombo*'s diesel lines have been cleared out – but I think that unlikely. I think he'll be heading for the military airfield just outside the town here and the fast way back to Rome. Ivan and I are just going out to the airport to check.'

'Check what?' Harrison asked.

'Whether there's air transport standing by for him.'

'Won't the airfield be guarded?'

'We are two Italian officers. I've just promoted myself to Colonel and will probably outrank anyone there. We'll just walk in and ask them.'

'That won't be necessary, Peter,' Josip Pijade said. 'My cousin, who owns a garage just outside the airport, works there as a part-time repair and maintenance engineer. Not, unfortunately, on the planes, but on the plant, otherwise the Italian air force would be experiencing mysterious crashes. I have but to lift the phone.'

'Thank you, Josip.'

Josip left. Lorraine said: 'Another solid and reliable citizen?'

'Yugoslavia is full of them.'

Josip was back in two minutes. 'There is an Italian plane on standby. *And* it's reserved for Major Cipriano.'

'Thank you.' He nodded to the small transceiver on the table. 'I'll take this with me. Call up if you hear from Imotski. We're almost certain of the route Cipriano will take into town so Ivan and I will go and select an ambush spot. We may take your car, Josip?'

'Take me, too. I know the perfect spot.'

Sarina said: 'We can go into town?'

'I think so. I won't be needing you until night-fall. The only attention you're liable to attract is wolf-whistles from the licentious Italian soldiery.' He looked at Giacomo. 'I'd feel happier if you went along.'

'No sacrifice too great,' Giacomo said.

Sarina smiled. 'We need protection?'

'Only from the licentious soldiery.'

The call came, inevitably enough, when they were halfway through lunch. Marija came in and said: 'They've just left They're heading for Posušje.'

'The Mostar road. Excuse us,' Petersen said. He rose as did Alex, Crni and Edvard.

George said: 'I wish I were coming with you. But everyone knows I'm not a man of action.'

'What he means,' Petersen said coldly, 'is that his jaws haven't even got out of second gear yet and he's barely touched his first litre of beer.'

Sarina said: 'You will be careful, won't you?'

Petersen smiled and said: 'Coming, Giacomo?'

'Certainly not. That's a public bar through there. The licentious soldiery might come in any moment.'

'There's your answer about being careful, Sarina. If Giacomo thought there was the slightest chance of shooting an Italian full of holes he'd be the first aboard the truck. He knows there's no hope. But thanks all the same.'

Alex, white handkerchief in hand, stood on a low knoll in the rough grazing field opposite the tree-lined lane which led off the main Lištica – Mostar road. In the lane itself, with engine running, Petersen sat in the cab of the Italian army truck which was parked only feet from the entrance to the road.

Alex raised the handkerchief high above his head. Petersen engaged first gear and waited, clutch depressed, accelerator at half-throttle. Alex brought the handkerchief sharply down and, clutch released, the truck moved forward under full throttle. Three seconds later Petersen jammed on the brakes, bringing the truck to an abrupt halt, fair and square across the width of the main highway.

The Italian army command car which, fortunately for its occupants, was travelling at only a moderate speed, had no chance: even as the driver stamped on the foot-brake he must have realized that his options were limited indeed: he could either keep to the road and hit the side of the truck head-on or swerve to his right into the field where Alex was – a swerve to the left would have fetched him up against the trees lining the lane. Prudently, he chose the latter course. Locked tyres screeching on the tarmac, the car bust through a low wooden fence, broke into the field while balanced on only two wheels, teetered for a couple of seconds then came to rest as it fell over on its left side, wheels still spinning slowly in the air.

Within seconds, rifle butts had smashed in the right-hand windows of the car but the need for haste was not there: the five occupants, unhurt except for cuts about their faces, were too dazed to recognize the presence of their assailants, far less offer resistance: when they did recover some sense of awareness, the sight of the four machine-pistol muzzles only inches from their heads made the thought of offering any resistance too ludicrous for contemplation.

When Petersen and Crni returned to the hotel they found George and his companions – inevitably, in George's case – in the bar. Equally inevitably, George was presiding behind the counter.

'Good afternoon, gentlemen.' George was at his affable best.

'You've finished lunch, then?' Petersen said.

'And it wasn't bad. Not bad at all. What shall it be? Beer?'

'Beer is fine.'

'Aren't you going to ask him what happened?' Sarina said indignantly.

'Ah. Alex and Edvard have been cut off in their prime?'

'They're in the truck and the truck is in the car park.'

'That's what I like. Solicitude. Making sure that the prisoners are not doing themselves an injury. When do you propose to bring them inside?'

'When it's dark. I can't very well march them through the streets, bound and gagged, in broad daylight, can I?'

'True.' George yawned and slid off his stool. 'Siesta.'

'I know,' Petersen said sympathetically. 'Go, go, go all the time. Wears a man down.'

George left in dignified silence. Sarina said: 'Doesn't go in much for congratulations, does he?'

'He postponed his siesta. That shows he's deeply moved.'

'So you got Major Cipriano. What do you think of that, Lorraine?'

'I suppose I should be weeping for joy. I am glad, I'm terribly glad. But I *knew* he would. I never for a moment doubted it. Did you?'

'No. It's very irritating.'

' "*Souvent femme varie*",' Petersen said sadly. 'Josip, would you send someone with your hotel wagon to pick up the prisoners' luggage and take it upstairs. No, not upstairs: I can examine it just as well down here.' He turned to Sarina. 'And you keep quiet.'

'I didn't say anything!'

'You were about to tell me that that was something else I was very good at. Examining other people's luggage, I mean.'

The five prisoners were brought in by the back entrance as soon as it was reasonably dark. The hotel doors were locked. Cipriano, Alessandro and the three others were settled in chairs and their gags removed. Their wrists remained bound behind their backs. The normally tranquil and civilized Major Cipriano had undergone a radical transformation. His eyes glared and his face was suffused in anger.

'What is the meaning of this – this abominable outrage, Petersen? Have you gone mad? Stark raving mad? Untie me at once! I'm an officer, an Italian officer, an *allied* officer!'

'You're a murderer. Your rank and nationality is of no importance. Not when you're a mass murderer.'

'Untie me! You're crazy! By God, Petersen, if it's the last thing I do –'

'Has it occurred to you that you may already have done your last thing on earth?'

Cipriano stared at Petersen. His lack of understanding was total. Suddenly, he noticed Josip for the first time.

'Pijade! Pijade! You – *you* are a party to this monstrous outrage!' Cipriano was so clearly nearly bereft of reason that he struggled futilely with his bonds. 'By God, Pijade, you shall pay for this treachery!'

'Treachery.' Petersen laughed without mirth. 'Speak of treachery while you may, Cipriano, because you're going to die for it. Pijade will pay, will he? How will he do that, Cipriano?' Petersen's voice was very soft. 'Your eternal curses from the bottom of hell where you'll surely be before midnight tonight?'

'You're all mad,' Cipriano whispered. The anger had drained from his face: he had suddenly become aware that he was in mortal danger.

Petersen went on in the same gentle tone: 'Hundreds of my comrades lie dead because of you.'

'You are mad!' His voice was almost a scream. 'You must be mad. I've never touched a Četnik in my life.'

'I am not a Četnik. I'm a Partisan.'

'A Partisan!' Cipriano was back to his husky whispering again. 'A Partisan! Colonel Lunz suspected – I should have listened –' He broke off and then his voice strengthened. 'I have never harmed a Partisan in my life.'

'Come in,' Petersen called.

Lorraine entered.

'Do you still deny, Cipriano, that you have masterminded the deaths of hundreds of my fellow-Partisans? Lorraine has told me everything, Cipriano. Everything.' He produced a small black book from his tunic. 'Lorraine's code book. In your own handwriting. Or perhaps you don't recognize your handwriting, Cipriano, I'm sure you never thought that you would be signing your own death warrant with your own handwriting. I find it ironic, Cipriano. I hope you do too. But irony isn't going to bring all those hundreds back to life, is it? Even although the last of your spies will have been trapped and executed by the end of the week, those men will still be dead, won't they, Cipriano. Where's the little boy, Lorraine's little boy? Where's Mario, Cipriano?'

Cipriano made a noise in his throat, a harsh and guttural and meaningless sound and struggled to his feet. Giacomo glanced at Petersen, correctly interpreted the nod and, with evident satisfaction, hit Cipriano none too gently in the solar plexus. Cipriano collapsed into his chair, harsh retching noises coming deep from his throat.

Petersen said: 'George?'

George emerged from behind the bar, carrying two pieces of rope in his hand. He ambled across the saloon, dropped one piece to the floor and secured Cipriano firmly to his chair with the other. Then he picked up the second rope, already noosed, and dropped it over Alessandro's chest before the man realized what was happening. Seconds later and he was trussed like the proverbial turkey.

'Cipriano isn't going to tell me because Cipriano knows that he's going to die, whatever happens.

But you'll tell me where the little boy is, won't you, Alessandro?'

Alessandro spat on the floor.

'Oh dear.' Petersen sighed. 'Those disgusting habits are difficult to eradicate, aren't they?' He reached behind the bar and produced the metal box of syringes and drugs he had taken from Alessandro aboard the *Colombo*. 'Alex.'

Alex produced his razor-sharp knife and slit Alessandro's left sleeve from the shoulder to where the ropes bound him at the elbow level.

'No!' Alessandro's voice was a scream of pure terror. 'No! No! No!'

Cipriano leaned forward and struggled against his bonds, his face suffused dark red as he tried to force words through his still constricted throat. Giacomo tapped him again to ensure his continued silence.

'I'm afraid I cut him a little,' Alex said apologetically. He was hardly exaggerating: Alessendro's arm was, indeed, quite badly gashed.

'No matter.' Petersen picked up the syringe and selected a phial at apparent random. 'Save the trouble of searching for a vein.'

'Ploče!' Alessandro's whispered. His voice was strangled with fear. His breath coming and going faster than once every second. 'Ploče. I can take you there!' 18 Fra Spalato! I swear it! I can take you there!'

Petersen replaced the syringe and phials and closed the lid. He said to the girls: 'Alessandro, I'm afraid, was psychologically disadvantaged. But I never laid a finger on him, did I?'

Both girls stared at him, then looked at each other. As if by some telepathic signal, they shuddered in unison.

When Alessandro's arm had been bandaged and Cipriano recovered, they made ready to leave. As Alex approached him with a gag, Cipriano looked at Petersen with empty eyes and said: 'Why don't you kill me here? Difficult to dispose of the body? But no trouble in the Adriatic, is it? A few lengths of chain.'

'Nobody's going to dispose of you, Cipriano. Not permanently. We never had any intention of killing you. I knew Alessandro would crack but I didn't want to waste time over it. A bit of a pragmatist, is our Alessandro, and he had no intention of sacrificing his life for a man he believed to be already as good as dead. We have every moral justification for killing you but no legal justification. Spies are shot all the time: spy-masters never. Geneva Conventions say so. It does seem unfair. No, Cipriano, you are going into durance vile. A prisoner of war, for however long the war lasts. British Intelligence are just going to love to have a chat with you.'

Cipriano had nothing to say, which was perhaps understandable. When the reprieve comes along just as the guillotine is about to be tripped, suitable comment is hard to come by.

Petersen turned to his cousin as Cipriano's gag was being fastened. 'Marija, I would like you to do me a favour. Would you look after a little boy for a day or two?'

'Mario!' Lorraine said. 'You mean Mario?'

'What other little boy would I be talking about. Well, Marija?'

'Peter!' Her voice was full of reproach.

'Well, I had to ask.' He kissed her on the cheek. 'The bane of my life, but I love you.'

'So we part once more,' Jossip said sadly. 'When do we meet again?'

'Dinner-time. George is coming back for the rest of that venison he couldn't finish last night. So am I.'

Edvard stopped the truck several hundred yards short of the entrance to the docks. Alex and Sava dropped down from the back of the truck followed by a now unbound and ungagged Alessandro – they were in the main street and there were a number of people around. The three men turned, without any undue haste, down an unlit side-street.

Crni, seated up front with Petersen, said: 'Do you anticipate any trouble at the control gate?'

'No more than usual. The guards are old, inefficient, not really interested and very susceptible to arrogant and ill-tempered authority. That's us.'

'Cipriano's wrecked command car is bound to have been found some time ago. And the people in charge at the airport must be wondering where he's got to.'

'If a Yugoslav found it, it will have made his day and he would have driven by without stopping. Whether the airport was expecting him I don't know – Cipriano seems an unpredictable fellow who does very much what he wants. Even if it's accepted by now that he's genuinely missing, where are they going to start looking? Ploče's about as unlikely a place as any.'

And so it proved. The sentry didn't even bother to leave his box. Beyond the gate, the docks were deserted – the day's work was over and the freezing temperatures were hardly calculated to encourage night-time strollers. Even so, Petersen told Edvard to stop two hundred metres short of where the *Colombo* was berthed, left the cab, went round to the back, called Lorraine's name and helped her down.

'See that light there? That's the *Colombo*. Go and tell Carlos to switch off his two gangway lights.'

'Yes,' she said. 'Oh, yes.' She ran a few steps then halted abruptly as Petersen called her.

'Walk you clown. No one in Ploče ever runs.'

Three minutes later the gangway lights went out. Two minutes after that the prisoners had made their unobserved way up the unlighted gangway and the truck had disappeared. The gangway lights came on again.

*　　*　　*

Carlos sat in his usual chair in his cabin, his good left hand tightly held in both of Lorraine's, the expression on his face not so much uncomprehending and stunned but comprehending and still stunned.

'Let me see whether I've got this right or whether I'm just imagining it,' Carlos said. 'You're going to lock up my crew and myself, abscond with Lorraine and Mario, imprison Cipriano and his men aboard and steal my ship?'

'I couldn't have put it more succinctly myself. Except, of course, that I wouldn't have used the word "abscond". Only, of course, if you consent. The decision is entirely up to you. And Lorraine, too. But I think Lorraine has already made up her mind.'

'Yes, I have.' There was no hesitation in her voice.

'I'll be dismissed from the Navy,' Carlos said gloomily. 'No, I won't, I'll be court-martialled and shot.'

'Nothing will happen to you. There is not a chance in the world. George and I have gone over it time and again.'

'My crew will talk and –'

'Talk? Talk what about? They're sitting in the mess-room with machine-pistols at their heads. If you had a machine-pistol at your head would you have any doubt whatsoever that your ship had been taken over by force?'

'Cipriano –'

286

'What of Cipriano. Even if he survives his captivity, which he unfortunately probably will as the British don't shoot prisoners, there's nothing he can do. There is no way your version and that of the crew – and this will become the official version – can be disproved. And he would never dare lay a personal charge against you – by the time peace comes you can call for the testimony of several solid and respected citizens of Yugoslavia who will testify to the fact that Cipriano kidnapped your son. The penalty in Italy for kidnapping is life imprisonment.'

'Oh, do come on, Carlos,' Lorraine said impatiently. 'It's not like you to dilly-dally. There *is* no other way.' She gently touched his chin so that his eyes came round to hers. 'We've got Mario back.'

'True, true.' He smiled at her. 'That's all that matters to you, isn't it?'

'Not all.' She smiled in return. 'You're back too. That matters a little. What's the alternative, Carlos? Peter doesn't want to kill Cipriano, and if Cipriano is free our life is finished. He *has* to be imprisoned in a safe place and that means in British hands, and the only way to get him there is in this boat. Peter doesn't make mistakes.'

'Correction,' Sarina said sweetly. 'Peter *never* makes mistakes.'

'"*Souvent femme varie*"' Petersen said.

'Oh, do be quiet.'

'If I'm locked up,' Carlos said, 'When will I – and my crew – be released?'

287

'Tomorrow. An anonymous phone message.'

'And Lorraine and Mario will stay with your friends?'

'Only a few days. Until we provide them with new identity papers. George is a close friend of *the* master forger in the Balkans. Lorraine Tremino, we had thought. In these troublous times you should have no difficulty in establishing a long-established family unit. A marriage certificate, George?'

George lowered his tankard. 'For my friend, a trifle. Venue? Rome? Pescara? Cowes? Wherever. We shall see what forms he has available.'

The door opened and Alex entered, Sava close behind him. Alex had a curly-haired little boy by the hand. The boy looked around him, wonderingly, caught a sight of Carlos and ran to him, arms outstretched. Carlos picked him up and set him on his knees. Mario wound his arms round his neck and gazed wonderingly at Lorraine.

'He's only a little boy,' George said comfortingly. 'For a little boy, Lorraine, six months is a long time. He will remember.'

Harrison coughed. 'And I am to go with Giacomo on this perilous voyage, this rendezvous with eternity?'

'Your choice, Jamie, but Giacomo has to have somebody. Besides, you know as well as I do that the Illyrian Alps are not your homeland and that there's no useful function you can perform here any more. More important, as a serving British officer you will lend credulity – total credibility – to Giacomo's story – apart from convincing the British of the true state of affairs out here, about which you feel so strongly.'

'I will go,' Harrison said. 'A twisted smile on my face, but I will go.'

'You'll untwist your smile when the fast Royal Navy patrol boat comes out to meet you. We will radio Cairo. I don't have their call-up sign but you do, don't you, Sarina?'

'Yes.'

'As a final back-up we will give you a letter explaining the situation fully. Do you have a type-writer, Carlos?'

'Next door.' Carlos had handed Mario over to Lorraine. The little boy, while not objecting, still had a suspicious frown on his face.

'This letter will be signed by the Generalmajor and myself. Can you type, Sarina?'

'Of course.'

'Of course. As if it were the most natural thing in the world. Well, I can't. You should, at least, be pleased. A chink in my armour. Come on.'

Carlos said, 'I don't like to say this, Peter, but I think you've missed something. It's a long long way to the south of Italy where I assume this ren-dezvous will be made.'

'Your diesel lines are cleared? Your tanks are full?'

'Yes. That's not my point. Oh, I'm sure that Giacomo can steer by the sun and the compass but a rendezvous has to be precise. Latitude this, longitude that.'

'Indeed. But there are some things you don't know about Giacomo.'

Carlos smiled. 'I'm sure there are. What?'

'Do *you* have a foreign-going master's ticket?'

'No.' Carlos smiled again. 'Don't tell me. Giacomo has.'

In the tiny cabin next door Petersen said: 'You liked Cairo, didn't you?'

'Yes.' Sarina looked puzzled. 'Yes, I did.' Her puzzlement changed to suspicion. 'Why?'

'Aristocratic young ladies like you are not cut out for this life. All the cold and ice and snow and mountains. Besides, you suffer from vertigo.'

'I'm coming with you.' The tone in her voice was final.

Petersen looked at her for a long moment then smiled. 'A Partisan.'

'I'm coming with you.'

'So is Michael.'

'I'm coming with you in a different way.'

Petersen pondered. 'If things like that have to be said I think that I should really –'

'You talk so much I'd have to wait for ever.'

He smiled and touched the auburn hair. 'About this letter.'

'Romance,' she said. 'Life is going to be full of it.'

'One little thing you've overlooked, Peter,' Harrison said.

'Peter never overlooks anything.'

Petersen looked at Sarina and raised his eyes. *'Souvent –'*

'Please.'

'Giacomo and I are going to be alone,' Harrison said. 'We have to sleep. Five dangerous men to be watched. How are we –'

'Alex?'

'Yes, Major?'

'The engine-room.'

'Ah!' A rare, a very rare smile touched Alex's lips. 'The oxyacetylene welder.'

Breakheart Pass

Alistair MacLean

'Explodes with action'
Daily Mirror

The Rocky Mountains, winter 1873...

Travelling along one of the most desolate stretches of railroad in the West is a crowded troop train, bound for the cholera-stricken garrison at Fort Humboldt. On board are the Governor of Nevada, the daughter of the fort's commander and a US marshal escorting a notorious outlaw. Between them and safety are the hostile Paiute Indians – and a man who will stop at nothing, even murder...

'Alistair MacLean is a magnificent storyteller'
Sunday Mirror

ISBN 0 00 615805 6

HMS Ulysses
Alistair MacLean

'A brilliant, overwhelming piece of descriptive writing'
Observer

This is one of the great war novels of our century and one of the finest achievements of Alistair MacLean's bestselling career. It is the story of Convoy FR77 to Murmansk – a voyage that pushes men to the limits of human endurance, crippled by enemy atack and the bitter cold of the Arctic.

'A story of exceptional courage which grips the imagination'
Daily Telegraph

'It deserves an honourable place among twentieth-century war books'
Daily Mail

'*HMS Ulysses* is in the same class as *The Cruel Sea*'
Evening Standard

ISBN 0 00 613512 9

Ice Station Zebra

Alistair MacLean

'Tense, terrifying . . . moves at a breathless pace'
Daily Express

The atomic submarine *Dolphin* has impossible orders: to sail beneath the ice-floes of the Arctic Ocean to locate and rescue the men of weather-station Zebra, gutted by fire and drifting with the ice-pack somewhere north of the Arctic Circle.

But the orders do not say what the *Dolphin* will find if she succeeds – that the fire at Ice Station Zebra was sabotage, and that one of the survivors is a killer . . .

'A thoroughly professional cliff-hanger'   *Sunday Telegraph*

ISBN 0 00 616141 3

Where Eagles Dare
Alistair MacLean

'A real humdinger. The best MacLean yet.' *Daily Mirror*

'There is a splendid audacity about *Where Eagles Dare* in which a handful of British agents invade an "impenetrable" Gestapo command post. . . MacLean offers a real dazzler of a thriller, with vivid action, fine set pieces of suspense, and a virtuoso display of startling plot twists.'
New York Times

'Alistair MacLean has done it again: produced another king-sized thriller of tremendous pace and excitement. The tension is almost unbearable at times, but you can't stop turning the pages in a feverish desire to know what happens next.'
Liverpool Echo

ISBN 0 00 615804 8

Circus

Alistair MacLean

Bruno Wildermann of the Wrinfield Circus is the world's greatest trapeze artist, a clairvoyant with near-supernatural powers and an implacable enemy of the East European regime that arrested his family and murdered his wife. The CIA needs such a man, and recruits Bruno for an impossible raid – on the impregnable Lubylan fortress, where his family is held.

Under cover of a circus tour, Bruno prepares to return to his homeland. But before the journey even begins a murderer strikes twice. Somewhere in the circus there is a communist agent with orders to stop Bruno at any cost . . .

Great reading'   *Sunday Telegraph*

'An action-packed story . . . finger-biting suspense' *BBC*

978-0-00-616735-8